Welcome to Natchez, home to whores, gamblers, and anyone out to make a fast buck, no matter what the cost…..

The untimely death of lovely young Rebecca Bennett's father forces the innocent girl from Savannah to live by her wits. Alone, penniless, and seemingly betrayed by the only man she has ever truly loved, she must live by her wits to stay alive and fulfil her dream: to buy her beloved Oliver's plantation and have a home of her own, even though he is miles away.

But though she tries to escape from her shady past, the powerful enemies at work against her and Oliver close in. Can she ever find happiness, safety, and the people responsible for her father's death and her ruin? And can she ever be sure of Oliver's love?

This is a novel full of suspense, excitement, advanture, and sizzling romance. Don't miss it!

Deb Crockett

Deb Crockett, at age eight, wrote a sequel to Peter Rabbit which her third-grade teacher thought was so good that she insisted Deb read it aloud to the class. The opportunity not only to write whatever her active imagination could conceive, but also to have an appreciative audience, ignited this author's enthusiasm. She hasn't stopped writing since. Deb writes mostly romances, all with strong elements of mystery, danger and excitement, enough to satisfy the most insatiable reader.

This novel is also available in disc book, e-book, and multimedia Cd-Rom format from Net Novels, http://members.xoom.com/NetNovels

NATCHEZ:

An Historical Romance

by Deb Crockett

Deb Crockett
8/3/99

Domhan Books

Copyright the author 1998

All rights reserved. No part of this book may be reproduced or transmitted in any form by any means, electronic or mechanical, including photocopying, recording, or by any information and storage retrieval system, without permission in writing from the copyright owner.

This is a work of fiction. Names, characters, places and incidents are the product of the author's imagination, and any resemblance to any actual persons, living or dead, events, or locales, is entirely coincidental.

ISBN: 1-58345-008-4

Published by Domhan Books

Domhan, pronounced DOW-ann, is the Irish word for universe. Our vision is to bring the reading public all genres of books from new writers all over the world.

In the United Kingdom:
3 Killyvilly Grove
Enniskillen
N. Ireland

In the USA
9511 Shore Road, Apt. 514
Brooklyn New York 11209

Printed and distributed by Lightning Print
part of Ingram Industries
La Vergne Tennessee 37086

CHAPTER ONE

"There are moments, Papa, when I fear that you have gone quite mad."

Henry Bennett's mouth fell open, and he stared at his daughter Rebecca with shock and indignation.

"What do you know about cotton farming?" she said, smoothing an imaginary wrinkle from the sleeve of her gown. "You're a merchant, Papa, not a farmer!"

"Of course I'm a merchant, or rather I was a merchant," replied Mr. Bennett. "And I was quite successful at it, too. Now I am determined to be a successful cotton farmer, and that is that."

"But Papa," Rebecca persisted, "why did we have to leave Savannah? Why couldn't you have bought some land and planted your old cotton in Georgia? Savannah is home! Why did we have to leave Savannah and come half-way around the world to Natchez just to grow some stupid old cotton!"

Mr. Bennett studied his daughter's face as she stood beside him on the dock at New Orleans, waiting to board the steamboat Sentinel that would take them upriver to Natchez, Mississippi.

She was so like her mother, same long, shiny hair the color of honey, same huge green eyes that could glitter like emeralds when she was excited, or soften the hardest heart when she was hurt. She was built like her mother, too, small of frame, dainty of figure. So like Mrs. Bennett, God rest her soul.

Activity on the docks increased as one steamboat departed and another landed. Rebecca looked up at the huge painted sign on the side of the boat that she and her father would soon be boarding: the Sentinel. It was not as large as some of the boats she had seen at New Orleans, but it was every bit as luxurious. This was the first boat that was making a stop at Natchez on which they had been able to secure passage.

Roustabouts, who made their living loading and unloading baggage and goods from the boats, picked up their pace as the great engines of the steamboat roared to life. When the boilers filled with steam, the boat would be ready to depart.

Passengers began boarding, and Mr. Bennett hastily took Rebecca's arm. "Come, my dear, let's get aboard."

Rebecca balked, giving her father a look that in any other circumstance would have instantly secured her heart's desire.

"But can't we stay in New Orleans for a few days? We only just got here yesterday. I've hardly seen anything of the city. Please, Papa? You know I've never been outside of Savannah before. I've never been anywhere before." She tilted her head up to him, with pleading eyes.

"You young girls are all alike," he teased, trying to coax back her usual good humor. "You want to go shopping, that's it. Dresses and millinery and ball gowns, that's all you ever think of."

Rebecca groaned with irritation. "That's not all I ever think of, Papa, and you know it. I've only been to one ball in my whole life, and that was Miss Meacham's Christmas Charity Ball for the Orphans. I had to dance with a thirteen-year old boy who kept stepping on my toes and wiping his nose on his sleeve! And I'm not a young girl anymore, either. I'm twenty, as you well know, and how do you expect me to find a suitable husband if I'm dressed in these old rags?"

Mr. Bennett gave his daughter a long-suffering look. He wasn't a terribly wealthy man, by most people's standards, but he had always kept his daughter decently and fashionably clothed.

Rebecca sighed and pulled petulantly at the brim of her felt hat, attempting to shade the warm afternoon sun. The brim was too narrow to offer much protection, although Mrs. Palatino, Rebecca's dressmaker back in Savannah, had assured her client that this was without doubt what all fashionable young ladies would be wearing by this time next year.

That might be true, Rebecca thought, but it wasn't nearly as glamorous as the large, gossamer-like confections that she saw on the New Orleans ladies. Their hats were specially designed to match their gowns, or was it the other way around? Lovely pastels, pretty florals.

Rebecca looked down at her plain russet-brown travelling suit that was neat and proper, but so dull. Since leaving Savannah, she had been nearly overwhelmed with the newness and novelty of everything she saw, and felt very plain and common compared to the exotic women she observed in New Orleans.

She pulled on his arm. "Oh, Papa, please, while we're here in New Orleans, please, can't we just spend a few more days? Please?"

When his daughter looked at him like that, it was hard to say no to her, but Mr. Bennett steeled himself.

"No, my dear, I'm afraid that's impossible. You know we are expected at Natchez. Oliver Sebastian specifically requested that we come as soon as possible, because he is anxious to get back to England, and I gave him my word that we would come without delay."

"Oh, bother Mr. Sebastian! Where is he, anyway? He was supposed to meet us here and accompany us, and now he's been detained and I don't think it's a good idea to go on without him, Papa. After all, it is his farm that you are going to buy."

"I told you before, Mr. Sebastian sent word to our hotel that he would meet up with us later in Natchez. I really don't see any purpose in waiting any longer. We might as well get on the boat. But, look..." Mr. Bennett wavered under his daughter's pleading gaze. "I promise you that as soon as everything is settled about the cotton farm, I'll bring you back to New Orleans, and we'll have a proper time of it, what do you say?"

She knew her father was anxious to get to Natchez, anxious to buy the farm and start the new life that they had come so far to find. If he promised to bring her back, then she could count on it. He was as good as his word.

"All right, Papa, but don't you forget! If I'm to be the daughter of a wealthy cotton-planter, then I'll have to have decent clothes. Look at this frumpy thing I'm wearing! And Natchez probably doesn't have one single competent dressmaker. I just know I'll have to buy all my gowns here in New Orleans."

"Don't you worry about a thing, my dear. This farm is going to make more money than that blasted mercantile store ever did. You shall have the finest gowns this side of Paris." He patted her arm, then took hold of it again. "Now, stop wasting time and get aboard."

Two stewards carried their trunks on board the Sentinel, and Rebecca and her father followed behind. When one reached for the small brass chest that Mr. Bennett was carrying, he quickly snatched the chest away from the steward's reach.

"No! I'll carry this myself, thank you."

"Do you see? Do you see, Papa? I believe you have gone quite mad! How could you be so careless as to carry every single dollar we have in the world in that one little chest? And in gold, too!" Rebecca sighed with exasperation and shook her head.

"Hush, child," said Mr. Bennett, "do you want everyone to know about it? Keep your voice down. That's why I'm carrying it myself, to keep it safe."

"Safe!" she whispered. "Bank notes would have been safe, Papa!"

"That's enough, Rebecca. We discussed this before we ever left Savannah. You know I don't trust banks. Banks can fail. Why, Grandfather Bennett himself lost everything -"

"-everything when a bank failed," finished Rebecca, sighing. "Yes, Papa, I know, you've told me that story a hundred times. But isn't carrying gold more dangerous, Papa?"

"You may be twenty years old, but you know nothing of these matters, my dear. Leave all that to your papa. The money is quite safe, I assure you. No one knows I'm carrying almost thirty thousand dollars in gold in this one little brass chest. Why, for all they know, I might have my shaving kit in here, or my shoe polish."

He patted the small chest and tucked it more firmly into the crook of his arm. "It'll be quite safe, my dear. Now I'm going to my cabin and lock it up securely in the trunk, and I'll meet you in the dining salon for supper, all right? Got a kiss for your old papa?"

Rebecca smiled ruefully, but gave him a peck on the cheek, then reluctantly followed a steward to her cabin on the second deck, the ladies' deck.

Every cabin door opened onto a large area designed specifically for the comfort of the female passengers. Rebecca discovered with a satisfied smile that the steamboat had much finer accommodations than the ship that brought them from Savannah to New Orleans.

In her room she had a wonderful view of the Mississippi River from a small window set just above the bed. A large calendar hanging near the door showed March, 1853. Rebecca peeled off the top page to reveal the next one, then put her finger on today's date, April 5. She pressed her fingernail firmly against the thin paper, making the impression of an X. It was a small way of leaving her mark here, on this boat that was taking them to a new life, and it was also her birthday.

"Rebecca Bennett stayed in this cabin on April 5, 1853, on her twentieth birthday," she murmured aloud, surveying her surroundings. The small cabin, while comfortably furnished, was stifling in the afternoon heat. She tried to open the window to let in fresh air, but it was stuck. The trip from New Orleans to Natchez would be much, much shorter than the voyage from Savannah, so she unpacked only a few things from her trunk.

It was a pity that Oliver Sebastian had not met them in New Orleans as arranged, to accompany them on the last leg of their journey. As yet neither Rebecca nor her father had met the man. Now that the trip was finally nearing its end, she was as anxious as her father to find out more about Natchez and the cotton farm and the new life he had promised her.

She left her cabin and ventured outside to stroll the deck, watching the activity around her with interest. Her father might be mad, with his idea of buying a cotton plantation, but at least she was seeing that there was more to the world than just Savannah, Georgia, and more for him than just a mercantile store. She had never seen him so excited about a prospect as he was about buying the farm in Natchez.

Until last month, Henry Bennett had been the owner and proprietor of a small mercantile store near the docks in Savannah. Bennett Mercantile had done a good business in that particular spot for many years, but now all the old businesses were gone, the buildings taken over by warehouses.

Since the sudden death of Rebecca's mother ten years ago, Mr. Bennett was concerned more and more about providing a secure future for his daughter. A mercantile store was good enough for him, and for his father before him, but then the business was quite successful in those early days.

Lately it was getting harder and harder to make ends meet. Most of the other businesses had moved farther inland, toward the center of town, and the empty buildings that were left were turned into warehouses.

Then came the offer from a group of local warehouse owners, seeking to expand their storage space near the docks. Mr. Bennett was offered a very handsome price for his building, and when he realized why they needed the extra warehouse space, his plan began to materialize.

Cotton! Bales and bales of it! Hundreds of thousands of bales of cotton arriving every year from the multitude of plantations in Georgia and the surrounding states, to be loaded onto ships bound for New England or to any number of ports in Europe.

The warehouses adjoining Mr. Bennett's property, once thriving businesses like his own, were now literally packed with millions of dollars worth of white gold. Cotton farming was by far the most profitable enterprise in which a man could engage, and fortunes could be made almost overnight.

Mr. Bennett didn't have to give it much thought. With his store fast becoming surrounded by cotton warehouses, and business virtually non-existent, the money that he could raise from selling the building and contents just might enable him to purchase his own cotton farm. That might be the opportunity, at last, to offer his daughter all the comforts of wealth that the mercantile store was unable to provide.

Standing on the deck of the steamboat, Rebecca thought of her life in Savannah as very far away. When Mr. Bennett explained to her that a cotton plantation could make them very wealthy, and therefore attract a suitable husband for her, Rebecca had been mortified. If a husband had to be bought and paid for, then she wanted no part of it!

Besides, she was not in any hurry to become a wife, not after the heartbreaking and disastrous results of her one and only engagement. Betrayal and abandonment were now linked in her mind with the word "marriage". She had taken care of her father since the age of ten, when her mother had died unexpectedly and left them to their own devices. She would be happy to live with him the rest of her life.

But Mr. Bennett had had other plans. He had accepted the offer made by the warehouse owners, sold the building and its contents, and began to inquire about purchasing land.

It was then that he had learned about Oliver Sebastian of Liverpool, who was giving up cotton farming and returning to England, and wanted to sell a plantation that he owned in Natchez.

Mr. Bennett had quickly sent word to Mr. Sebastian and asked him if he would be good enough, if the property was not yet sold, to give him next option.

Mr. Sebastian had answered that the property was still available, the plantation was fully-equipped and highly successful, and he would be happy to oblige Mr. Bennett, but he was rather pressed for time, so could Mr. Bennett visit the farm as soon as possible?

Thus it was that they found themselves on the final leg of their journey, docked at New Orleans aboard the steamboat Sentinel, bound for Natchez, Mississippi, and a new life.

Rebecca now was caught up in the excitement as she watched the final passengers boarding, some with children, most with servants or slaves. Each one had an air of importance, as if knowing that these were times of change, that they were all a part of the fabric of history in the making.

Beneath her feet the deck began to tremble slightly as the boat's great engines roared and boilers filled with steam which would serve as the fuel to propel them upriver. Very smoothly, as if barely moving at all, the huge steamboat began to edge its way clear of the dock.

Rebecca watched as passengers on deck waved good-bye to loved ones on shore, and wished she had someone to wave to. When they left Savannah, there was only her father's lawyer to see them off. No family waved goodbye. No young man came running up to the ship declaring his undying love for her and demanding that she stay and become his wife. There was nothing, really, to hold them in Savannah.

So it was not difficult, despite her protestations to her father, to wave good-bye to the old life and to embrace the new.

Excitement began to rise in her, tempting her to raise her arm and wave, too. No one would know that she was not waving at anyone in particular, only waving because she felt like it.

She caught a glimpse of a tall man in a dark suit and hat, a very striking figure, running up to the edge of the dock. Could she wave at him? The thought made her smile.

Was it all right to flirt if the object of the flirtation was unaware of it? It was safer that way. It allowed her to have romantic notions and thoughts about men without risking being hurt or embarrassed.

She watched as the man frantically waved both arms, apparently trying to get the attention of someone on the boat. Failing that, he turned and began running down the dock as the Sentinel pulled slowly away from the wharf and began to turn her bow upriver. Rebecca quickly walked around the deck to the opposite side, curious to see what would happen.

Yes! There he was, making some expressive gestures to a man in a small flatboat, gesturing toward the steamboat. He reached into a pocket and handed the boatman something, at which the boatman tipped his cap and helped him aboard.

By now the Sentinel was out into the main part of the river and moving upstream at an accelerating pace. Rebecca watched as the flatboatman began to row his boat out toward the Sentinel, and suddenly she realized that the gentleman in the dark suit was actually racing to catch the steamboat before it got away.

The crew and passengers, watching from the deck, started up a cheer to urge the man on.

But the Sentinel was fast gaining headway, and the flatboat was falling behind. In desperation the gentleman picked up another pair of oars from the bottom of the flatboat and began rowing for all he was worth, straining muscles bulging underneath his dark coat.

Even from that distance, Rebecca could see the strength in those long arms, those broad shoulders. With both of them rowing, the small boat began to come alongside the steamboat, nearer and nearer.

The crowd on deck cheered them on. Other passengers on board heard the commotion and hurried over to see what all the excitement was about.

"What's happening?"

"That fellow appears to be trying to catch this boat!"

"He'll never make it, we're moving too fast."

"Would you like to place a wager on that? I've got a twenty-dollar gold piece that says he'll make it."

"I'll take that bet. Come on, 'Sentinel', faster, faster!"

Two crewmen from the steamboat threw a rope to the smaller boat but missed, and had to haul it back in before they could try again.

The second time it was thrown, the man caught the rope and began to pull toward the steamboat.

Rebecca joined in as the crowd on deck started chanting "Pull! Pull!"

Several crewmen rushed to help bring the small boat alongside. Now it was close enough to see the man's face, and she caught her breath.

He was by far the most handsome man she had ever seen. A hot flush tingled through her body, and involuntarily she leaned farther out over the rail, as if to get closer to him.

His tall black hat somewhat shaded his eyes, making them appear very dark, but she could see excitement twinkling in them, and something like amusement.

His long black hair brushed in stark contrast against the crisp white of his shirt collar around his neck. A firm jawline and aquiline nose set off a strong chin and full lips to appealing advantage.

The thought that she had almost waved to him, flirted with him, brought stinging heat into Rebecca's cheeks.

But only for an instant, because as she watched, the man suddenly jumped from the smaller boat, hanging on to the rope, and the crewmen began pulling him up.

In their excitement they forgot to pull in unison. The man dangled precariously on the rope.

A gust of wind lifted his hat from his head and threatened to carry it away over the water, but he grabbed it at the last instant and tossed it toward the steamboat.

Rebecca leaned against the rail, and was almost too shocked to react as the hat flew up right to her. But she caught the hat and held onto it, her fingers tingling as she stroked the sleek material.

Without his hat she could see his eyes: they were black, or at least a very dark brown, and they yet twinkled with something very like amusement, the same something that threatened to curve the straight line of his lips into a smile.

The crewmen yanked the rope again, and for one heart-stopping moment, the man came dangerously close to being swung into the paddlewheel on the side of the boat. The crowd on deck gasped with horror.

A fraction closer would have meant certain death. But by his own agility he managed to gain the deck safely, and a great cheer from the appreciative crowd went up for him.

He smiled brilliantly, as if the whole ordeal had been immensely entertaining.

Rebecca was crushed against the railing as the crowd gathered closer to the mysterious man. Then suddenly she felt warm, strong hands grasping hers as she held the hat tightly and she looked up into those same fascinating dark eyes.

For a long moment the man looked at her, smiling, then nodded a silent thank you. Taking his hat from her reluctant fingers he swept her the lowest, most elegant bow Rebecca had ever seen.

The crowd applauded his achievement as he shook hands with the crewmen in thanks for their help and waved good-bye to the flatboatman who was already far away as the steamboat gained speed and left New Orleans behind.

The man was lost to her sight as the crowd gathered around him, with much backslapping and handshaking. She craned her neck to see over their shoulders, but she was just too short. In another moment, most of the men in the group entered the bar, no doubt to buy the handsome, brave young man as many whiskeys as he could swallow.

Rebecca stood at the rail, staring at the river and listening to the slosh-slosh of the paddlewheel, feeling something that she had not felt in a very, very long time: an attraction to a man.

It frightened her, actually. Old memories that she had tried so hard to forget intruded upon her thoughts. She had believed herself to be cured of romantic inclinations after the incident with Samuel. Now this dashing figure had reawakened those long-forbidden desires.

When would she find the man who was right for her? Was there a man anywhere in the world who would love her and cherish her as she was? Her father was persuaded that a large dowry would lure the proper match, but Rebecca had serious doubts about that. Besides, even a dowry wouldn't make amends to a husband for receiving a wife who was not as pure as she should be.

She naively expected that when she fell in love, birds would sing and rainbows would appear. That had not happened because she had not yet fallen in love. When the right man came along, the world would be perfect, and the deep yearning in her heart would be put to rest.

But where was he, this perfect man? She had waited all her life for him. As inexperienced as she was in matters of the heart, she realized just how foolish it would be to accept a marriage proposal that would provide her with security, no doubt, but not a hint of passion.

But it was passion, she reminded herself bitterly, that hadled to her downfall. She had thought she was in love, once. Samuel had been a fine young man with excellent prospects in a local Savannah bank. He'd been rather attractive, and had easily turned Rebecca's head to fanciful notions of marriage and a future together. Mr. Bennett had not objected to the alliance because Samuel was from a good family and was making his own way in the world. Besides, he would not have denied his daughter any happiness that she desired.

An old, unforgettable bitterness washed over Rebecca as she clutched at the railing of the steamboat, her knuckles white from the pressure. Although she had talked to her father about marrying Samuel, it was never officially announced. On the night that Samuel had asked her to set a date, she'd happily began making plans. Samuel had been so glad that he ordered a bottle of wine to celebrate.

And then ordered another bottle, and another. When Samuel insisted that she prove her love for him, to "seal the bargain" as it were, she'd been young and naive and intoxicated enough to go along with him. After all, he was to be her future husband. How could she deny him anything now, when marriage was just a formality?

Tears welled up in Rebecca's eyes, but didn't spill. She had cried all she was going to cry over Samuel. What a rogue he had turned out to be! After giving in to his persuasive urging, after having intimate relations with him before marriage, after giving herself completely to him, he had disappeared without a trace.

She had wanted to think him gentleman enough to be so ashamed of his behavior that he couldn't bear to face her. But if he were a real gentleman, she thought, he would have married her because of it. Rebecca would always believe that he had run away because he had finally gotten what he wanted. He had never wanted her as his wife. All that talk of marriage had been just a ruse, just a way of coercing her into giving Samuel what he really wanted. And once he had had that, there had been nothing left of the relationship.

She had been so ashamed that she hid herself away in her room for nearly a month, ashamed to face her father's questions, ashamed to admit that she was lying when she explained that Samuel had left to go find his fortune in the California gold mines.

The truth was that she didn't have a clue what became of him. She never saw or heard from him again. Ruined and unfit for anything but becoming an old maid, Rebecca had decided then that she would never marry, that she would carry on as usual, and take care of her father for the rest of his life.

That was the reason why all this talk about a dowry and a proper match only increased her unease. She had never told her father what happened between Samuel and herself. She simply let him think that his daughter had changed her mind about the young man, which was certainly her right. She would rather die than to have her father know the truth.

But her father was determined that she would find the right man and be happily married and raise a family of her own. If fortune and social position would help further that conclusion, then he would do everything in his power to help her.

Although she tried to put all thoughts of romance out of her head, Rebecca still yearned in her heart for something she considered out of her reach. Time might eventually heal the wound that Samuel had inflicted on her, but she believed in her heart that only another man, the right man this time, could heal her heart completely. Hiding away from men was not the solution, was not what she truly wanted.

It would take an extraordinary man to capture her heart, however. When she said yes to a man, he would not be a milquetoast bank clerk. He must be someone daring, and brave, and a little reckless. Someone who could hold her in his arms and make her heart soar. Someone like the heroes she had read about in popular books. Someone like the handsome stranger who had very nearly missed the boat.

Yes. Someone like him.

She could not get him out of her mind. He was nearly killed in the paddlewheel but laughed about it. Was life such a grand adventure to him? How she wished she felt the same!

Maybe she did, in her heart of hearts. Her simple, sheltered existence in Savannah had offered little excitement. After Samuel's disappearance, she had kept to herself. She had felt more excitement just watching that handsome man catch up with the boat than she had on the entire journey, and she yearned for more.

Her eyes lit up with the thought that, at any rate, he was now on board. To think that she had wanted to spend another day or two in New Orleans, waiting for Oliver Sebastian! Why, if they had, she would never have seen this man, might never have known that such men even existed.

Perhaps he would be going as far as Natchez.

Perhaps she might see him again, maybe even at supper.

Rebecca returned to her cabin, stopping in the ladies' salon for a cool drink of water from the huge, ornate silver water cooler that stood on a marble-topped table in the center of the floor. There were silver drinking cups attached to it by chains, and she filled one of these from the spigot.

The water was slightly yellow but delightfully cool, and had a sort of sweet, nutty taste that she found to her liking. She filled the cup again and drank.

Several ladies in the salon were talking about the tall man in the dark suit who had given them all such a thrill. More than one of them remarked, with a little laugh, upon his fine form and good looks, and as Rebecca went into her cabin, she silently agreed with them.

Perhaps the possibility of seeing him again was what prompted her to put on her loveliest gown, a peach-colored confection of dainty floral print with lace at the short sleeves and a rather daring décolletage. She piled up her long honey brown hair into cascading curls decorated with peach ribbons and hoped Mrs. Palatino was right when she said the color would set off her ivory complexion and vivid green eyes.

Since leaving Savannah, she had worn nothing but plain, serviceable suits and gowns. There had been no reason to dress up, her father being her only male company on the long trip. Now, however, things might be different.

It might be time, at last, to stretch her wings, to start experiencing some of the things that up to now she had only read about, or dreamed about. She was no longer a schoolgirl. She was a woman, a woman full of passion and love and no one to bestow them upon. Samuel wasn't the only man in the world, she reminded herself. Maybe she was ruined for ever finding a proper husband, but she was not dead yet, not by a long sight.

Secretly she wanted to live the life of one of the heroines in those popular novels, falling in love with such a man as the world had never seen. But so far the only male attention she enjoyed came, in the main, from her father.

But what if her luck should change? What if her prayers were being answered even now? She must be ready.

When she found her father waiting for her at the entrance to the dining salon, the look of appreciation on his face was gratifying.

"My dear, you look exquisite! But, er..." Mr. Bennett looked disapprovingly at her daring décolletage, but she squeezed his arm before he could protest, and implored him to introduce her to the men who were with him.

"Oh, yes, Mr. Patten, Mr. Greenfield, and Mr.-"

"Latimer," supplied that one, as he swept Rebecca a short bow.

"Latimer, yes. Gentlemen, my daughter, Rebecca."

She smiled her most charming smile. Patten and Greenfield seemed to be about her father's age, but Latimer was younger, perhaps in his thirties. The older two seemed like friendly gentlemen, but this Mr. Latimer made her uncomfortable under his gaze, which she could only describe with a word she had read in one of those novels: lecherous.

More than once she caught his eyes glued to her bosom, and unconsciously she fluttered a hand there, clutching at the fabric that should have been there but wasn't, and thinking that perhaps she had made a mistake. Perhaps she was not as ready to experience life as she thought.

She should have had a coming out. It was her own fault that she hadn't. Her father had wanted to give her one, of course, a great, wonderful party when she turned eighteen, to announce her arrival into the adult world. It was Rebecca who had insisted that she really didn't feel comfortable having a debut, especially after the disaster with Samuel.

Her mother was not there to help, and although her father was as kind and generous as one could wish in a father, she didn't want to put that burden on him. Boots and yard goods he knew, but young ladies and their debuts were beyond his expertise.

So she had missed that important event in every young girl's life. Even harboring her horrible secret, if she had had a debut, perhaps she might now be a bit more socially astute, more confident, more outgoing. She might be a young woman of twenty, who had experienced more than most unmarried girls of her age, but Latimer's unsavory glances brought home to her all the more sharply just how unsophisticated she was.

Mr. Bennett suggested that they all go in to supper, and to her dismay Mr. Latimer offered her his arm. There was no way around it. They must all dine together.

She accepted his arm and allowed him to escort her to an empty table, where he seated her between her father and himself.

Immediately whiskeys were ordered, and from her father's rather flushed face, Rebecca guessed that this was not the first whiskey for him since he had come on board.

"Tea for me, please," she told the steward.

Mr. Bennett and his companions talked amiably, and Rebecca was glad for his sake that he was making some new friends.

But Latimer, she noticed, seemed more interested in her than in cotton farming.

He kept asking her silly questions and "accidentally" touching her whenever possible in a way that repulsed her. Latimer's blue eyes seemed cold as they raked over her. Somehow she had taken an immediate and irreversible dislike to him, and avoided his talk and his touch as much as possible.

Rebecca looked around, pretending to be interested in her fellow passengers. Really she was avoiding Latimer, and also trying to catch a glimpse of that handsome man in the dark suit for whom she had so carefully dressed. It was wasted on Latimer, that was certain.

Suddenly her attention was drawn, captured, and held by a force that seemed almost physical.

He stood in the doorway, tall and handsome, surveying the crowd. Rebecca's heart leaped again as it had done at first sight of him. She could not have explained it if her life depended on it, but she was drawn to him almost magnetically.

The boat's purser stood at his side, and they both appeared to be searching the crowd. The other passengers noticed him, too, for suddenly a great cheer went up, in obvious appreciation for his daring stunt and the entertainment it had provided for them.

The man smiled and gave them a short but elegant bow.

"Eh?" muttered Mr. Bennett as he turned to see. "Is that the fellow, there?"

When her father turned to look, Rebecca saw the purser point directly to him and say something in the man's ear. The man nodded his thanks, and to her amazement began to walk in their direction.

Her heart began to pound. Surely he would walk on by. What possible reason could he have for stopping at their table?

But he kept coming, and when he saw her she noticed something change in his eyes. A spark leaped between them when first their eyes met. He held her gaze as he came up to the table, and she could not have looked away if she had tried.

"Bravo!" said Patten and Greenfield in unison.

"That was quite some excitement you gave us!" said Mr. Patten.

"Yes, quite!" said Mr. Greenfield.

The man finally tore his eyes away from Rebecca's to give them a short bow.

"So this is the fellow who caught the boat, then. My dear sir," said Mr.

Bennett, rising from his seat, "I did not witness the event myself, but my friends here tell me it was extraordinary. I wish I had seen it, 't'would have been a keen story to tell over a brandy, eh? Won't you join us for a drink so that we might toast your success?"

"Hear! Hear!" said Patten and Greenfield. Latimer sulked. Rebecca held her breath.

"It would be an honor, Mr. Bennett," the man replied.

An uncomfortable lump leaped into her throat. She stared into her empty teacup. The man had spoken in a deep voice with what was unmistakably an English accent. Her head began to spin.

"Eh? What - You know me, sir?" sputtered Mr. Bennett.

"You are Mr. Henry Bennett of Savannah, are you not?"

"Well, yes..."

"Then this must be your lovely daughter, Rebecca."

The blood pounded in her ears. She could not look up. She could not even breathe.

"I'm afraid you have me at a disadvantage, sir."

"I beg your pardon. Allow me to introduce myself. I am Oliver Sebastian."

CHAPTER TWO

Rebecca was astonished, but somehow she had known it all along. While he had spoken only a few words, the English accent gave him away.

"What!" gasped Mr. Bennett. "Why, this is astounding! We thought we had missed you in New Orleans. Well, well, this is a surprise! Please, sit down. Rebecca, my dear, what do you think of this? Isn't it amazing?"

She could not look at him. Surely he must see how flushed her cheeks were.

"Yes," she murmured, "amazing."

"I am very sorry that I was unable to meet you in New Orleans, but I was unavoidably detained. You will forgive me, I hope?" He said the words to her father, but Rebecca had the distinct impression that they were directed at her.

"Of course, of course, think no more of it. Gentlemen, can you believe it? This is the very man I was on my way to meet. Allow me to introduce my friends, Mr. Sebastian."

The other gentlemen were delighted to make his acquaintance, except for Latimer, who seemed to shake hands with him only because the occasion required it. Rebecca could sense an undercurrent between the two men that she didn't understand.

"And of course, my daughter Rebecca."

"My pleasure, Miss Bennett. I believe we almost met, earlier. I must thank you for saving my hat. I'm rather fond of it, you see. Good hats are hard to come by." His voice held more than a touch of amusement, but she knew somehow that he was not mocking her, but rather trying to put her at ease.

However, she was not at ease, not the least bit. Her tongue was stuck to the roof of her mouth. She could say nothing, could not even look up.

"Hats? Yes, indeed, good hats are hard to come by. I must confess," said her father, "that I was expecting a much older gentleman, sir."

"And I must confess," said Mr. Sebastian, "that I was expecting a much younger daughter, Mr. Bennett. Your letters spoke of a daughter, of course, but I rather expected freckles and braids, not a beautiful young lady."

The man had paid her a compliment. Was she supposed to thank him? Her father saved her from having to reply.

"Then we are both surprised, are we not?"

"Indeed we are, sir. I trust your journey was a happy one, Miss Bennett?"

Now she must reply. "Yes, thank you," she murmured, staring at her lap.

"And how did you like New Orleans?" he asked.

Slowly she raised her face to his. The connection between them was undeniable as their eyes met.

But looking him in the eyes somehow made her less anxious. She found something there that welcomed her.

"Actually, Mr. Sebastian, I saw so very little of it that I cannot give you an objective opinion."

He smiled, his eyes twinkling. "Perhaps we could have remedied that if I had known you wished to see more of the city before leaving for Natchez. One day, I would like to show you what you missed."

A shiver went through her, which was not caused by the breeze from the river. Somehow she believed him. She lowered her gaze again.

But he was not so easily daunted. He tried several times to draw her out, to get her to speak to him, to look at him, but she could not. She was quite unable to account for it, but the man upset her extremely.

Not the way Latimer did, to be sure. Nonetheless, she was almost beside herself with feeling, and it confused her down to her toes.

She was not an overly shy person, generally, but this man made her feel conscious of herself in ways she had never felt before.

He paid her flattering little attentions, like passing the sugar for her tea as soon as it was poured, and handing her the salt cellar before she hardly knew herself that she wanted it.

It made her feel wonderful, but also uncomfortable. This was nothing like what she had felt for Samuel. It was all so new and strange to her. She needed time to think about these new sensations.

She was almost glad when supper was over and the gentlemen talked about going to the bar for a game of poker. Mr. Sebastian was pressed to join them for another whiskey. He gave her a long look before accepting the invitation.

Rebecca excused herself and retreated to her cabin.

But she didn't stay there long. Her cabin was still warm from the afternoon heat, and besides, she was so restless that she nearly wore out the carpet, pacing back and forth.

Fresh air was what she needed, she decided, so she left her cabin and went to stroll on deck.

Waves lapped against the steamboat as it pushed gently but firmly upriver. The bow of the boat speared into the current, causing little crested waves on either side to rise and splash with rhythmic repetition.

Fireflies lit up the night, dancing like sprites over the silvery, moonlit river.

The breeze from the water was soothingly cool. Soon she was lulled into a dreamy reverie, broken only by the occasional bangs and clunks as the boat encountered drifting pieces of wood.

For a long time she stood, leaning on the rail, feeling the soft spring breeze on her face, gazing at the water and the reflections cast by the lights of the boat and the full moon riding on the horizon.

"It's a beautiful night, isn't it?"

She turned quickly and saw Mr. Sebastian standing at her side. Her heart did somersaults.

"Yes...lovely."

"I'm glad to see you don't care to be confined to your cabin. Shows an adventurous spirit."

Was he paying her another compliment? "It was too warm," she replied.

He leaned against the rail and stared out over the water. "Look." He pointed upriver. "There's another steamboat headed this way."

She looked in the direction he pointed, but could only see what looked like a tiny pinpoint of light in the darkness far upriver.

"How can you tell it's a steamboat?" she asked, her shyness slowly beginning to fade underneath the growing excitement caused by the close proximity to this fascinating man.

He shrugged. "Just instinct. I've lived on this river for enough years to know when there is a steamboat coming. When the boats are the only available sensible transportation for getting from here to there, you learn to recognize the signs."

She stole sidelong glances at him, noticing how the lights reflecting off the water caused dancing sparks in his dark eyes. It was an appealing effect.

"I don't believe you."

He turned and stared at her in surprise. "What?"

Her self-consciousness was fading quite away, replaced by a heady intoxication.

She repeated, "I don't believe you. It's probably a light on shore somewhere."

He smiled, showing perfect teeth. "You think so? Well, then, would you care to place a small wager on that?"

"A wager? Let me think. Since you are a foreigner, Mr. Sebastian, you cannot possibly know this river like you say you do. Therefore the odds should be pretty heavily in my favor, shouldn't they?"

He grinned. "I learned a long time ago, Miss Bennett, not to judge a book by its cover. Do not underestimate my resolve."

She grinned back. "All right, what shall we wager? As long as it isn't money. Papa keeps all the money, and I haven't a cent. On the other hand, I could use some pin money of my own. How much did you have in mind to wager?"

"You seem pretty sure of yourself," he mused. "Maybe I shouldn't bet with you after all."

"What? Are you afraid that you may be wrong? Come, come, Mr. Sebastian, you're the one who has lived on this river for years. I'm the newcomer. Why back down from a wager you're sure to win?" Her eyes twinkled. She was enjoying this!

His eyes danced over her face. "Very well, then, let's see. If I win, we dispense with the formalities and you must call me Oliver. And if you win, you must still call me Oliver."

She pretended to consider this for a moment, then shook her head. "No, no, that will not do. What sort of a wager is that, Oliver? No, we must think of something else."

He laughed playfully, as if enjoying her particular brand of humor. "All right, Miss Bennett - "

"What! Call me Rebecca, after all, we are on a first-name basis."

"Very well, Miss – er, Rebecca. How about this? If I win, you must have a drink with me."

"Oh, but I don't drink whiskey," she protested quickly.

"Not old enough?" he teased.

"Of course I'm old enough, I'm twenty!"

"I have you beaten by ten years. I'm thirty." He grinned. "Now, back to the wager."

"Yes, by all means...but no whiskey!"

"Well, then, how about champagne? You do drink champagne?"

She meant to say of course! but told the truth instead. "I've never had champagne."

"Then that's my wager. If I win, you join me for a glass of champagne."

"And if I win?"

He smiled. "You won't."

"Really!"

"But to show you what a good sport I am, if you win, you shall name your wager."

"Anything?"

"Anything."

"Now that's the sort of wager I like," she replied mischievously. What was happening to her? She was enjoying this little flirtation!

"I can almost taste the champagne now..." he teased.

But she refused to be baited. Instead she demanded that he show her once again exactly which light he was referring to, so that there would be no mistake.

They watched in anticipation as the light drew nearer and nearer, and grew bigger and bigger. It was becoming apparent that if it was simply a light on shore, as she thought, then it was an awfully bright light.

"Let's call off the bet," he said suddenly.

"Why? Afraid you'll lose?"

"In the ridiculous event that you do win, I'm curious as to what sort of punishment for me you have in mind?"

"What makes you think I would punish you?" she asked.

"Oh, to bring me down a notch, for being so presumptuous as to know a steamboat when I see one. Besides, anyone who has never tasted champagne has no real conception of pleasure."

Her reply was interrupted just then when the Sentinel's whistle blew three short, sharp blasts.

"Listen!"

From a distance upriver came an answering three blasts from another steamboat. The rumble underneath her feet as the big boat slowed made her grab for the rail. Excitement began to rise within her.

"Guess I'd better go tell the bartender to put that bottle of champagne on ice," he said.

"You haven't won yet," she reminded him, but he was gone.

She stared with fascination as the light up ahead turned slowly into one huge spotlight and several smaller lights, revealing another steamboat nearly as large as the Sentinel.

Several passengers crowded to the rail as the other boat came into shouting distance, and people on both boats began to wave and yell back and forth.

The boats passed with only a scant few feet between them. A gentleman on the other steamboat tipped his hat to Rebecca and shyly she waved her hand. There were several remarks passed back and forth to do with weather, destinations, and the condition of the river, along with a few bawdy jokes that made Rebecca blush.

Then almost as suddenly as it had appeared, the other boat disappeared into the night.

"You missed it," Rebecca said as Oliver joined her again at the railing.

"Missed what? Don't tell me," he gasped, "another steamboat just went by?"

"You're impossible!"

"And you're a sore loser." He smiled brilliantly. "Next time maybe you'll listen to me."

"You're the one who wanted to bet."

"Ah! But you see, I only bet on a sure thing. Just like I'm willing to bet that you're going to love champagne."

"Is that a sure thing, too?"

"I believe so, yes."

"Then I am determined to hate it."

He laughed brightly. "You are delightful!"

The way he said that made her knees turn to butter.

She blushed. "Well, where is the abominable stuff?"

"It's on ice. Champagne should be served chilled."

"In that case I shall take it warm, as I shall have all the more reason to despise it."

"Can't wait to taste the only real pleasure you've ever known, eh? Very well, then, come with me and we'll fetch it now."

"You mean...to the bar?"

"I believe that is usually where it is kept, yes."

"But I can't go in there."

He stared at her. "And why not?"

"Because...it just isn't proper, that's why."

"Proper? Oh. Well, in that case, wait here and I shall be right back." He turned and walked down the deck and entered the bar.

She meant to stay there, truly she did, but finally her curiosity got the better of her.

Maybe just a tiny peek wouldn't hurt. She had never been in a bar before. If she were determined to experience more of life, to spread her wings, then she must know about such things.

She moved over to the door and looked in through the glass window. The room was hazy with cigar smoke, and crowded. She saw Oliver talking to the bartender, and just over there was her father, engaged in a game of poker with Patten, Greenfield, and Latimer.

That was nothing new. He had occasionally played poker with his friends back in Savannah.

She was glad that Mr. Bennett was in such good spirits. He was even smoking his pipe, which he did only when he was relaxed. That pipe had been packed away in his trunk since leaving Savannah, so he must be feeling less anxious about the trip now that they had finally met Oliver Sebastian.

There were women in there, too, she noticed, but did not get a chance to examine them closely, as Oliver approached the door with a bottle in his hand.

She moved quickly back to her post at the rail, not wishing to be caught spying.

As Oliver came out of the bar, Rebecca saw that he was not alone. A very pretty red-haired woman was tugging at his arm, as if to invite him to come back inside, but Oliver gave her a crooked smile and shook his head.

The redhead sighed deeply, gave him a sad smile in return, and released him a bit reluctantly. Her gaze followed him as he walked over to Rebecca, then she gave another sigh before going back inside the bar.

"It's not a vintage year," he said, "but it's the best I could do."

He tore the wrapper off the neck and looked at her. "Since you've never had champagne, then I suppose you wouldn't know the correct way to open a bottle?"

"No, how?"

"Like this!" he said, and shook the bottle vigorously.

Suddenly the cork popped off with a loud bang and she feared that the bottle had exploded, because the champagne inside spewed out in a tall, cascading fountain that showered them both. She felt it hit her in the face, and laughed with him at the unexpected champagne shower they received.

He held the bottle at arm's length, and the fountain stopped, but now it was foaming from the neck and falling over his hand.

He took the bottle in his other hand and was about to shake off the champagne when she impulsively grabbed his wet hand and brought it to her lips, eager to have her first taste. She licked his fingers, and the bubbly liquid tickled her tongue.

When she looked up again, smiling with delight, he was staring hard at her.

"You shouldn't have done that," he said huskily.

"W-why not?"

"Because now you have the advantage over me. And that will never do."

He gazed deeply into her eyes and she felt herself becoming a little dizzy as he came closer to her, grasped her by the back of the neck, and pulled her head toward him.

She thought...she was sure he was going to kiss her.

Her eyelids fluttered closed. Then to her utter astonishment she felt not his lips but his tongue as he licked a drop of champagne that had splashed right between her eyes.

"Now we are even," he said, withdrawing his hand.

She was so amazed she could hardly breathe. The spot on her forehead tingled from his touch, sending little shivers all through her body.

"Damn me, I forgot glasses," he said casually as if nothing had just happened.

"Glasses?" she repeated, dazed.

"Of course, we could use my lady's slipper."

"My what?"

"Your slipper. Oh, it's all the rage in Paris. The latest fashion, drinking champagne from a lady's slipper. But I've never tried it myself. What do you think of such an idea?"

"I think it's the most...ridiculous thing I've ever heard," she lied.

He smiled at her. "Then I'll just have to run back for a couple of glasses, won't I?"

"Never mind the glasses. Let's just drink from the bottle, shall we? I am anxious to have my first taste of the only real pleasure I have ever known," she teased.

"You've already had that," he said, and the smoldering look he gave her sent fresh, tantalizing shivers wracking through her body.

CHAPTER THREE

Oliver offered the bottle to Rebecca and she took a sip. The bubbly wine fizzed on her tongue and tickled going down. It had a pleasant, rather sweet taste. She took another sip. "I like it!"

He laughed. "I was sure you would."

"But I thought champagne was supposed to be for special occasions, like christening ships or something."

"Well, isn't this a special occasion?"

"What do you mean?"

"I mean, this is your first steamboat trip, and your first time on the Mississippi, and your first visit to Natchez, and...what else?"

My first love? she thought, and blushed fiercely. This was no storybook hero, this one was flesh and blood. She could, she realized with a tingle of excitement, very easily fall in love with this man.

"My first bottle of champagne?"

"Right!" he exclaimed. "That's as good a reason as any. Here's to your first bottle of champagne! May it be the first of many!"

He took a healthy swallow, then offered the bottle to Rebecca.

"I'll drink to that," she said as she accepted the bottle and took another, larger sip.

They continued to toast the river, the night, the driftwood, the moths and other insects incessantly buzzing around the lamps on the boat, until finally they toasted the last drink left in the bottle, which they very companionably shared.

"I think I like this thing called champagne," Rebecca said as she took the empty bottle and held it bottom up over her tongue. One drop fell, she swallowed, then the final drop left in the bottle dangled precariously on the rim, and she licked it, rolling her tongue over it until not a single bit of the liquid remained.

"I can't imagine why I never tried this before, it's delicious. Thank you." She tossed the empty bottle into the water and watched it float away.

"You really are very special, do you know that?"

"How do you mean?" she breathed.

"I've never known anyone who could draw so much pleasure from a simple bottle of champagne."

"Oh, well, it's all your fault, you know. You said it would be the only real pleasure I've ever known, remember? You insisted. As a matter of fact," she continued, the bubbly wine and the ease with which they flirted with each other making her a bit reckless, "I believe you manipulated me into that wager. You knew that there was another steamboat coming all the time, didn't you?" She laid a hand on his arm. "Was it your intention to get me intoxicated and take advantage of me?"

Before the words were out of her mouth, she realized she had not meant to say that. Yes, she was flirting with him, and in a brazen fashion, but she wished she could take back the words.

He gazed at her with smoldering eyes. "I assure you the wager was entirely legitimate. As for getting you intoxicated, yes, I will take responsibility for that. But as for taking advantage of you..."

She waited with held breath.

"I assure you, Miss Bennett, that I am a gentleman. I have not the slightest intention of doing anything of an unseemly nature, regardless of how I may be tempted or... invited."

"Invited?" Why was he speaking to her in that way? And why had he called her Miss Bennett? "I - I didn't..."

"I was only trying to make up for not meeting you and your father in New Orleans, and to pass a pleasant evening. Nothing more. If I gave you the impression that I had designs on you, then I must apologize for that. Since you and your father are travelling alone, I only thought to keep you occupied until we reach Natchez. Now have I made myself clear?"

His words struck her almost physically, and his dark eyes had turned stormy.

"Yes, of course. I'm sorry, I didn't mean -"

But the smoldering passion was still there in his eyes. He grasped her by the shoulders and crushed her body to his, a movement that sent a plethora of mixed emotions through her.

"Is this what you want?" His lips crashed down on hers in a savage kiss that jarred down to her toes.

"And this?" His mouth sought and found the soft underside of her jaw and ravaged the skin from there down to the neckline of her gown, sending mixed shivers of delight and fear through her body.

When his mouth reached the soft mounds of flesh barely concealed by fabric, he found her cleavage and explored that crevice with his tongue.

Rebecca moaned from the depth of her being. This was beyond anything she had ever known, beyond anything she could have imagined. Her fingers tangled themselves in his hair, silky to her touch. Her senses reeled. Maybe it was the champagne, or maybe it wasn't, but Rebecca wanted more of this fascinating man.

An inarticulate sound came from his throat as he jerked his head up and glared fiercely at her. "Did that satisfy you, or do you need more?"

She answered his question by pulling his head toward hers, until their lips met in sizzling desire. Her head spun wildly and she made small moans of pleasure. Oliver suddenly broke the kiss, looking at her in astonishment. His breathing was ragged. "What have you done to me, you sorceress?" he whispered. "Do you need to know just how much I desire you? Does this tell you anything?"

With that he placed a hand in the small of her back and pulled her firmly to him, molding their bodies together.

At first Rebecca didn't fully understand him, until he moved his thigh against hers, and she could feel a rock-like presence of another sort. When realization dawned, she blushed a fiery crimson, her eyes wide in amazement.

He noticed her discomfort and suddenly released her, staring unbelievingly at her for a long moment. His tone was conciliatory when he said, "I'm sorry...I thought...but you've never known a man, have you?"

Rebecca couldn't speak. How could she tell him the truth? The truth wasn't so cut-and-dried, so black-and-white. She had known a man, once. But she had never, never known a man like Oliver Sebastian. She shook her head slowly.

He raked a hand through his glossy black hair. He seemed almost as embarrassed as she. "I feel like a fool. Please, please, can you forgive me?" he pleaded.

"There is nothing to forgive, Mr. Sebastian. Think no more of it." Her calmness surprised her as much as it did him. Inwardly she was a wreck, but outwardly she displayed cool control in the face of heated passion.

His dark eyes went soft. "Then there is no more to be said?"

Oh, there is plenty more to be said, she thought to herself, but only replied, "No."

He sighed deeply. "You will forgive me, I trust, but I feel the urgent need to stroll around the boat and...cool down."

She nodded slowly. "I think it is time I retired to my cabin. It must be very late and the night air has turned brisk. Thank you for the champagne. I shall see you tomorrow?"

"Of course. We should reach Natchez around mid-afternoon. Until then."

He bowed deeply to her, turned, and walked away.

Deep in thought, Rebecca watched until he was out of sight. This was all very strange to her. Of course she had been kissed before, but never had she felt this kind of passion for a man. Oliver had fanned a spark within her into a raging fire, one that could quickly, she realized, get out of control.

She desperately needed someone to talk to, someone to give her some advice and an explanation of what was happening to her. Her father loved her very much, but he could not possibly understand.

She shook her head, as if to shake off the odd feelings that engulfed her, but to no avail.

She turned to go back to her cabin, when she saw her father and his friends just coming out of the saloon.

"Rebecca! My dear, what are you doing out here so late? You'll catch your death of cold. You should be in bed asleep," said Mr. Bennett as she joined them.

"Yes, Papa, I was just on my way, but I needed some fresh air first. Has the poker game broken up?"

"Oh, no, not yet. We just came out to stretch our legs. This young whippersnapper Latimer, though, has taken my last dollar from me. How did I know he would have four jacks, eh? I was betting on a flush. How can one man be so lucky, eh, Latimer?"

Latimer smiled, and pulled something from his vest pocket.

"Well, now, I like to think that it's because I carry this here good luck charm."

"Charm? What have you got there?"

"Just a little old possum's foot, that's all. But I reckon it has brought me good luck. Yessir, real good luck."

Latimer held up the object and Rebecca gasped. It was the most hideous-looking thing she had ever seen.

"I was damn near to starvin' once, when this little old possum come strollin' right up to my camp, and so I cut off this foot to carry with me for good luck. I reckon it works, too. I didn't starve, and I'm mighty lucky at cards."

Rebecca averted her eyes. She disliked this man even more, if that was possible.

"Well, you may have something there. It's certainly brought you good luck tonight, at any rate. Now if you gentlemen will excuse me, I must go to my cabin for some more money. And more pipe tobacco, too. Damn me if I'm not having the best time in years, even if I am losing. But I warn you, Latimer, I shall play more carefully now that I know you've got some sort of charm working for you. Good night, my dear."

"Good night, Papa," she said, kissing him on the cheek. "Don't stay up too late, please? We have a big day tomorrow."

"Just like her mother," muttered Mr. Bennett to his friends as Rebecca turned away. She could hear their laughter as she walked away toward her cabin.

Just then she felt a hand touch her elbow.

"Might I have the pleasure of walkin' you to your cabin, Miss Bennett?"

said Latimer. "It ain't fittin' that a young lady should be walkin' these decks alone this late at night, especially a beautiful young lady like yourself. You never know what kinda rogues and rascals you might run up against."

"Yourself, for example, Mr. Latimer?" she remarked archly.

He laughed. "Now, Miss Bennett, if I didn't know better, I'd think that was a mighty unkind remark. But I like my women with a little spunk, I sure do."

Rebecca cringed at the touch of his hand on her elbow, but the easiest way out of the situation was simply to let the man walk her to the ladies' salon and then say a firm good night. She could not put a finger on why, but she did not like him, not at all.

As they reached the upper deck, the steamboat suddenly blew a long shrill blast on its whistle and the rhythm of the paddlewheel slowed to a near stop. The boat began to edge nearer to shore, and Rebecca could see a group of lights on land. "What's happening?"

"Probably just pullin' over to wood up. Nothin' to worry about."

"Wood up?" she repeated.

He grinned. "This must be your first steamboat trip, if you don't know what wood up means."

"Yes, as a matter of fact, this is my first trip," she replied almost angrily.

"All it means is that the boat is pullin' over to buy some more wood to burn in them big furnaces to make them boilers boil and make steam to make this thing run. That's all. She cain't carry more than a few cords of wood at a time, and that don't last hardly no time. There'll be a few more of these here stops along the way before we make it to Natchez."

"How did you know that my father and I are going to Natchez?" she asked warily.

"Why, Mr. Bennett told us all about the cotton farm and all. Said he was aimin' to get filthy rich so as to provide you with a decent dowry to get you hitched. Why, shucks, Miss Bennett, I'd take you without a cent."

Obviously he meant it as a compliment, but Rebecca could only shudder at the thought. So her father was telling everyone that he had to get rich to get her married off in fine fashion! How humiliating!

The boat had come to a complete stop alongside the shore and now Rebecca could see a great storeyard of cut wood, cords and cords of it, and a man standing near a small floating dock.

"Now listen and you'll hear the captain say, got any wood for sale? and that old man over there will say, reckon it's possible. Listen."

Rebecca waited, and sure enough, from the pilothouse above, she heard a loud voice call out, "Got any wood for sale?"

The old man on shore looked over at the mountains of wood, spat into the river, and replied, "Reckon it's possible."

The captain yelled, "How do you sell it a cord?"

The old man answered, "Two dollars."

"Two dollars! That's a dollar a cord too much."

The old man spat again. "When you gets me out of bed this time of night, you pays premium."

As Rebecca watched, several deckhands and crewmen and even what appeared to be passengers disembarked at the floating dock and began to haul wood by the armful onto the boat, to be stored in an empty area near the engines.

"Are those passengers helping to load wood?" she asked. "Why do they do that?"

"Oh, just to stretch their legs and get in a bit of strong exercise," Latimer replied. "On a long trip, a boat can be mighty confinin', and sometimes a man just natural has to do something physical to take his mind off of...things..." He glanced at her bosom.

Rebecca thought of Oliver, taking a stroll around deck to "cool down", and couldn't control a secret smile. Luckily, Latimer did not notice it.

"It's sorta the way things are done, gettin' off to help load wood, I mean. And it speeds up the trip. The more hands, the better. But it's also a good way to sneak on board without payin'."

"What do you mean?"

"I mean a fella could hide in the woodpile and wait for the next steamboat, which wouldn't be a very long wait, I can tell you that. Anyway, he would wait and when one stopped to wood up, commence to haulin' wood with the passengers and crew, then go on board as if he'd been there the whole time. No one ever notices, especially at night."

"You sound as though you speak from experience, Mr. Latimer."

"Well, let's just say I've known it to be done."

For several minutes the loading continued, until not another inch of storage space for the wood could be found. The captain himself went on shore and paid the man, then reboarded the boat. Presently the paddlewheel began to turn again, slowly edging the huge vessel away from the shore and into the main channel.

Latimer escorted her to the entry to the ladies' salon, his hand never leaving her elbow, until finally she turned to him and held out her hand. "Thank you, Mr. Latimer. I can manage from here."

She only wanted to get his hand off her elbow. But he took her outstretched hand and brought it to his lips, in what he thought was a gallant gesture, kissing it with much more relish than she liked.

"Are you sure you don't want me to see you to your cabin, Miss

Bennett? That there poker game won't take up again for a little while, so I've got some time to kill. How about let's you and me go to your cabin and - "

"No!" she nearly shouted, extricating her hand from his grip. "No, thank you, Mr. Latimer, it is late and I am going to bed."

He grinned, showing bad teeth. "Well, now, since you mention it, that there is just what I had in mind. Come on now, honey, be good to ol' Harvey, and ol' Harvey will be good to you."

Brazenly he put a hand on her bosom and squeezed one breast. She swatted his hand away in horror. His touch made her skin crawl.

"Good night, Mr. Latimer," she said firmly and moved to retreat toward the safety of her cabin.

Boldly he grabbed her arm and jerked her toward him. She collided against him, nearly losing her balance, and he put his arms around her body and pulled her roughly to him.

"Mr. Latimer, please!" she cried, trying vainly to break free of his grip.

Latimer smothered any further outcries as he smashed his mouth down hard on hers. His rancid whiskey breath almost made her gag. She struggled in his arms, but her protests only seemed to fan the flames of his ardor.

With his left hand he pinned both her wrists painfully behind her back, and with his right hand he began to dig beneath the scanty fabric for her breasts. He was so rough his fingernails scratched her tender skin, doubling her desperate efforts to free herself.

Rage and fear washed over her in shattering waves. Rage was getting her nowhere, he was far stronger than she. Fear eventually won over, as Rebecca was sure this man wanted more from her than a mere kiss and a fumble at her breasts.

Latimer moved forward, shoving her body with his, pressing her on into a small alcove on the upper deck. When she realized this she knew she would be trapped, helpless. There was a small ripping sound as he pulled at her dress.

She couldn't scream. His mouth was still clamped tightly to hers. The dark night and late hour meant there were not many passengers strolling the decks, no one to see her predicament and come to her rescue. Desperately she wrenched away with all her might, and managed to slide her mouth away from his.

"Help—!" was all she got out as he found her mouth again with his own.

"Let her go."

Rebecca's heart leaped with hope when she recognized the British accent.

Latimer took his time releasing her, and slowly turned around to come face to face with Oliver Sebastian.

"And just who's gonna make me?" he sneered.

Rebecca wiped her mouth with shaky fingers and tried vainly to cover her nearly-exposed bosom with the shreds of thin fabric that were dangling where Latimer had ripped her gown.

Oliver glared at the other man and held out his hand to Rebecca. "Are you all right, Miss Bennett?"

Before she could take his hand, Latimer stepped between them.

"Who the hell do you think you are?" Latimer spat, swatting Oliver's hand away from Rebecca.

Rebecca could tell from how his jaw tensed that Oliver was trying very hard to control his fury. Oliver's eyes glittered dangerously as he surveyed his opponent.

"I have no wish to fight with you, Latimer, but I will, if you push me. Now move aside and let Miss Bennett pass."

Latimer stood his ground, hands clenched into fists at his sides. After a moment he chuckled. "What makes you think Miss Bennett here wasn't enjoyin' my attentions? How about it, darlin'. Tell the man to mind his own business."

"Miss Bennett, if this fellow has harmed you in any way –"

"I am perfectly all right, Mr. Sebastian, thank you," she answered quickly. She had no wish to see these two fight. She only wanted the safety and comfort of her own cabin. She shoved her way out of the alcove, past Latimer, who put out an arm to stop her.

He never touched her, because Oliver grabbed his arm and in a swift, smooth movement had turned Latimer completely around, his face smashed into the clapboard siding of the steamboat, his arm twisted at a painful angle behind his back.

"If you bother this young lady again, you'll regret it. I give you my word," Oliver said in a low voice into Latimer's ear. "Now run along before you get into more trouble."

He gave Latimer's arm another painful twist to emphasize his intent, then released him. Oliver held out his hand to Rebecca. "I'll see you safely to your cabin, Miss Bennett."

Latimer turned, nursing his hurt arm, eyes blazing with fury. "I'll kill you, you son-of-a…"

Oliver Sebastian punched him once, hard, in the stomach. Latimer doubled over and groaned in pain.

"That took the ill wind out of him," said Oliver as he again offered his hand to Rebecca. "Come, my dear, you are not experienced enough in the ways of the river to know that it's not safe for you to be out here alone, at night. You will be all right now, I can promise you that."

She believed him. Apparently there was not any occasion that Oliver could not handle, except, perhaps, when he was in her presence, because as she took his hand and moved away from Latimer's writhing, groaning body, she felt him tremble at her touch.

Or maybe it was Rebecca who trembled.

They walked quickly toward the door to the ladies' salon. Oliver opened it, spilling light from inside onto her, showing him the effects of Latimer's "attentions" upon her clothing and face. His expression visibly softened.

"I'll send your father to you. He may want to take action against Latimer himself."

"No!" Rebecca said, a little too quickly. "No, please, I'm all right now. I don't want to upset Papa."

"You've had a rather horrid night, haven't you?" he said in a tone just above a whisper. His eyes searched hers, looking for something.

She managed a thin smile. "I had heard this part of the country was wild. But I never dreamed it would be like this."

He gave her an apologetic grin. "I assure you, not everyone around here is as vile as Latimer. Or myself."

"What do you mean?" she asked, puzzled.

"I mean – " He hesitated. "Miss Bennett – Rebecca - I must apologize for my behavior earlier. I cannot think what came over me. It is all my fault, of course. If I –"

"Oliver," she interrupted. "You just saved me from the Lord knows what. I can never thank you enough. You owe me no apologies at all. It is I who must apologize to you." She squeezed his hand reassuringly. "If the truth be known, it was my fault. You see, I've never known anyone quite like you. You fascinate me in many ways."

A pleased twinkle lit his eyes. "And you fascinate me, Rebecca. I confess I am not myself when I'm near you."

A thrilling wave of pleasure shot through her. Her cheeks flamed. "Perhaps we had better say good night now. I'll be fine in my cabin. There's a lock on the door." She grinned at him.

"If I'm any judge of men, a lock won't deter the likes of Latimer. But as you wish. Good night, Miss Bennett."

"Good night, Mr. Sebastian."

She extended her hand to him, to shake good night, but instead he brought it to his lips and placed a very soft, gentle kiss there. Very gallant, she thought approvingly, and nothing at all like Latimer. Maybe all men weren't alike, after all.

* * *

She should have gone straight to bed. She should have, but she didn't. Somehow she knew sleep would be elusive. After securely locking the door, Rebecca grabbed a woolen shawl from her trunk and wrapped it around her shoulders. The fabric at her breast was in shreds, but she tucked the ragged ends into her corset. She sat down on the bed, her back against the headboard, to think.

Rebecca had no idea what time it was. The night was quiet except for the slosh of the paddlewheel, which she could still hear even in her cabin. She wondered how the steamboat was able to run at night, in the darkness. There were huge lights on the front of the boat, she had seen that when earlier Oliver had pointed out the oncoming boat. But was that enough light to navigate?

She pushed the thought from her mind. She would leave all that to the captain and pilot. That was their job. She had something far more pressing to think about, like her growing feelings for Oliver Sebastian.

It confused her. Rebecca had believed she was immune to masculine charms. After what had happened with Samuel, she had thought she never again would have romantic notions toward a man. She had deliberately subdued that part of her emotions, thinking that she would save herself from any further harm. Now Oliver was reawakening all those dormant feelings, and she wasn't exactly sure she welcomed them.

She feared she would be hurt again. But Oliver Sebastian was a gentleman, wasn't he? Or was he? The way he had acted earlier confused her. But then she had thought Samuel was a gentleman, too, and he had proved her wrong.

At least Oliver hadn't forced himself on her, like Latimer had. She shuddered again at the thought of what might have happened if Oliver hadn't come along when he did. It was men like Latimer and Samuel that made her determined never to trust a man again. But Oliver was different.

Wasn't he?

Rebecca sat on her bed thinking for a very long time. When the night air got cooler and she felt a chill run through her body, she discarded the shawl and changed from the now ruined peach gown into a plain blouse and skirt from her trunk.

Sleep was not an option, not with her emotions so topsy-turvy. She would rather sit up all night than toss and turn in her bed, unable to rest. She paced back and forth in the confines of her cabin, restless and confused. When later she heard the Sentinel's whistle give three short, sharp blasts, she realized that the boat must be pulling over again to take on more wood for fuel.

Rebecca left the safety of her cabin and ventured out once more to the deck. The night air was quite cool, and she wrapped her arms around herself as she stood at the railing, alone, watching as the crewmen worked, loading wood from the woodpile where they had stopped.

Before she even realized what she was doing, she had descended the stairway between decks and was peeking surreptitiously through the glass doors of the bar.

Rebecca's throat closed painfully around a lump that rose unbidden there when she spied Oliver sitting at a table with the lovely red-headed woman she had seen earlier. They were drinking, and talking, and laughing, and the redhead placed her hand intimately on his arm, and squeezed, and smiled brightly into his face. When Oliver smiled back at her, and laughed, and placed his hand over hers, the pangs of jealousy that rose in Rebecca were more than she could control.

She turned quickly away from the bar. She couldn't watch any more. She hadn't even had time to look to see if her father was still there, because after seeing Oliver and the woman together, nothing else mattered.

Rebecca walked blindly to the railing, and clutched it until her knuckles turned white. She didn't hear the man approach until he was by her side.

"Well, Miss Bennett, I shoulda known you wasn't through with ol' Harvey. Back for more, are you?"

She turned and stared at Latimer coldly. He leaned beside her against the railing, and ran a hand over her fingers. She snatched them away.

"Please leave me alone, Mr. Latimer," she told him firmly.

"You ain't got that damned Englishman around to save you now," he said.

The crew had finished loading wood, and the boat began to edge slowly away from the shore.

Suddenly the night air was rent by the shrill blast of the Sentinel's whistle. Rebecca lurched against the railing, grabbing for support, as the steamboat jerked almost to a stop. The whistle kept up its shrill sound in short, sharp blasts.

"What's happening?" Rebecca cried in alarm.

"I don't know," Latimer replied, then let out a frightened gasp. "Oh my God..."

Rebecca looked in the direction where Latimer stared, and to her horror saw, out of the darkness, another steamboat bearing directly down upon them.

The Sentinel had not yet made it away from the woodyard into the main part of the river. Another boat was apparently also stopping for wood. The pilot of that boat had either misjudged the distance or miscalculated the speed at which the Sentinel was moving away from the shore, because the two boats were headed for a collision.

Rebecca bit into her fingers to stifle a scream. The Sentinel's whistle kept up the alarm, trying in desperation to alert the other boat of the danger.

But the current of the river at this place must have been treacherous. She watched with dread as the other boat stopped its paddlewheel and attempted to reverse it, but the current carried the boat relentlessly on.

"We're going to hit!" she cried, clutching at Latimer's arm.

"Sweet Jesus," Latimer whispered. "I'm gettin' outta here!" He peeled her clutching hands roughly from his arm and fled.

Rebecca stared in horror as the other boat loomed closer and closer. She could see frantic crewmen on both boats, running and yelling.

"Get away from the rail!" She heard Oliver Sebastian yell and felt him grab her around the waist. He hauled her backwards and she crashed into his body, nearly spilling them both to the deck.

"If we hit, you'll be catapulted over the rail into the water," he explained as she clung to him, frightened.

Now the boats were within scant feet of each other, and Rebecca could see the pilot of the other boat in the pilot house frantically turning the huge wheel, trying desperately to turn the vessel away from the Sentinel.

The pilot of their own boat did the same thing, turning the Sentinel into the shoreline to keep from colliding with the other steamboat.

Rebecca breathed a sigh of relief as the two steamboats passed harmlessly, with only inches to spare.

"Thanks be to God," she whispered, and looked up at Oliver.

But he was staring dead ahead, and there was no look of relief on his face. His expectant expression brought new fear into her heart.

"Brace yourself," he said tersely and grabbed her so tightly and pulled her body so close to his that he almost knocked the wind out of her.

As much as she relished being held in his arms, she could hardly breathe, and she struggled, but to no avail. He did not loosen his grip, but planted his feet firmly on the deck and held her.

In the next instant, the deck seemed to be snatched from under their feet, and they tumbled wildly through the air. Rebecca clung to Oliver with all her strength, but she needn't have. He held her tight and didn't let go.

They were tossed like toys as the great boat shook. She could hear the sound of glass shattering, and passengers screaming, and wood breaking. Something that felt like sharp nettles scratched across her cheek, but she kept her eyes tightly closed.

A tremendous groan of creaking, breaking wood filled her ears, and after one final violent shudder of the boat, everything was still.

Oliver slowly loosened his grip on her, and Rebecca raised her head cautiously to look around.

Something large and dark loomed right in front of her face, and after a moment she realized it was a tree branch. She could hear the sound of water very close. The deck railing where she had stood moments earlier was now in splinters. A huge tree trunk jutted out from a gaping hole in the deck. The boat tilted at an awkward angle and water rose quickly over the deck.

"W-what h-happened?" she stuttered.

Oliver didn't reply right away, but stood up on the debris-littered deck, pushing the tree limb away to make room, and pulled her up beside him.

"It looks like we ran into a snag near the shore," he answered finally. "Come on. We have to get off now. This boat is sinking."

CHAPTER FOUR

Glass crunched under their feet as Oliver and Rebecca made their way carefully down the deck toward the rear of the boat. They had to shove aside some of the gingerbread trim that had fallen from upper decks, and duck under tree branches that stuck out from the bank of the river.

Rebecca heard screams of pain and fright, and she wondered where her father was. She was all right, with a few scrapes and scratches, but no broken bones. Fervently she prayed that her father was all right too.

People were scurrying frantically in sheer panic. Children cried and women wailed. Rebecca felt like she was in the middle of a chilling nightmare. But when she saw a young slave girl trapped under some fallen rubble, blood covering her face, she knew this was no dream.

Rebecca pulled her hand from Oliver's grip and went to the young girl's aid. She tugged desperately at the wooden beam that had the girl trapped, but didn't have enough strength to budge it. She gasped in horror when she noticed the water that had risen onto the deck and was licking at the hem of her skirt.

"Oliver! Help!" she screamed.

Suddenly Oliver was at her side with a crewman and together they managed to lift the beam just enough for the girl to crawl from under it. In gratitude, the young girl hugged Rebecca around the waist, clinging to her. Rebecca wiped at the blood on the child's face, and noticed an ugly wound at her hairline.

"This girl needs a doctor," she said to Oliver.

"No time for that now," he replied gruffly. "We have to get off this boat or we'll have no need for doctors." He grabbed Rebecca's arm and forced her to follow him. The slave girl clung to Rebecca's skirt.

The boat was tilting crazily now, and water was getting deeper and deeper on the deck. Oliver led her around the end of the boat to the other side, where the other steamboat had pulled alongside. He began helping the frantic passengers of the Sentinel aboard.

Rebecca rushed across the short, narrow gangplank that had been improvised between the two boats, the girl still clutching her around the waist. Once safely on board the other boat, Rebecca sighed with relief when the girl ran into the arms of another black woman, who said a very loud, fervent prayer in thanks for the deliverance of her child.

It appeared that most of the passengers were now on board the other boat. Rebecca scanned the faces in the crowd for her father's, but could not spot him. The captain of the boat was bellowing orders to everyone to move toward the rear. The original passengers of the second boat were all crowded on the decks as well, and all the people at one end of the steamboat made it list dangerously with so much weight.

Crewmen started herding them back toward the rear, and Rebecca reluctantly went with them. But when she saw Oliver running across the gangplank, she thrust her way through the crowd and ran to him.

"Help me find my father," she pleaded. They turned and began to look through the crowd, Rebecca taking one side of the boat and Oliver taking the other.

When they met again at the rear, and neither had found Mr. Bennett, Rebecca's heart lurched in panic. "He must be still on the boat! Oliver! Please! Help him!"

Oliver gave her a quick hug and shoved his way past the passengers, back toward the front. Rebecca followed behind. He dashed across the makeshift gangplank and disappeared around the corner of the dangerously listing Sentinel.

Agonizing minutes ticked by. The river water by this time had nearly covered the lower deck. The boat's purser rushed across the gangplank with a sheaf of papers in his hand, and once aboard, began taking a tally of all the passengers, to be certain that everyone had gotten off.

Rebecca chewed her fingernails anxiously, her eyes glued to the Sentinel, looking for a sign of her father or Oliver. Just when she thought she could stand it no longer, she saw Oliver making his way carefully across the crooked deck of the Sentinel, supporting her father, who looked dazed.

"Papa!" she yelled. Oliver helped the older gentleman across the gangplank and Rebecca rushed to them.

"I'm all right, I'm all right," Mr. Bennett repeated in response to his daughter's pleas.

"He was trapped in his cabin. The door had jammed shut. I had to break the door down to get him out," Oliver said.

Rebecca and Oliver helped him away from the gangplank and sat him down. She began to inspect her father for injuries, but aside from being dazed and a little confused, and a nasty cut on his forehead, he appeared unhurt.

"I'll get a doctor to look at that cut," Oliver said. But Mr. Bennett grabbed his arm and pulled him closer. Oliver had to bend his ear to Mr. Bennett's lips to understand what the man was saying.

"Trunk... Chest... Gold..."

"I don't understand. What does he mean?" Oliver looked at Rebecca.

"The money to buy your farm," she explained. "It's in a little brass chest in his trunk, in his cabin." She looked back at the Sentinel, which was beginning to disappear quickly beneath the dark, murky water of the Mississippi.

She put a fist to her mouth to stifle a sob. Tears welled in her eyes. Bravely, she forced a calm expression on her face. "We're alive, Papa. That's all that matters."

"No!" cried Mr. Bennett with his remaining strength.

Oliver glanced at each of them, then looked at the Sentinel. "I'll do my best," he said simply, and quickly rose and ran back across the gangplank to the sinking steamboat.

"Oliver!" Rebecca cried out, but he paid no heed. Water was now nearly up to his knees over the deck as he rounded the corner and was lost from sight.

The captain, pilot, and last remaining crew members rushed across the gangplank. Rebecca heard the captain telling the crew of the other boat to back it away, quickly, because the boilers were about to blow.

She didn't know exactly what this meant, but it sounded ominous. Nervously she watched for Oliver to reappear. The gangplank was yanked up hurriedly, and the steamboat's paddlewheel turned in reverse, backing slowly away from the Sentinel.

"No!" Rebecca screamed, and flung herself at the crewmen who took up the gangplank. "Oliver is still on board! You can't -!"

She was thrust away, and could do nothing but grip the railing hard and stare at the sinking boat.

Someone pulled at her arm and said something about being checked for injuries, but she pushed them away. Behind her she could hear the pursers of the two boats shouting instructions to the passengers. They would have to double up in the cabins, but there should be enough room for everyone. Those who were not hurt would please do whatever they could for those who were injured.

She heard all this behind her as if it was far in the distance. Nothing mattered now except Oliver. Her gaze swept the boat from right to left, then left to right, looking for him.

All of a sudden one of the boilers on the Sentinel exploded with a mighty boom. The shock sent her toppling to the deck. On her knees, she looked up and saw a huge fireball explode from the steamboat, sending ash, soot, and debris flying through the air. Burning fragments fell into the river, and some fell onto the steamboat. Crewmen and passengers alike rushed to put out the flames.

The Sentinel was now on fire.

"Dear God," Rebecca prayed aloud, "save him! Forget the gold. Just save him."

The paddlewheel stopped turning. The boat was still. Rebecca could no longer hear anything but the beating of her own heart. Her eyes scanned the boat, scanned the water, looking for a sign of Oliver. But there was nothing.

And then, when she thought her heart would break with desperation, she saw his head break the surface of the water just a few feet from her.

Oliver gasped for air, breathing in huge gulps, then slid down below the water again, only to struggle back to the surface for another breath.

"There!" Rebecca yelled and pointed. Crewmen rushed to his aid. One or two jumped into the water to help him, and brought him alongside the steamboat.

Almost fainting with relief, she did not notice the leather strap around Oliver's neck, until one of the crewmen in the water with him tugged it free and handed it to another on board. The small brass chest flashed in the light from the fire.

Rebecca rushed to Oliver's side as he was brought aboard, but she was pushed roughly aside as the crewmen turned Oliver over and began pulling his arms up from behind, between his shoulder blades, pumping water out of his lungs.

"Dear God! Don't let him die!" she cried fervently, watching in horror as Oliver's pale face turned paler. Then suddenly he coughed violently, dirty river water spewed from his mouth, and he gasped for air.

The crewmen rolled him back over, and he lay there, weak and exhausted. Mr. Bennett walked unsteadily toward him, leaned down and placed a hand on his shoulder, and mumbled his thanks. Mr. Patten and Mr. Greenfield, who had escaped any injury at all, came out of the crowd and helped her father to his feet.

"We'll look after Mr. Bennett," one of them said to Rebecca. The other took the brass chest and they both supported her father as they led him away.

Rebecca fell to her knees beside Oliver. She pushed wet hair out of his face, then took his cold, limp hand in hers. He was breathing steadily, but still coughing up water.

"Let's get him into bed," said a female voice. Someone gently took her hand. She looked up and recognized the redhead she had seen earlier with Oliver when he came out of the bar.

Several men gingerly picked up Oliver's limp body and carried him toward an open cabin door.

Rebecca followed. But at the door to the cabin, one of the men put out a hand to stop her. "The doctor will tend him, miss. There's nothing you can do."

She ignored him and shoved her way into the small cabin. Oliver was laid gently on the bed, and extra quilts and blankets were piled on top of him, to keep him warm.

She squeezed into a corner and watched as a doctor came in and examined him. "Let's get these wet clothes off him before he goes into shock," the doctor said, and immediately Oliver was undressed.

She should have averted her eyes, that much she knew, but there was no need. This was not the time for niceties. His bare chest was the same color as his face, pale and ashen. The covers were pulled up to his chin.

"Brandy," ordered the doctor, and someone left to fulfill that request. "Clear this room, and try to keep him warm. Who is she?" asked the doctor as he noticed Rebecca. "Are you his wife?"

She gaped at him. "I – ah – "

"Keep him warm. Get some hot soup into him. Keep him quiet, and he should be all right. I'll check back later."

Rebecca was left alone in the cabin with Oliver.

She had no idea whose cabin it was, but in such an emergency it really didn't matter. She rummaged until she found a clean cloth, then poured water into the porcelain basin and brought them to Oliver's side. She bathed his forehead with the wet cloth, wiping away mud and grime and soot.

He was lucky to be alive, she thought, and gave silent thanks to God.

A crewman brought in a bottle of brandy. She asked for some soup for him, and also asked the man to find out if her father was all right. When he left, she found a glass and poured some of the amber liquid into it, then held it to Oliver's lips, urging him gently to take a drink.

Oliver's eyes had remained closed the whole time. When she finally forced a few drops of brandy into his mouth, he sputtered and coughed and spit the brandy out, along with more brown, dirty river water.

Gently she wiped his lips and chin. Then she made him drink some more. This time it stayed down. After a moment, he slowly opened his eyes. She could tell when they finally focused on her by the expression on his face.

"Rebecca," he whispered faintly. Her spirit leaped. She almost cried with happiness.

"Yes, Oliver, I'm here. You're going to be all right. Just rest."

He sighed and closed his eyes again, briefly, then looked at her. "What happened?"

"You went back for the gold," she explained, "and nearly drowned yourself. You ought to be whipped, you foolish man."

He gave her a weak grin. "Did I... did I get it?"

Her eyes misted. "Yes, you did. Everything is all right now."

"Good," was all he said. His eyes closed, and his breathing became regular and rhythmic as he drifted into sleep.

In a few minutes, someone brought in a bowl of soup and a bit of bread, but Oliver was sleeping so peacefully she didn't disturb his rest. It was reported that her father was fully recovered and doing fine. Apparently there were few injuries incurred during the disaster. They had all been very, very lucky indeed.

The doctor came in again and examined Oliver briefly. "He'll be all right. Just keep him warm and let him sleep."

Rebecca nodded, and when the doctor left, made herself comfortable in a chair. Examining her torn, filthy skirt, it finally dawned on her that all her clothes were gone. Everything was gone. Except the gold. She heaved a heavy sigh of relief. If they had lost the money, too, God only knew what would become of them.

She remembered how disturbed she had been to discover that her father was carrying all that money in gold. He deserved a good dressing-down for his foolishness. It might have been a tragic mistake, for surely it was the weight of the gold that had been such a burden to Oliver Sebastian when he had to swim back to the boat after the Sentinel's boilers had exploded.

Rebecca offered another silent prayer of thanks to heaven. All would be right now. They were alive, the gold was recovered, and clothes could be replaced. She closed her eyes and was soon sound asleep.

But her sleep was disturbed with nightmarish images and sounds, and she thought she could hear Oliver calling her name. She awoke with a start to realize that Oliver was indeed calling her name.

She hurried back to his side on the bed, re-wet the cloth towel and began mopping perspiration from his forehead. Oliver groaned and writhed under the covers, then began shivering violently.

Alarmed, Rebecca pulled the quilts more tightly around his neck, then tucked them in all along the length of his body. The shivers didn't stop. His teeth began to chatter.

"S-so cold..." he whispered.

Quickly she searched the cabin for more quilts, but found none. She flung open the door to see if she could find a crewman or someone to get more quilts, but there was no one in sight just then. What should she do? Should she leave him alone and go get help? What if he needed her while she was gone?

Making up her mind, she closed the cabin door and, on second thought, locked it. Rebecca looked down at Oliver, helpless and quivering, then pulled back the quilts just enough for her to slide into bed next to him.

Remembering something she had read in one of those popular novels, Rebecca wrapped her arms around him and pressed her body to his. His violent shivers shook her as well, but she clung tightly to him. She had read that the quickest way to warm someone was to share body heat.

It was the very least she could do for him. Of course it wasn't the proper thing to do, she knew that. But this was an emergency, and "proper" was the last thing she was concerned with.

For a long time, she held him like that, held him close, their bodies pressed together. Oliver seemed oblivious to her presence, as he groaned and shook with cold. But eventually, his shivering subsided, his body relaxed, and he slept.

Rebecca must have slept a while, too, for the next thing she knew, Oliver was kissing her.

CHAPTER FIVE

Rebecca opened her eyes, and Oliver tenderly kissed her again on her forehead. He gazed at her with tired but clear eyes, and gave her a gentle smile. Then he kissed her again, on the cheek, then on the other cheek, then on her forehead again, then on her nose, which made her giggle.

"Hello, love," he said.

"Hello," she returned, with another giggle. "Are you feeling better?"

"I feel grand," he answered.

"You gave me quite a fright. I thought you were going to come undone, you were shaking so with cold."

"And were you cold? Is that why you're in bed with me?" he asked, grinning wickedly.

She could feel hot color rushing into her cheeks. "N-no. I th-thought I could warm you up with my own body heat."

"You amaze me. Wherever did you learn that?"

"From a novel. You'd be surprised what you can learn from books. And it must work, too, because you stopped shivering."

He sighed. "I thought I was still dreaming when I found you next to me. If it is a dream, please don't wake me." He wrapped his arms around her and pressed his face into her neck, nuzzling her skin gently.

A hot flush rushed over her. The feelings, not just physical but emotional as well, that he incited in her were extraordinarily delicious. She wanted nothing more than to lie in his arms forever.

But the worst was over now. He was better. There was no reason now to continue to lie in bed with him. Besides, the nuzzling at her neck was causing such sweet sensations she was afraid of her own response to him.

Gently she squeezed her hands between their two bodies and pushed on his chest, but he resisted.

"This is my dream," he said, "and in my dream, you don't push me away."

"B-but I was only trying to keep you warm," she protested lightly.

"I'm warm," he replied, again nuzzling her neck and placing soft kisses there. "It worked. It worked too well. I'm not just warm. I'm hot."

Suddenly he moved on top of her, his body stretched the length of hers. He gazed deeply into her eyes. "Thank you from the bottom of my heart. I would gladly risk freezing to death again and again if I knew that you would be there to warm me."

Rebecca smiled a bit nervously. "My pleasure," was all she could think of to say.

"No," he asserted. "Mine."

Then his lips descended on hers in a wonderful kiss that began tenderly but quickly escalated into fiery passion. Rebecca's head began to spin deliriously. She reciprocated when his tongue invaded, and she marveled at the deliciousness she found. Her toes curled, her arms wound around his neck, and she pulled him close, closer. Like a woman dying of thirst, she drank from him.

"Do you know how much I want you?" he whispered against her lips.

"As much as I want you?" she asked, and guided his hand to her breast, reveling in the delicious sensation as he began to stroke gently.

"Oh, God," he groaned. "You don't know how good this feels."

But she did know. Her body was on fire with desire for him. This was nothing, nothing like what had happened with Samuel. She had only wanted to please Samuel. There had been no pleasure in it for her. This was different. She wanted this man.

Slowly she unfastened her blouse, untied the thin chemise underneath. At the sight of her tender, innocent breasts, he groaned again.

She threw her head back against the pillows and savored the thrill of his touch. Expertly his tongue circled the fleshy mounds, drawing ever closer to the rapidly hardening peaks. The anticipation had her clawing at his back, until finally, finally, when she could bear it no longer, his tongue completed the teasing madness and assaulted the nipples, capturing them fully, in turn, until she moaned with pleasure and began to writhe beneath his body.

Oliver lifted her skirt. Through the thin fabric of her undergarments, she suddenly felt his hand exploring the delicate area between her thighs. She gasped as his thumb found and gently massaged the secret bud until a volcano of white hot lava threatened to burn her alive.

She moaned his name over and over, as his hand pulled away the hindering garment and sought her again, flesh to flesh, sending an exploratory finger into the warm, fluid depths. He began to rock gently back and forth, his thumb still mercilessly teasing the tiny mound that by now was sending sparks of white hot fire through her body. The rhythmic motions were driving her to ecstasy, and just when she feared she might explode with pleasure, he covered her mouth with his, his tongue sending dizzying sensations that, matched with his hand, propelled her right over the edge.

The volcano erupted with an intensity that shook her to the core of her being. Her body was consumed by a white hot deliciousness and she arched her body hard against his. His mouth on hers stifled her gasps of pleasure, but filled her with his own moans of passion.

For a long moment, the fine throbs of fulfillment shook her, as his fingers maddeningly teased every tremor of pleasure from her.

Then she lay still, sated for the moment, and opened heavy eyes to gaze lovingly into his. She found her love returned, there could be no mistaking it. She smiled at him and he smiled back.

"I've been wondering what you taste like," he said, then he removed his hand from under her skirt and, in a move that astonished her, he licked the fingers that had brought her to such heights of pleasure.

A thrill of expectation shook her. He lowered his head to rain a soft patter of kisses all along her stomach, and circled her navel with his tongue. Her head spun with the delicious new sensations he forced upon her, and when he thrust his tongue gently but firmly into her navel, she arched her body against his mouth. When she did this, he grabbed her soft round buttocks in his hands and held her slightly aloft, then touched his tongue to that throbbing place between her thighs.

She cried out in amazement at the delicious, white-hot sparks of pleasure that seared her with their intensity. Her head rolled from side to side, as his mouth descended and seemed to want to devour her. She clutched at the clothes beneath her, at his hair, at the very air, clutched and released, her body beginning to shake violently under the mastery of his tongue.

"Oliver!" she cried, gasping for breath. The white-hot lava flow that she thought had consumed her alive already, consumed her again. The explosion of ecstasy bombarded her with a torrent of sparks shivering over her body. Convulsions shook her, leaving her breathless and giddy with delight. Laughter, sheer, abandoned, unstoppable laughter bubbled up from inside and forced its way between her lips.

And still his mouth was upon her, drinking her, drinking every last drop of rapture from her body, prolonging the moment when she must come back to her senses. But finally, finally, the convulsions subsided, and the sweet throbbing under his tongue was all that remained.

He placed one final, sweet kiss there before he looked up into her love-filled, wondering eyes. He licked his lips. "Mmmm, nectar fit for gods."

Oliver moved slowly until he lay full length on top of her, his hard body nearly crushing her soft one. He propped his arms beside her, cradled her head in his hands, and kissed the tip of her nose, then began kissing her neck and breasts again, all the while Rebecca laughing with uncontrollable glee.

Through her near-delirium, she was aware of his hard, naked body lying on hers, aware of his manly desire for her, aware that if he wanted anything from her, anything at all, she would give it, gladly.

She moved her hips seductively beneath him. He looked into her eyes, and she saw unmistakable passion there. She put her arms around his neck and brought his lips to hers, kissing him with all the pent-up emotion of twenty years.

He groaned into her mouth. "Stop that," he managed to say.

"Stop what?" she said.

"Driving me mad," he replied.

"I want you," she said, grinding her hips harder against him.

"And I want you," he said. "But are you not just a little bit frightened?"

"Yes," she admitted in a small voice.

"So am I."

"You! Why?"

"Because I have waited a long time."

"I have waited all my life," she replied.

He smiled, his eyes very soft. "It is not the same thing, my sweet. The first time should be very slow, and gentle, and not like this." He pressed his hard body urgently against hers to show her what he meant.

She did not flinch.

"I have not made love to a woman for a very long time."

"Then perhaps you have forgotten how to do it," she answered, as she moved her body suggestively beneath his, and began to maneuver them both expertly into position. His eyes widened in surprise.

"I thought you were new to this."

"I am learning from an expert," she said, and again brought his mouth down to hers.

"I'm dreaming," Oliver whispered, "that's it. I'm still dreaming. This isn't real."

"I'm real, Oliver," she whispered back, kissing him again.

Rebecca lay beneath him, tenderly tracing her fingers along the muscles of his strong, broad back, reveling in the touch of him, the smell of him. She buried her face into his hair and breathed in the mingled scents of soap, leather, and something so utterly masculine that it turned her insides buttery, all over again.

He burrowed his face between her breasts, turning first one cheek then the other against the soft flesh, and the hint of beard stubble grazed deliciously against her tingling skin. "God, I could die happy in your arms," he murmured.

A thrill went through her at these words. He loved her. She knew it. And in that instant, she knew she was in love with him, too.

But a stout knock at the cabin door brought them both quickly back to their senses. Oliver rolled off her and she hastily rearranged her clothing. The door handle was tested from the outside, but luckily she had thought to lock it earlier. In another moment she was presentable, and after glancing quickly at Oliver, who was lying beneath the covers and smiling at her, she opened the door.

The doctor entered and began his examination of Oliver. Rebecca took the opportunity to slip outside for some fresh air. It was still dark. She had no idea what time it was, or even where her father could be. The night air was fresh, but cool. She rubbed her arms briskly and strolled down the deck.

A crewman passed her, then came back. "Miss? Are you all right, miss? You shouldn't be out here at this time of night."

"I'm all right, thank you very much."

"Where is your cabin? You're from the wreck, aren't you? Do you have a place to sleep?" he asked.

"No, I suppose I don't. I'll be just fine."

But he wouldn't take that for an answer. He insisted on escorting her to the ladies' salon, where she found other women unable to sleep, as well.

"I'll find you a cabin," the crewman said, and left. Rebecca sat down wearily in a plush velvet chair, surprised at how languorous her body felt. Was it just exhaustion? Or was it Oliver and all they had shared?

After a short while, the crewman appeared again and led her to an empty cabin. She thanked him, and he departed, but she had no intention of sleeping. She had to return to Oliver.

But it wouldn't hurt to take just a short moment to rest. The bed looked so inviting. She lay down across it, fully clothed, and closed her eyes.

Rebecca awakened some time later. She had no idea what time it was, but she could hear sounds of activity outside her cabin, and sunshine was streaming in through the small window.

The mirror on the wall above the washstand showed the harsh evidence of a difficult night. She looked a sight. There were smudges and scratch marks on her cheeks, and her hair looked like a blue jay had made a nest in it. She noticed with a little embarrassment that her blouse was buttoned wrong, and hoped that no one else had noticed. Her eyes were slightly swollen, but in the depths of their greenness lay something that hadn't been there before. She couldn't quite put her finger on it exactly, but it most certainly had something to do with Oliver Sebastian.

She poured water from the pitcher into the wash basin and splashed cool water onto her cheeks. Using her fingers as combs, she quickly rearranged her hair until she was suitably presentable, then left the cabin.

The warm April morning sunshine did wonders to revive her. A grumble in her stomach reminded her that she had not eaten for a long time.

She strolled down the deck, nodding to the people who nodded to her, and spotted Mr. Greenfield and Mr. Patten sitting in chairs smoking cigars.

"Good morning, gentlemen."

They rose and tipped their hats. "Good morning, Miss Bennett."

"Have you seen my father this morning?"

"Why, no, I haven't," said Mr. Patten. "Have you, Mr. Greenfield?"

Mr. Greenfield replied that he had not. "We left him sleeping peacefully in his cabin. He looked like he could use the rest. Lucky for us this steamboat was only half full of passengers, otherwise I'm sure most of us would have been sleeping on the decks."

"Yes, very lucky," agreed Mr. Patten. "That Mr. Latimer would have had to share your father's cabin if the purser hadn't found him one of his own."

An unexplainable chill went through Rebecca. Hadn't Latimer caused enough trouble already?

"Which cabin is he in? I'd like to go see that he's all right."

The two gentlemen exchanged a look. "That wouldn't be quite proper, Miss Bennett. Ladies aren't allowed in the men's quarters," said Mr. Greenfield.

"Especially unmarried ladies," added Mr. Patten.

Rebecca smiled, remembering the night she had just spent with Oliver. "Then would you gentlemen be so kind as to go and check on him for me, please? I'm sure he's all right, but I would like to know for certain."

"Of course, Miss Bennett. Anything to oblige." They tipped their hats again and she walked on down the deck.

Just then the steamboat whistle blew another long shrill blast, and when she looked upriver, she saw the inevitable woodpile and knew that they were stopping to wood up again. She leaned against the railing and watched as the man who tended the woodpile came down to the floating dock and took up a pose, whittling on a piece of wood. When the boat had docked, she heard the captain call out the ritual greeting.

"Got any wood for sale?"

"Reckon it's possible."

"How do you sell it a cord?"

"Two dollars."

"Two dollars! That's a dollar a cord too much!"

The man continued to whittle. "Well, on up yonder ways, there's a man what sells his wood at two and a quarter a cord. And he's the last stop afore Natchez. Take your pick."

Rebecca smiled as she saw the crewmen and deckhands swarm off the boat after this last remark. It didn't matter what kind of argument was given, or even what price was asked, although she guessed that two dollars was the going rate. It was a ceremony that they performed without fail. And the loaders would not leave the boat until it had been done, even though they all knew that they must have wood, at whatever the cost.

When she saw some of the female passengers leaving the boat, she was surprised. But they were not going to help load wood, they were going to stretch their legs on dry land.

That was exactly what she needed, so she headed down the stairway and joined the troop on solid ground, relishing the feel of hard earth under her feet.

She knew she should not wander too far, as the steamboat would be leaving soon. But there was a peach orchard in bloom just over there that beckoned her with its loveliness.

She reached up to an overhanging branch and cradled the delicate blossoms in her hands and inhaled their rich perfume

"Ain't this a purty sight?" She knew the voice, without turning to see. "You look mighty purty standin' there, Miss Bennett, mighty purty."

As she didn't turn around, Latimer came and stood in front of her, much too close. He grabbed a low limb and jerked a group of blossoms from it. Then he presented it to her, but she refused his offer.

She could smell whiskey and cigar smoke on his breath and it nearly gagged her. Couldn't this man take a hint? Did she have to be brutal with him to get it through his thick skull that she did not relish his company? That she despised him and his crude attentions?

She sighed. "You will excuse me, I'm sure. I want to take a walk before the boat gets under way again."

With that she turned and began to walk away from him, but he was not to be so easily snubbed.

"Well, that's the very thing I had in mind all along, Miss Bennett. You won't mind if I join you. I'd like to stretch my legs."

I'd like to stretch your neck, she thought, at the end of a rope.

"Miss Bennett, is there some trouble here?"

She looked up in surprise. Oliver Sebastian stood in their path and the way his eyes blazed at the other man made it obvious that he was aware of her difficulty.

She breathed a sigh of relief. "Oh, good morning, Mr. Sebastian. No, there's no trouble at all. I am just on my way back to the boat and Mr. Latimer here is just going off for a walk to stretch his legs. Aren't you, Mr. Latimer?"

Latimer looked a bit confused but would not give in. "Well, now, I thought we might take a little walk together, Miss Bennett -"

"Miss Bennett does not wish to walk with you," Oliver said firmly.

The other man bristled visibly.

"And just who are you to say -"

"Miss Bennett does not wish to walk with you," Oliver repeated. Then he offered her his arm. "May I see you safely back to the boat?"

"Why you lowdown sorry English bast -"

Oliver stopped him in mid-speech with a quick blow to the mouth which busted his lower lip and sent a trickle of blood flowing down his chin. He dabbed a finger at it, stunned. Then his eyes blazed in dangerous fury.

"I'll kill you for that."

"What seems to be the problem here?" said a stern, authoritative voice. They all turned to see that the captain of the steamboat had joined them.

"This here bloody English dog just busted my lip," whined Latimer.

The captain nodded. "Well, you probably deserved it. Now look here, Latimer, I've had trouble out of you before, and I don't want any more. Now do you behave yourself or do I have to put you off my boat in this God-forsaken territory?"

"But he -"

"Make up your mind. I have a schedule to keep. Now if you will all be so kind as to go back on board, we'll get underway."

The captain turned to go back to the boat. Oliver gestured that he wanted Latimer to go next, which he reluctantly did. Then Oliver offered Rebecca his arm again and murmured, "Never show your back to the enemy."

When they were once again steaming upriver, Rebecca said, "You seem to be fully recovered."

He smiled. "I had a most excellent nurse. Yes, I feel fine. How about you? And your father? Is he all right?"

"I don't really know. I haven't seen him since last night. Mr. Patten and Mr. Greenfield were going to check on him for me. I'm sure he's just fine." Her voice ended on a tiny quaver of doubt.

"Let's go find out for ourselves, shall we?"

He offered his arm again, and as they walked down the deck, she caught a glimpse of Latimer skulking in the shadows, nursing his wounded lip and eyeing them both with open hostility.

Rebecca saw Greenfield and Patten walking toward them. But her father was not with them.

"Did you find my father well, gentlemen?" she asked politely.

"Why, no, Miss Bennett, not yet. He didn't answer our knock at his door. We assumed he had already gone out. Now you have us concerned, Miss Bennett. Is your father given to sleeping late?"

"Absolutely not. He is an early riser. Something must be the matter." She turned to Oliver. "Something is wrong, I know it. My father would never sleep this -"

Oliver squeezed her arm to calm her.

"Please, Rebecca, the situation can be easily remedied. Sit down here and I will go and inquire after him." Oliver made her sit in a deck chair, and squeezed her hands in his. "I will find out, never fear. I'm sure he's perfectly all right." Then he turned to the other men. "Would one of you be so kind as to show me which is his cabin?"

After several minutes of nervous waiting, Oliver still hadn't returned. Rebecca was becoming more agitated by the second. Something was wrong, terribly wrong, she could feel it in her bones. Mr. Patten was quite unable to calm her with his periodic attempts at reassurance.

Then just when her nerves were at their most tense, the steamboat whistle blew several short, sharp blasts, and the paddlewheel slowed almost to a halt. She could hear running footsteps and shouts, and a bolt of sheer terror struck her. Not again! Dear God, hadn't they had enough trouble?

She jumped to her feet and rushed toward the stairway, but just as she got there, Oliver caught her in his strong arms and held her firmly. She looked into his eyes, searching, finding only a clouded, somber expression there.

"Well? Is he all right?"

A grievous look crossed his face. "Miss Bennett... Rebecca..."

"What?" she nearly screamed. "What is it?"

"Your father...I'm afraid there's been..."

"Tell me!" she shouted.

He sighed mournfully, and tightened his grip. "Your father is dead."

The shock of his words sent an icy chill through her. "Did you say...no, you can't be serious. What a cruel joke! Where is he? Where is my father? Tell me it's not true!" But her body began to shake, and she knew in her heart that he was telling the truth.

"Rebecca..."

He held her tightly, to quell the shaking, and looked at her with the most piteous sympathy. Tears sprang into her eyes.

"How - ?" she choked, "He seemed perfectly fine last night. Did he die in his sleep? Were there injuries we were unaware of? How - ?"

Oliver made a gallant effort to take control of the situation. "You've had a terrible shock. Let me take you to my cabin. We'll talk about it there. Gentlemen, would you be so kind as to fetch a bottle of brandy from the bar and have it sent to my cabin?"

She pummeled his chest with her fists. "I don't want brandy! I want you to tell me! What happened? Is there a doctor with him? He may only be ill... Dead! I can't believe it! I want to see him. Take me to him!

Please!"

"You can't see him, Rebecca."

"Can't? Can't see him? Why can't I see him? He's my father, for God's sake!"

"Please, Rebecca, trust me."

With a violent jerk she thrust him off. Before he could recover, she bolted down the stairs to the lower deck.

A crowd of people had collected outside one of the cabins, and she shoved her way into the room.

The captain was standing beside the bed, and he turned with a look of grave uneasiness. When he moved toward her, exclaiming, "What is she doing here? Get her out!" she saw her father lying on the bed.

Mr. Bennett looked as if he was asleep, but his eyes were open, and then she saw the ugly red-black wound on his neck, and a spreading pool of blood under his head.

Rebecca screamed, a wailing pitiful sound that surely must have been heard all the way to New Orleans.

She lunged for him. He was her father. If she could hold him in her arms it might bring life back into that still body.

But she was prevented from going further into the room by the captain, who gently but firmly made her turn her face away and leave the cabin. She was jostled by many hands, and voices all around her increased the madness in her brain.

"What's going on?"

"Someone's been killed!"

"Killed!"

"Who's been killed?"

"His throat's been cut!"

"Good God!"

"Murdered!"

"You don't say!"

"Who's been murdered?"

"The girl's father!"

"Poor thing!"

Rebecca felt as if the world had been destroyed under her very feet. She collapsed against someone's body and through teary eyes she saw the face of the red-haired woman from the bar looking at her compassionately.

"I'll take over from here," she heard Oliver Sebastian say and felt his hands take hold of her, felt his strong arms lift her off her feet. "I need your help," he said simply to the redhead, who nodded and followed as he carried Rebecca to his cabin.

Rebecca fainted long before he got there.

CHAPTER SIX

Rebecca came to with a scream on her lips.

Someone pressed a cool damp cloth to her forehead and soothed her with soft words. She opened her eyes and saw the redheaded woman bending over her, dabbing the perspiration from her face.

"Where - where's Oliver?"

"He's with the captain. Now you just relax and -"

"Relax!" She thrust the cloth away. "My father! Oh, dear God! Papa!" Rebecca covered her face with her hands, weeping uncontrollably.

"I know you've had a terrible shock, sugar. They shoulda never let you see the body. Men think they know everything about women, but they don't know beans when it comes to somethin' like this."

"Oh, dear God! What shall become of me?" She looked up into the woman's pretty face and saw kindness there.

"Everything's gonna work out, you mark my words, it always does. Here, take a little sip of this brandy. It's damn near rotgut, but it's the best they got on this old tub. Come on, now, sugar, this'll make you feel much better."

She held a glass to Rebecca's lips, and Rebecca reluctantly allowed a small amount to spill into her mouth. The fiery liquor seared her throat as it went down, and she coughed.

The woman laughed softly. "Guess you ain't so used to fire water, huh? The thing is, see, you don't take it and roll it around your mouth. Just tilt your head back and throw it down the hatch."

Rebecca did as she was told, and belted down the remainder of brandy, grimacing as she felt it hit her stomach.

"That's it! You're gettin' the hang of it! Now just lie real quiet and in a minute or two you'll feel this kinda warm glow all over, like you ain't got a care in the world. Come to think of it, I could use a little myself right about now."

Rebecca watched as the pretty redhead poured nearly half the glass full of the amber liquor and threw it down her throat, then smacked her ruby lips, her blue eyes twinkling. "Well, it may be rot-gut, but it's still better than the pig swill I get in my saloon."

"Saloon?"

"Yeah, sugar, I got me a dandy little place at Natchez-Under-The-Hill. Red's Place, they call it, though the official name is the Elysian Fields. Found that in a book I read once. Thought it kinda had class. Guess that may be the only class that old joint will ever have. But it's a livin'."

"Red? Is that your name?"

"Well, that's what they call me. Cain't imagine why." She twisted a stray lock of her coppery hair and rolled her eyes. "My real name is Mary. Mary Frazier. But what kinda name's that for a saloonkeeper, I ask you!"

Rebecca couldn't help but smile.

"Now that's more like it! Didn't I tell you that brandy would make you feel a whole heap better?"

A soft knock came at the door. When Red opened it, Oliver came in. "How is she?" he asked her.

"See for yourself," Red answered and started to leave.

"No, please, don't go. I only wanted -"

"She's been callin' for you ever since you brung her here, like she was delirious or somethin'. Now you tend to her a while so I can take a breather."

He grabbed her arm. "You can't leave us alone!"

"For heaven's sake, why not?"

"Because...Because it isn't proper."

She laughed in his face. "Proper be damned!" she retorted, dismissing his objections, and left, closing the door behind her.

Oliver stared at the door for a long moment before he finally turned his gaze to Rebecca. He looked so stricken, so at a loss, she momentarily forgot her own tragedy and wanted to hold him in her arms.

"How are you feeling?"

"I'm all right, thank you." Her voice sounded calmer than his.

He picked up the brandy bottle and poured himself a stout drink. "I've been with the captain. It appears that robbery was the motive. We searched but didn't find the gold."

"H-he was murdered for his gold?" she asked, shaken.

He looked at her sadly. "Apparently. It's gone."

Tears streamed down her cheeks. "I told him it was foolish. But he was so adamant. He didn't trust banks at all. I told him he shouldn't be carrying around so much gold."

Oliver sighed deeply. "Then it will be damned near impossible to find the villain who murdered him."

"What?"

"Well, if it had been bank notes, say, on a bank in Savannah, then it would be fairly simple to wait and see if anyone tries to pass them in this part of the country. But gold! Impossible!"

"You mean you don't know who murdered my father?"

"Not a clue. Even if the person is still on board, we haven't any evidence. Unless we could find that gold. But I don't believe the murderer is still on this boat."

Something nagged at Rebecca's brain. "Mr. Latimer. I'll bet he had something to do with it."

"Oh?"

"They were playing poker last night, Papa, Mr. Latimer, Mr. Greenfield, and Mr. Patten. Before the wreck. Have you talked to them?"

"I've talked to everyone but Latimer. I was hoping to avoid him, if possible."

"But they all knew about the gold, I'm sure of it. In fact, I think my father was rather bragging about the plantation he was going to buy. He told everyone who would listen."

"But that's not proof, Rebecca. You can't convict a man without proof. We'll just have to make a thorough search of the boat, and see if that brass chest turns up. But you must be prepared for the worst. The gold and the murderer are probably long gone by now."

"Prepared for the worst! What could be worse than losing Papa? The money isn't important, Oliver. My father is dead!"

He gently took her shoulders in his hands. "I know, my darling. But the fact is that he is dead and the money is gone. What will you do now?"

That thought really hadn't occurred to her. Fresh tears stung her eyes. "I don't know. It was all we had. I don't have a cent, Papa always provided. Now it's gone. Everything is gone. The hopes, the dreams. Even you. He was going to buy your farm, and now..." She burst into wracking sobs and he wrapped his arms around her, holding her tightly.

"I should be the least of your worries. I can sell the farm, there's no problem with that. It's you I am concerned about. I suppose you'll be going back to Savannah?"

"No!" she cried vehemently, and threw her arms around his neck. "I can't go back there. There's nothing to go back to."

"But surely you have family back there?"

"No," she sobbed. "No one. No one."

Her sobs shook her so violently that Oliver gathered her into his arms, lay beside her on the bed and held her hard against his body, absorbing part of the shock.

"What will I do?" she cried.

"Shhh, we'll think about it later."

"Oliver, can't I stay with you?"

For a moment he was silent, then he said simply, "No."

Her blood chilled. "But why not?"

"Because I'm going back to England. Didn't your father explain it to you?"

"Oh, I don't know..." she sobbed. "Yes, I guess. I guess he did. Must you go back to England?"

"Yes."

"But why? I don't want you to go! Please, can't I stay with you?"

His voice had a slightly hard edge. "I'm afraid that's impossible."

"But why? Don't you know that I've fallen in love with you?"

His body became rigid against hers. "You mustn't say that."

"But it's true!" She raised her head and took his face in her hands. "I think I fell in love with you when I first saw you, running down the dock, trying to catch the steamboat. I caught your hat." She tried to laugh, but what came out was a funny little gasp.

His eyes grew suddenly dark. "Rebecca, you mustn't say such things."

"I love you!"

"You don't know what you're saying."

"You're wrong, I do know. I know that I love you." And with that she pressed her lips to his, tears streaming from her eyes.

For a moment he did not respond. Then a groan came from deep inside him and he opened his mouth to hers.

Her tongue darted in to taste the sweetness that she knew she would find there. When his tongue sought and found hers, it sent a shock through her down to her toes. For a long, breathless moment, they lay locked in sweet embrace, exploring each other's mouths, finding all the deliciousness that was there.

Then suddenly Oliver wrenched his face away. His eyes were dark and stormy with passion. "This has to stop. You don't know what you're doing."

"Oh, yes, I do. You showed me before, remember?"

She moved her thigh against his, and knew the depth of his desire for her.

He tried again to warn her. "Rebecca, this isn't proper."

"Proper be damned!" she said, echoing Red's words. "I've just lost my father, and my future, and I don't know what will become of me. All I do know is that you are here with me right this moment, and that's all I care about."

He made a motion to get up from the bed. "Maybe I'd better call Red to come back in."

"No! Please, Oliver, please? Just hold me? I need to feel your arms around me. I have no one to comfort me now."

He squeezed her tighter, but she could feel his body rigid as stone beside hers.

"Kiss me again."

"Rebecca, I -"

She cut him off as she pressed her lips against his, but he pulled away, his eyes dark with passion.

"You don't know what you're doing to me."

The steamboat gave several long, loud blasts of its whistle. Oliver sighed with relief. "We've arrived in Natchez. We'll discuss your situation later. All right?"

Before she could protest, he was gone.

A glance in the mirror made her wince. Her eyes were puffy and bloodshot from crying, but that was understandable. She splashed water on her cheeks, vowing that she would find a way, somehow, to make Oliver change his mind about going back to England.

* * *

Natchez! The name itself sounded exotic to her ears.

She stood at the rail and watched as the steamboat maneuvered into port, butting up against the floating wharf that could rise and fall with the temperament of the river as no stationary pier could.

There was hustle and bustle everywhere. Wagons and drays were loaded with all sorts of merchandise waiting to be shipped up or down the river, mules, donkeys or horses straining against the weight.

People were everywhere, men, women, children, black, white, Indian, of nearly every race and nationality, walking, running, playing, shoving, brawling, drinking, or just watching the steamboats coming into port with a curious excitement, as if every boat might hold some new entertainment for them.

Rebecca could feel her own excitement rising.

"Hi, sugar! Guess you're over your cryin' spell, huh?"

Rebecca smiled at Red, who had joined her at the rail. "I want to thank you for being so kind to me."

"It wasn't nothin', sugar, I was happy to oblige. I've faced a mite of sorrow in my day, and all it takes is time, believe me. My granny always told me, no matter how devastatin' a thing might seem, the good Lord never gives you a burden you cain't carry. And you know what? Granny was right, bless her ornery soul. It's never somethin' you cain't handle. Oh, you can holler and carry on all you want to, and say you just cain't go on livin', but you always do."

Red adjusted her fashionable ostrich-plumed hat to just the right angle, and cocked her head toward Rebecca. "I should know. I've been down on my luck so many times I thought the Lord had a special vendetta against me, for leadin' the kinda life I do and all. But it ain't that way at all. No, sir, been my experience that everything happens for a reason. You either brung it on yourself, or it's a test to see how you gonna act. Or sometimes it's just, well, destiny, you might say. Now I know you're all sorrowful about your pa and all, but mark my words. Somethin' good will come of it. Look right up there."

She pointed behind them to the colossal sign on the side of the boat that said, "Lucky Star".

"See? You ain't got a thing to worry about."

Rebecca smiled ruefully. This was the first time she had been told the name of the steamboat that had rescued the passengers of the Sentinel last night. "I certainly hope you're right, Red."

"I'm never wrong, sugar. Seldom right but never wrong. Just remember what my granny said. Well, looks like we're home."

The boat was secured against the wharf and passengers began streaming off. Several men were apparently waiting for Red on shore, because when they saw her, they let out a whoop and tossed their hats into the air.

"My admirin' public," she said wryly. "I was in New Orleans to round up some new talent for my saloon, but they won't be gettin' here until next week. Them boys will be itchin' like skeeter bites. I'll have to think of somethin' to keep 'em happy until the ladies get here. Lucky for me, they ain't that hard to please. Good-bye, sugar, take care, and come see me sometime, you hear?"

"Elysian Fields, right?"

Red gave her a grateful smile. "Right!" Then she was gone down the gangway and into the arms of the boisterous men who hugged her and whirled her around in the air, so happy were they to see her.

"Miss Bennett."

She turned at the sound of her name and saw the captain standing before her with Oliver at his side.

"My deepest condolences, Miss Bennett. And my sincerest apologies. Nothing like this has ever happened on my boat before. You may be very sure that I did all that was humanly possible to discover who did it, but I'm afraid it must be turned over to the local authorities now. You do understand?"

Her mouth was dry. "Yes, captain, I understand. Thank you for all you have done."

He bowed to her, evidently glad to have that particular chore over. Then he turned and began bellowing instructions to some of the crew who carried something wrapped in a blanket down the gangway and placed it on a wagon. She put a hand to her mouth as she realized that it was her father's body. She turned to Oliver questioningly.

"I have given orders that your father shall be taken to my farm and buried there. With your permission, of course."

She nodded dumbly.

"I though it only fitting that he should find his final rest there. It shall be put into the deed of sale that his grave will never be disturbed."

She didn't know what to say to this. "Thank you. I'm sure he would have appreciated your kindness."

Then he was still planning on selling and going back to England? In spite of the fact that they loved each other? Or was she mistaken? She was in love with him. Wasn't he in love with her?

"Come," he said, and gently took her elbow and led her down the ramp to shore.

"Where are we going?"

"To my home. You'll be more comfortable there."

To his home! Rebecca's heart leaped with joy. Then he was in love with her!

Oliver helped her into a waiting buggy then climbed up beside her. Deftly he took the reins and whipped the fine black horse into motion.

Rebecca stared around her at the many buildings and houses crowded onto the rather small stretch of land that was right on the river beneath a very high bluff.

"Doesn't look like much of a town," she murmured in a small disappointed voice.

"What? Oh," he laughed, "this isn't the real Natchez. The real town lies up above us, on the bluff. This is what is ignominiously called Natchez-Under-the-Hill. Or just Natchez-Under, to the residents above. This is the only blight on an otherwise beautiful town."

She stared at the several saloons and gambling houses, and at the myriad of people coming and going from them. A feminine voice from somewhere called out something very suggestive. Rebecca looked up to see a woman in what would politely be called dishabille lounging in an upper story window of one of the saloons, tempting the men below with promises of what she would do for them if they had twenty dollars to spend and legs to climb the steps.

"They say that if it can't be found here, then it hasn't been thought of. It's not the sort of place for a lady," Oliver said, then amended, "or a gentleman."

Rebecca saw several of what looked to be gentlemen just going into one of the saloons. "Though of course they still come," continued Oliver. "Those proud, sanctimonious people on the bluff click their tongues and say something should be done about Natchez-Under-the-Hill, but they are the ones who frequent it the most. Sin on Saturday, repent on Sunday." His voice held a stinging sarcasm.

"You disapprove?" she asked with a smile.

"It's not that I disapprove of their coming. I despise them for being hypocritical about it, that's all."

"Have you ever heard of the Elysian Fields?"

He gave her an odd look. "Do you mean mythically?"

She laughed. "No, I mean the saloon."

"Then you mean Red's Place."

"She prefers to have it called the Elysian Fields, thank you. Says it gives the place class."

"Ha!" he snorted, then, "well, it is one of the nicer establishments down here. But it's no place for you."

His proprietary manner was flattering. "Do you speak from experience, sir?"

He gave her a sidelong glance. "Maybe."

"I just thought it might be nice to visit Red sometime. She's the first real friend I've made here yet."

"Red is a peach, a real gem, but she can't protect you in this place. Anything goes, here. The law almost never comes down here. They just let them settle things their own way. And what they can't settle, the river can."

Suddenly out from an alley burst two men locked in battle, fighting and rolling around on the ground, and they rolled right into the path of the buggy.

"Whoa!" Oliver shouted as the horse shied and tried to rear, but he kept the animal under control.

With a start, Rebecca saw Latimer standing on the porch of a saloon, staring hard at her. He reached a hand up to his hat, as though he would tip it to her, then arrested the motion, with the effect of an arrogant insult.

Rebecca looked quickly away, a bitter taste in her mouth.

It seemed they would never get away from Natchez-Under. Oliver drove the buggy up the treacherous incline that was called Silver Street and was the only way up to the bluff from the landing. "Street" was a misnomer: it was nothing more than a wagon trail full of ruts and mud holes. Finally they reached the summit and turned south, driving along a shady willow-lined drive that ran along the edge of the bluff.

On her right Rebecca could see the brownish-yellow river and the thick green forests on the Louisiana shore. On her left she could see a beautiful old Spanish plaza right in the middle of a collection of grand houses and buildings built in every conceivable architectural style, but most of the older ones still retained their Spanish heritage. It was every bit as charming as New Orleans, but not nearly so crowded.

Here there were broad streets and wide expanses of lawn and park ground, making a very pleasing sight. It was old and it was new, offering the advantages of both.

Rebecca smiled. She thought she might like it here.

Oliver was very quiet. He had not said two words since leaving Natchez-Under-the-Hill. The town proper was left behind as they continued their journey out into the countryside. They passed several magnificent plantations, houses with grandiose, multi-column facades and tree-lined drives. Slaves were everywhere, working the fields for their masters, and doing the myriad jobs required to keep a large plantation running smoothly.

Something tugged at Rebecca's heart as she observed the back-breaking toil these people performed, for little more than food and board, and an occasional whipping from their owners. There had been slaves in Savannah, to be sure, but the ones she had seen had worked on the docks, or had been domestics in private homes. She had never seen them working in the fields as they did here.

So this was how men became millionaires! They bought land, and slaves to work it, and sat back and reaped the profits. In a way she was almost glad her father was not here to see this. She was sure he had had as little comprehension of slavery as she.

"Do you own slaves, Oliver?" she asked suddenly.

His body jerked at the sound of her voice, as though his mind had been a million miles away. "No," he replied after a moment. "I hire people to work in my fields. Not all the blacks you see here are slaves, Rebecca. Many of them are free."

"Free? Then where do they live?"

"It depends. Some live on the plantations that they work, doing extra jobs like shoeing horses for room and board. Others have their own cabins on a small parcel of land that they sharecrop. And still others have their own businesses, like merchants, or barbers."

"I didn't know that," she replied. "I guess I just assumed that all colored people were slaves to somebody else."

"Many of them have bought their own freedom. Or were manumitted by previous owners. Even some freedmen of color own slaves."

She shook her head. "I'm sure my father had no real idea what slavery means. I think he just had a romantic notion in his head. He wanted to be a country squire, not a slaveholder."

But she said nothing else, because that was all gone, now. Best to forget it and look to her own future.

She glanced at Oliver, but he was looking straight ahead. A funny tingling sensation began between her thighs and she unconsciously fidgeted in her seat.

She longed to talk to him, but he seemed strangely uncommunicative.

Presently they had left all the grand mansions behind, and were on a narrow dirt trail that wound its way between fields and stands of forest.

"Is that the river over there?" She pointed off to her right, where water glimmered like gold through the trees.

"Yes. We've been driving south from Natchez, right along the bluff."

"You live this far from town?"

"Yes."

"I've only lived in Savannah, right in the middle of town. All this openness scares me a little." She waited for him to say something else, but he remained silent. Why wouldn't he talk to her, for goodness sake?

"Oliver... is something wrong?"

Abruptly he reined in the horse, bringing the buggy to a sharp halt, and turned to face her. The tension in his body was almost palpable. "Yes. Something is wrong," he gritted.

"What?" she whispered, hardly daring to speak.

The knuckles of his hands whitened as he gripped the reins, and the look in his eyes sent tremors down to her toes.

"What happened back there, on the boat... That should never have happened. I knew better, God help me, I knew better." He reached up to remove his hat and wipe the sweat from his brow, and Rebecca noticed that his hand shook.

"Wh-what do you mean?"

"I mean it should never have happened. You were so...I was just..." He was truly at a loss for words. Her heart went out to him, even though she suspected that she was the cause of his torment. Gently she laid her hands on his, but he snatched them away as if he'd been burned.

"Don't. Please. I can't..." Gulping huge breaths of air, he tried to steady himself. "You don't understand. I'm sorry. It has nothing to do with you. No, that's a lie, it has everything to do with you..."

"You don't love me, do you?" she said. Tears threatened to spill from her eyes, but she held them back bravely.

He dropped the reins into his lap and grabbed her shoulders, gripping hard. "This has nothing to do with love!" he rasped. "I simply couldn't resist you."

A slow smile broke over Rebecca's face. So that was it. He was in love with her, after all, only he wouldn't admit it, even to himself.

"Stop smiling like that, damn it!"

"Kiss me," she demanded.

"No," he answered, giving her shoulders a rough little shake. "No more kisses. You've got to understand. This must stop."

"Kiss me," she repeated, and with a groan that held all the agony of love denied, he did.

Quickly, passionately, then he pulled away. "No! This can't go on..."

She pulled his mouth to hers again. Her fingers dug into his neck, pressing his lips hard against hers.

He groaned into her mouth, making her head spin with delirium.

His hand sought her breast, and it didn't take much teasing to bring the hard little peak to rigid attention. Her whole body was on fire with desire for him.

"Rebecca, Rebecca, Rebecca..." Oliver repeated her name over and over.

There was nothing to worry about. He did love her, he did.

Her father was gone, but Oliver was here. Perhaps Red had been right about the "Lucky Star" after all.

Abruptly he picked up the reins again and whipped the black horse into motion.

This time it was Rebecca who had nothing to say. She was still digesting all the wonderful new things that he had introduced to her. She hugged herself, as if holding him to her heart, and smiled.

Suddenly up ahead, in a clearing surrounded by magnificent oaks and weeping willows, she caught sight of a small white house, small compared to the huge mansions, but still grand in its own way. As they drew nearer, she saw that it had eight tall white columns running along the front of the house, supporting the roof and providing shade for the long verandah which also ran the length of the house.

A lump formed in her throat. She felt sorry again for her father who would never see this, never know that his hunch had been correct.

"Mister Sebastian! Mister Sebastian!" A small black boy of about nine years came running up to the buggy before Oliver could bring it to a halt, and grabbed the horse by the bridle.

"Hello, Jeremiah! Did you keep everything in order while I was gone?"

The boy grinned a wide, white smile. "Yessir, I took care of Miss Charlotte, just like you told me. And I done killed a big fat hen for your supper."

"Very good, Jeremiah. I knew I was leaving the place in good hands." He jumped from the buggy and rubbed the boy's shoulder affectionately, then helped Rebecca down from the buggy. "Jeremiah, this is Miss Bennett. She is our guest. I want you to show her every courtesy that you would to Miss Charlotte."

"Hello, Jeremiah," she said.

The boy eyed her carefully, then said, "Pleased to meet you, ma'am," with all the dignity that nine years could muster.

Oliver guided her toward the front door, then turned. "Oh, Jeremiah, before you put up the horse, go and find Big Ben. I have an important job for him."

"Yessir. Cain't I help too, sir?"

Oliver smiled. "Not this time, I'm afraid. Unless you want to help dig a grave."

The boys eyes grew wide in wonder. "Nosir, I'm too young to be diggin' no grave, thank you just the same."

The front door flew open and a middle-aged black woman beamed a toothy smile at them. "Lord, here you are at last! Miss Charlotte and me been nearly delirious listenin' for your buggy comin' up that drive! I reckon this must be Miss Bennett. Welcome, Miss Bennett, mighty pleased to finally meet you. Where's Mr. Bennett?" She glanced behind them as if to see someone else standing there.

"Mr. Bennett will not be coming, Portia," Oliver said. "I'll explain in a moment. Where is Charlotte?"

"In the library, as usual. She spends all her time readin' them books you brung her last time you went down to N'Orleans."

Oliver opened two wide doors on the left and walked inside. Rebecca moved over to the entrance but did not go in until invited.

"My darling, how are you feeling?" Oliver said in the warmest voice she had yet heard from him. He knelt beside a chair on which was seated a beautiful but rather pale blonde woman, and kissed her full on the lips.

"I'm fine, darling, just glad to have you home."

She spoke with a cultured English accent.

"You don't look fine to me. She looks rather paler than she did when I left, don't you think so, Portia?"

Portia stood at the side of the door and nodded her head. "Yessir, I sure do think so. I cain't hardly get her to eat enough to keep a bird alive."

"Darling, you must eat, to keep up your strength."

"I know, dearest. It's the heat, that's all."

He gazed lovingly at her for a long moment.

Rebecca was starting to feel extremely uncomfortable with confusion. Then he looked up.

"I beg your pardon. Where are my manners? Darling, you know that the Bennetts were supposed to arrive today to look over the farm. Well, there's been a terrible tragedy. Mr. Bennett was killed on board the boat, but I have brought his daughter here. This is Miss Rebecca Bennett. Miss Bennett," he stood, "allow me to introduce Charlotte Sebastian. My wife."

For the second time that day, Miss Rebecca Bennett fainted.

CHAPTER SEVEN

A cool, damp cloth was pressed to her forehead, and for a moment Rebecca thought she was back on the riverboat. But when she opened her eyes, it was not Red that she saw bending over her, but Charlotte Sebastian.

My wife, Oliver had said. Emotion flooded her again, bringing hot stinging tears to her eyes.

"I think she's coming around, Portia," said the pale blonde woman.

Portia looked over her shoulder at Rebecca and sighed deeply. "Praise the Lord!" she said. "That poor child looked nigh unto death! Here, Miss Charlotte, let me freshen that rag." She took the cloth and dipped it into a porcelain basin of water, then handed it back. Mrs. Sebastian again pressed it to Rebecca's face. It felt refreshing.

Rebecca noticed that she was lying in bed, on a very soft feather mattress. Had Oliver carried her here?

"Are you feeling better, Miss Bennett? You gave us all such a fright. But then you've had a terrible shock, I know." Her voice was very soothing, but not at all like Red's. Maybe it was the English accent.

"Oliver told me what happened. How dreadful! I am so very, very sorry for you. I understand that your father was your only family. It will take time to get over this terrible tragedy. You are lucky to be alive. Please, Miss Bennett, please accept my warmest welcome, and feel free to remain here as long as you like. Until you are able to take up your life again, my home is your home." She smiled at Rebecca.

Rebecca didn't know what to say, except, "Thank you," which came out in a very small voice.

"I expect Miss Bennett might want to rest, now, Miss Charlotte. She's had a long trip and a bad shock, and she's probably more than a mite tired." Portia laid a hand gently on Mrs. Sebastian's shoulder, but the woman did not move until Rebecca said, yes, she was feeling very tired, and if they would please excuse her, she would like to rest for a while.

Mrs. Sebastian smiled again, and said, "Please come and talk to me when you feel better, Miss Bennett. Now we'll leave you alone. Come, Portia."

When they had gone, Rebecca could hold back no longer, and the tears came hot and heavy. She buried her face into the soft feather pillows to cushion the body-shaking sobs that wrenched from deep inside.

It just didn't seem real. None of it was real. It was all a dreadful nightmare, and in a moment she would awaken back in her bedroom in Savannah, safe and sound. This was all just a terrible, terrible nightmare.

She told herself over and over that it wasn't real, that the steamboat hadn't been wrecked, that her father wasn't dead, that she hadn't seen him with his throat cut, that she hadn't fallen in love with Oliver, that he hadn't made love to her, that he hadn't brought her to his home, that he hadn't introduced her to his wife.

She told herself this over and over, but she could not make herself believe it. When she raised her head and looked around, she was not in her small, safe bedroom in Savannah, but in a large, strange bedroom in Natchez. The room was really very nice, with pretty ruffled curtains and lacy bedspread and heavy mahogany and marble furnishings. It would have been a wonderful room, had it not felt so cold.

Or was it Rebecca who felt so cold? There was no welcome warmth here, as she had thought there would be, but then she had thought that Oliver was bringing her here to be near him, because he loved her. He had said nothing about a wife. Not a word.

Rebecca turned her face to the pillows and cried herself to sleep.

She must have slept very soundly, for when she awoke, she noticed, lying on a beautiful damask chaise, a black dress, which she knew was not hers, because all her clothing had been lost in the wreck. It must have been Mrs. Sebastian's, then, loaned to her in her time of sorrow. However else the two women differed, they were about the same dress size. Rebecca could not help but feel grateful to her.

Black was the traditional color for a woman in mourning, and she was certainly a woman in mourning, for more reasons than one.

It was turning dark outside, and must be late evening. The shadows were lengthening in the room, and despite the urge to crawl back into the bed and sleep until she died, Rebecca knew that there were things to be done. Her father's funeral, for one.

She chided herself severely for being so selfish. Red was right. Her life was not over, not yet. She might still salvage some bit of happiness, but to do so she must finish up all the loose ends. She struck a match and lit the lamp on the dressing table.

Then she inspected the dress. Yes, it would fit her just fine.

Several minutes later, she left the room and made her way down the staircase in the center of the house to the hall below. She could hear voices, masculine voices, coming from the library, and could see several shadows thrown from that room onto the hall floor. She smoothed out the black dress and, gathering up all her courage, slowly descended the stairs.

The voices stopped suddenly as she appeared in the doorway to the library. Oliver turned from where he stood at the hearth and came quickly to her.

"Miss Bennett, I'm so glad you are feeling well enough to come down. Please, come in, sit down." He took her arm gently, and she wanted to tremble at his touch, but couldn't find the strength. She sat on a dark blue velvet chair and stared at the other men in the room.

Oliver introduced them. Mr. Brown was the sheriff of Natchez, Mr. Winslow was Oliver's lawyer, and Mr. Beckworth was a friend and neighbor. Each man presented himself to her and offered his condolences, and she accepted them all gracefully.

Oliver poured her a glass of brandy and pressed it into her hands.

"Thank you, Mr. Sebastian," she murmured, not looking at him. She took a sip as the men began to talk again of the tragedy of her father's murder. The brandy was sweeter and smoother than what she had had on the boat, and felt warm and comforting going down her throat.

Sheriff Brown came and stood near her, twisting his hat in his hands. "Miss Bennett, I know this has been a terrible time for you, but if you could just answer a few questions for me. Oliver has told us all he knows, but there may be some little thing that may help to solve this mystery. If you don't mind?"

"No, not at all, sheriff. But I'm afraid I know as little as you. My father was murdered for his gold, this I do know."

"He was carrying a rather large sum of money with him?"

"Yes. I don't know how much exactly, but it was a large sum. About thirty thousand dollars, I believe. He sold his store in Savannah and took all the payment in gold. He didn't trust banks, you see."

Rebecca told them everything that had happened up until the time she herself had seen his lifeless body, everything, that is, except for the part about her falling in love with Oliver. That part now seemed like a bad joke.

"You say the boat was thoroughly searched?" Sheriff Brown asked Oliver.

"Yes, the captain assured me that it was. No chest of gold was found, nor any large amount of gold at all. It had obviously been removed from the boat already."

The sheriff sighed. "Well, if there are no clues, and no witnesses, and nothing whatsoever to go on, I'm afraid there is nothing I can do. If the murderer did jump ship, then he is long gone by now, and no amount of searching is apt to turn up anything."

"I'm afraid you are right," Oliver sighed.

"I know who killed my father," Rebecca said simply and drained the brandy from the glass. They all stared at her. "That Mr. Latimer did it. I know it."

Oliver explained. "Mr. Latimer is that rather repugnant fellow I was telling you about. But there is no proof - "

"I don't need proof," Rebecca interrupted in an icy voice. "I know he did it."

"But Miss Bennett, he was still on the boat, and where is the gold?"

The sheriff could not believe she was serious, and the look that Oliver gave the others said that he put no stock in her intuition.

"He had an accomplice, I'm sure, to remove the gold from the boat. He killed my father, took the gold, and then his accomplice left the boat and they will probably meet later to divide the spoils." Her voice had been calm, but now it rose stridently, with the force of her conviction. For deep inside, she believed it herself. "He stayed on board just for the purpose of having an alibi."

"But Miss Bennett, everyone on the boat was accounted for. No one was missing."

"So? What does that prove? The person could have gotten on when we stopped for wood, and gotten off the same way. Mr. Latimer himself told me it was possible to board a boat without being detected when it stopped for wood. It would therefore be possible to leave a boat without being detected. Carrying a chest full of gold. In the middle of the night. Gentlemen, I tell you, that is how it happened!"

The four men shared a look that made Rebecca's blood boil. "You don't believe me!"

"Oh, it isn't that, Miss Bennett. It's certainly - ahem - possible, but there is no evidence to suggest it."

"But you do believe that it is possible?" she pressed.

"Oh, yes, indeed, the way you describe it, it could very well have happened that way. The problem is, Miss Bennett, that if the murderer did jump ship, he is long gone by now. And all you have on this Mr. Latimer is a feeling. No, I'm sorry, Miss Bennett, I wish there were more we could do but the simple truth is, we have absolutely nothing to go on."

"Then you will do nothing?"

"There is nothing to be done."

"Very well," she said in a strangely calm voice, "then I shall have to take matters into my own hands."

Oliver turned to her with a concerned look, and came quickly over to refill her glass with brandy. As he leaned over her to pour, he whispered warningly, "Careful." She looked at him in surprise. Why should she be careful?

"Why, what do you mean, Miss Bennett?" the sheriff said in a rather unpleasant voice.

Oliver shot her another meaningful look. Now she was confused.

"I...I only mean..."

"Miss Bennett means that since her father was her only family, and the gold her only fortune, and she so accustomed to having someone to take care of her, naturally she is a bit concerned about having to make her way in the world. Isn't that what you meant, Miss Bennett?" Oliver asked and all eyes turned to her.

She searched Oliver's face, and found a message there that said, please, enough of this for now. "Yes...that is what I meant."

Oliver let out a soft sigh, and the sheriff was satisfied with this answer. Oliver offered the men another brandy, which they declined. She sat quietly, deep in her own thoughts.

"Well, gentlemen, it's getting late, and I would invite you all for supper, but I'm sure you are all anxious to get home to your own tables, eh?"

Mr. Beckworth, the neighbor, said, "Ah, yes, Sebastian, that Portia of yours is a fine cook, I can vouch for that. But the missus will be worried if I don't show up for supper at home. You know how peculiar wives can be."

Yes, they all agreed, they knew indeed. Mr. Winslow the lawyer said something Oliver about seeing him tomorrow in his office? Oliver replied that he would be there. Sheriff Brown said he would get back to town and file his report on this case, what little there was to file, and then without further ado, they made their good-byes to Rebecca and were escorted out.

Rebecca sat very still for a long time, until she felt the hairs on her neck bristle and she looked up to see Oliver staring at her from the doorway.

"You little fool," he murmured almost inaudibly.

She started in surprise. He paced into the room and stood by the hearth, his eyes blazing into hers. "That was a stupid thing to tell the sheriff."

"What?"

"That you would take matters into your own hands! If I hadn't explained for you -"

"Thank you very much," she said sarcastically, then wished she hadn't. He was right. It was a very stupid thing to say, and if it hadn't been for his quick intervention, she would have told them all that she planned to bring that murderer Latimer to justice if she had to do it herself.

He stared coldly at her. "Just what do you intend to do?"

"I intend to see that justice is done," she replied calmly.

"And how do you intend to do that?"

Something inside her broke under the strain, and she pressed a shaking hand to her feverish brow. "I don't know. I don't know anything anymore."

Oliver came over and stood before her, hands clenched at his sides, as though he wanted to take her in his arms, but could not. She looked up at him, her eyes questioning.

"Why? Why didn't you tell me?"

He looked stricken. "Tell you what?" he said, but he knew. He must know.

"About her. About your wife."

"I thought you knew. Didn't your father tell you?"

"No, he never mentioned the fact that you were a married man. If he had, I -"

"Yes?"

She wanted to say, if he had, she would not have fallen in love with Oliver. But that was absurd. She would have fallen in love with Oliver if he had been a leper, and she knew it. "I would have remembered it," she finished lamely.

"Miss Bennett – Rebecca - we have to talk." He reached for her hand and drew her to her feet. "But not here. Let's go for a walk, shall we?"

The springtime night air was warm. Rebecca began to feel better away from the house, and perhaps out in the open she could think more clearly. They walked for a long time in silence, Oliver's hand on her arm to guide her feet along the unfamiliar ground.

The moon hadn't risen yet, but there was just enough starlight to light their path. They walked slowly, each wrapped in private thoughts, listening to the sounds of crickets and frogs. Far off in the distance a steamboat whistle blew, sending a shudder of remembrance through Rebecca's body.

What was she doing here in this strange place? Once again she had the feeling of being somehow in the middle of a bad dream, from which she hoped to awaken safe and sound back in Savannah. Natchez! It might as well have been the moon! Whatever had possessed her father to leave behind everything that they had ever known, to come here to this unknown place, chasing the promise of fortune?

Dowry for his daughter, indeed! That was the part that really appalled her. To think that her father actually believed that he must provide her with an attractive inheritance to insure that she would marry a proper gentleman!

And where was he now? Why had he brought her here and then abandoned her? It was all his fault, really. If he hadn't been so old-fashioned in his insistence on a dowry, if he hadn't been carrying so much gold, if he hadn't told everyone about it. It was all his own fault...

A sob involuntarily escaped from her lips, and the man at her side squeezed her arm in comfort. No, that was unfair, she couldn't blame her father for his own death. And he had done all this for her, she knew that.

They could have had a nice, dull but safe life in Savannah, but he wanted to give her more. Out of his love for her he had given up his orderly existence and set out in search of fortune, a fortune that would have been hers, too. He had wanted to provide her with something more than a rundown mercantile store that was slowly being surrounded by warehouses and surely couldn't prosper for much longer under those conditions.

No, she certainly couldn't blame him for loving her. Now the best way that she could repay him was to take hold of this new life that was so suddenly thrust upon her and make him proud of her. How she would go about doing that was still unclear, but she was resourceful. She would find a solution.

Oliver would have been the perfect solution - but she immediately suppressed that thought before it took hold of her imagination. Even that option was removed, now.

Oliver was already married.

He turned off the dirt path and headed up a small incline, Rebecca following, her feet sinking into the soft cushion of grass covering the hill.

They made their way up to the top where there was a small crescent-shaped grove of trees. In the midst of the crescent was a small, round, white wooden building with nothing more than a roof and a floor, open on all sides, but with beautiful gingerbread trim on the eaves and along the waist-high railing. It was utterly charming.

"Oh!" Rebecca exclaimed, finally breaking the silence. "What is this?"

"It's called a gazebo, though around here I believe it is known as a summerhouse." He led her up two short steps onto the floor and she noticed that there was a narrow bench running around the inside of it. She sat down, and he stood and leaned against one of the support posts. "There's the river," he said softly and pointed to the west.

She looked and indeed it was the river, not so very far away, glistening in the dim night like a silver thread.

"This is an enchanted place," she said almost in a whisper. "I'll bet if we are very quiet and still we shall see fairies dancing with the fireflies."

He turned to look at her, but she could not see his eyes. "I built this place for Charlotte," he said softly, almost apologetically. "I thought it would be a cool place to escape the heat of the house, but she never comes here. She says the mosquitoes drive her mad."

"It's beautiful," Rebecca replied simply.

He turned back to gaze at the river, and was silent for a very long time.

All of a sudden he jerked around to face her and said fiercely, "I love my wife!"

Rebecca was startled, and a shiver went through her that had nothing to do with the soft cool breeze blowing off the river. She stared at him as he convulsively clenched his fists. Then he was at her side on the bench, having cleared the space between them in one long stride. He grabbed her hands in his and held them tightly. His eyes bored into hers, seeking understanding there, finding only more questions.

"Surely your father told you why I want to sell this farm," he said urgently.

"No, he only said that you were going back to England."

"And he said nothing about why I was going back to England?"

"No."

Oliver sighed. "Then I beg your forgiveness. I thought you knew. You see, the reason..." He let out a short, tortured little laugh. "The reason I have to sell is because Charlotte is in very poor health, and I am afraid that if she stays here much longer she will die."

Rebecca's eyes grew wide in understanding. So that was it. Her father hadn't told her that little item of information. Or maybe he thought he had told her, and had forgotten. At any rate, she understood now, and squeezed his hands in sympathy.

"I'm sorry that Mrs. Sebastian -" - funny how easily she could say that now - " -is ill."

"I've been such an idiot," he said vehemently. "She wasn't in the best of health before we came over here. When she lost the baby, she nearly died. I should have taken her home then. But no, I had to stay and make a fortune in cotton, just to prove that I could, and it almost cost me my wife."

He took a deep breath, staring at his hands. "She never wanted to come in the first place. We had a lovely little home in Liverpool, but I thought it was too small. And I thought Liverpool was no place to bring up children. How stupid of me. I was born in Liverpool myself, it's a wonderful old town. But then when I started working down on the docks and began to see the money that could be made from cotton if a man could only find some land and work it for a few years, there was no stopping me. I wanted to give Charlotte everything that she deserves, that she was born to have. She comes from a very old family, did you know that?"

Rebecca was silent, knowing that he did not expect an answer, only needed to talk.

"Royal blood flows in her veins. And believe me, for her to marry a poor man's son like me was something, I can tell you. I wanted to prove to them all that I was worthy of her. So I brought her over here, and bought this farm, and I've been so busy making money hand over fist that I neglected her to the point of -"

He stopped and rubbed a hand roughly across his eyes. "I couldn't see what was happening to her. She lost the baby in her fourth month, and it nearly killed her. Since then, I've been reluctant to touch her. I didn't want to risk it again."

Rebecca stroked his hands gently.

"She never fully recovered from that, not really. Her health has been steadily going from bad to worse. She's lost a lot of weight. She is so pale. She won't eat."

Rebecca could feel the torture he was going through, as he blamed himself for his wife's condition.

"The weather here is bad for her. It's too hot and too damp. She is very delicate, she should be back in England. And always, always, there is the threat of yellow fever. Don't you see, I must get her out of this place before she dies!"

His eyes begged for her understanding, and strangely enough she could give it. "Yes, of course you must," she replied soothingly.

"I have no choice!" he cried. "Yes, I've made my fortune, now I can go home in triumph, now I can show those upper-class bastards that I'm good enough for her."

He broke off almost on a sob, which tugged painfully at Rebecca's heart. The class structure was very much an issue in England, this much she knew, and if Charlotte did indeed have royal blood, then her marrying a commoner would have been reason enough for her society to reject them both.

She reached up and gently pressed her hand against his cheek. He closed his eyes and leaned against it with a groan, as if this were the only comfort he could find.

"You poor man," she murmured softly, sincerely. "Of course you must take your wife home. I'm only sorry that my father was not able to fulfill his obligation to you to buy your farm. Had he been, it would all be settled now. It's a wonderful place, and he would have loved it. But now I'm afraid it will mean several more days delay until you can find another buyer. I'm terribly sorry."

Oliver looked at her sadly, and she thought she saw a wetness about his eyes. "Oh, my darling child, you mustn't think such things. Don't feel sorry for me because of what happened. You are -" He tried to laugh, but it sounded more like a gasp. "You are a beautiful child." He touched her face gently the way she touched his, and smiled at her. "You have your own tragedy to deal with, I should not have burdened you with mine, too. Forgive me?"

"I love you," she answered simply. He closed his eyes for a moment, then opened them again.

"You don't mean that."

"But I do! I do love you, can't you see that? You are the only thing that I have left in this world, and now -" But she couldn't finish, couldn't say that now he must take his wife back to England, that now she would lose him too, just when she had found him.

He grabbed her by the shoulders. "I love my wife!"

"I know! I know you do. But could you love me, too?"

Oliver pulled her hard against his chest, held her tightly. "My little darling," he whispered into her ear.

He crushed her harder against him, rocked gently back and forth for a long moment, then suddenly he raised her face to look into her eyes. She could barely see him in the pale moonlight through the haze of tears.

"I love my wife," he repeated, as if to make that very clear to her, "but I think I love you, too."

And with that he lowered his lips to hers and took possession of them in a gentle kiss that turned into a fiery embrace as she returned his kiss, passion for passion. Stars exploded behind her eyelids as their mouths opened and they attempted to devour each other with their hunger. Feverishly she clung to him, pulling him closer, until he could come no closer, and still it was not close enough. His tongue sent sweet raptures through her body, making every nerve alive to his presence.

He tore his lips away from hers, breathing raggedly. "I must get Charlotte back to England."

She ran her fingers through his hair, loving the texture and the way the moonlight made it look streaked with silver. She imagined him as an old man with gray, silver hair, and was pleased with the picture. He would never lose those handsome good looks. He could only get better with age.

Suddenly Rebecca was gripped with a sadness that threatened to engulf her, and he felt her body stiffen. He looked questioningly into her eyes, and tears welled there but did not spill. "What is it?"

"I was just thinking this will be the last time you and I will be together. Would it be proper for me to say...thank you?"

His eyes clouded. "Proper be damned!" he hissed, and crushed her lips with his. But even in the middle of his fiery kiss, she could not help thinking that they must soon part, never to see each other again, never to soar to such heights as they were capable of reaching together, never to share the joy of simply being in love.

When he lifted his head, his eyes were stormy with emotion. "It is I who should be thanking you, for giving me the only real moments of true pleasure that I've had in a long time. I would give anything -"

He broke off, and she knew that he did not mean that, he would not give anything, for there was still something that stood in their way - his love for his wife. She could not deny him that. In fact she honored him for it, for his devotion to Charlotte. If he felt that strongly about a woman he could no longer touch, what limits would there possibly be to his love for a woman he could love as he had her?

How very tragic, that Rebecca's first love must be a forbidden love!

If she had never met Charlotte Sebastian, maybe she could have hated the woman, could have stolen her man away from her. But it was not that way at all. She had seen how frail and weak Charlotte was, how even Portia agreed that she was wasting away to nothing. It meant giving up the man she loved, but a life might be saved because of it. Rebecca was no martyr, by any means, but she knew in her heart that it must be this way.

"Shhh." She pressed a finger to his lips to quiet him. "We have had this time together. No one can ever take that away from us. Wherever you go, whatever you do, just remember that I love you, and I will always love you. My beloved Oliver."

"My beloved Rebecca."

They embraced one final time, then walked slowly back to the house.

CHAPTER EIGHT

Lights blazed in the windows downstairs in what should have been a welcoming sight, but it meant that there were persons inside who would be wondering where they had disappeared to, and why. She took a deep breath and tried very hard, without success, to still the quavering inside, lest she give them both away. Their private moment was over; now they had to face the real world again. He opened the door and she stepped inside.

"Oliver? Is that you, darling?"

"Yes, dearest," he replied, closing the door behind them and preceding Rebecca into the library.

"Oh, there you are, Miss Bennett, I went in to check on you but found you had gone." Her voice was as calm as her face. "I was concerned. Are you all right, my dear?"

Rebecca went to her side and took her outstretched hand in hers. It felt very cool and limp. "Yes, thank you, I am now. I was in need of some air, and Mr. Sebastian very kindly offered to walk with me." She felt ashamed at the ease with which she could lie.

"How thoughtful of you, my darling," she said to Oliver as he bent over her and placed a light, quick kiss on her forehead.

"Not really," he replied nonchalantly, "when you consider that Miss Bennett has never been in this part of the country before and was apt to go falling into the river in the darkness. One tragedy at a time, please." He threw himself into a chair and picked up a newspaper, pretending very hard to become engrossed in it.

Rebecca could feel color coming into her cheeks. She smiled at Mrs. Sebastian to distract her attention. "I want to thank you for lending me this dress."

"My dear, you are very welcome. I understand that you lost all your things in the accident. It was the very least I could do to aid you in your time of sorrow. And it fits even better than I had hoped. We must be the same size."

"It really was very thoughtful of you. I should have had to have one made otherwise, though without funds -" She broke off, embarrassed. "Well, thank you again."

"Please, think no more of it. Now, would you care for something to eat? Portia has kept supper warm, and I believe I could eat something myself."

Rebecca glanced up at the mantel clock. After nine! "I'm so sorry to have kept you waiting, I didn't realize it was getting so late. Yes, please,

I would like something to eat. Now that I think of it, I haven't eaten in a very long time."

"Then let us go at once." She rose from her chair. "Oliver, my darling, will you be coming in to supper?"

"Hmm?" He lowered his paper. "Oh, no, thank you, dearest, I'm not hungry. You ladies go ahead. I want to catch up on all the news since I left Natchez." Then he hid behind the paper again.

Rebecca could see it so plainly, why couldn't she, his own wife?

"Shall we, Miss Bennett?"

"Please, call me Rebecca."

"Very well, Rebecca, and you must call me Charlotte."

Portia served them roasted chicken with a delicious stuffing of cornbread and pecans, along with several vegetable dishes so uniquely flavored that Rebecca found herself complimenting Portia on every dish and helping herself more than once to some of them. She had not noticed, but she was ravenously hungry, and ate with a relish which seemed to gratify the cook.

The best gratification, however, came with seeing the way Mrs. Sebastian - Charlotte - ate a little of everything, and seemed to gain a bit more color and vivacity. She plied Rebecca with questions, about her life in Savannah, about the trip to Natchez, about everything. Rebecca answered all her questions between mouthfuls.

After supper, they went back to the library where Charlotte showed Rebecca a piece of needlework that she was doing, a very fine copy of a medieval tapestry. Rebecca was impressed with her talent. Needlework was not one of Rebecca's skills, but they passed a pleasant hour with Charlotte attempting to teach her the rudiments of embroidery, and entertaining her with stories of her life as a young girl in one of the oldest families in Britain. Maybe she did have royal blood, but she certainly didn't flaunt the fact. Her good breeding was evident in everything she did.

Rebecca was acutely aware of Oliver's presence in the room, though outwardly she gave no sign of it. He sat very quietly during the whole time they talked, occasionally rustling his newspaper or relighting the cigar that kept going out. Was he listening to them, or merely deep in his own thoughts? More than once she stole a glance at him and caught him staring into space.

But Charlotte soon began to tire; that was obvious from the way she kept dropping the small pointed embroidery scissors. At length she pushed it all aside.

"I hope you will forgive me, Rebecca, but I think I shall retire now. Do you mind?"

Rebecca stood up. "Oh, no, of course not. In fact, I didn't want to be rude, but I'm really very tired myself. Shall we go up together?"

She extended her hand to Charlotte, who took it and leaned on Rebecca's strength to rise and cross the room. Oliver came to them at the door. "Going to bed, my sweet?"

"Yes, dear, I'm afraid Rebecca and I have exhausted each other with all our talk. Will you be up soon?"

"In a little while. I have some papers to go over." He kissed his wife softly on the lips. "Good night, darling."

"Good night, Mr. Sebastian," Rebecca said as they turned to leave the room.

"Oh, Miss Bennett, may I have a word with you?"

She stopped, but did not turn. "Yes?"

"About the funeral arrangements tomorrow," he said, waiting for Charlotte to go on without her.

Rebecca kept her hold on Charlotte's hand. "Yes?" she repeated.

There was a long pause during which she did not look at him. Finally he said, "I have asked Reverend Dockery to preside over a small graveside ceremony tomorrow morning. I hope this meets with your approval." The tone of his voice told her that it was not her approval he was hoping for.

"Yes, that will be very nice, I'm sure. My father would have appreciated your kindness, as I certainly do."

He was silent for so long, that finally she turned to look at him. "Is there something else, Mr. Sebastian?"

He gave her a pained look that spoke volumes. She only hoped that Charlotte did not see it. "No, that was all I wanted," he lied. "Good night, Miss Bennett."

"Good night, Mr. Sebastian."

"Reverend Dockery is a fine man. Oliver could not have chosen better," said Charlotte as they went up the stairs together.

Rebecca smiled at her. "I can't thank you both enough for the kindness you have shown me. I only wish my father could have lived to meet you, Charlotte. You would have charmed him right off his feet."

Charlotte returned the smile. "You are too kind. Good night, my dear."

"Good night." They exchanged small pecks on the cheek and Rebecca went into the bedroom that had been given to her.

She slept very deeply that night, and though she dreamed about her father, about Oliver, about Charlotte, about them all, her dreams were all sweet. No nightmarish qualities intruded anywhere, for which she was thankful when she awoke the next morning, rested and serene.

Portia knocked on her bedroom door and then entered, carrying a pitcher of water. "Good mornin', Miss Bennett."

"Good morning, Portia. Is Miss Charlotte up?"

"No, ma'am, Miss Charlotte is still asleep. She must have been mighty tuckered out last night."

"I'm afraid that's my fault, Portia. We stayed up late talking. Where is Mr. Sebastian?"

"He went into town early this mornin'. They buryin' your papa this mornin', are they?"

"Yes. Mr. Sebastian has given a small plot here on his property for the grave. Papa would have liked that."

"He sure is a good man. They both are mighty good people. And if you don't mind me sayin' this, Miss Bennett, you sure are good for Miss Charlotte. I ain't seen her lookin' so healthy or eatin' so well in a long time. This place been hard on her, and livin' so far out from town she don't hardly never see no womenfolks her own age. I hope you'll be stayin' on here for a while, Miss Bennett. You is a tonic for Miss Charlotte, I reckon."

"Why, thank you, Portia. But I don't know how long I can stay. You see, I have no family anywhere, and no money, and I don't really know what I'll do now..."

Suddenly emotion choked her, and tears filled her eyes. Rebecca stuffed the edge of the sheet into her mouth, to quell the sobs that threatened to overtake her.

Portia sat beside her on the bed, and gently took Rebecca in her arms, rocking back and forth and soothing her with soft murmurings.

"It's all right, honey child, everythin' will be all right. You poor little lamb, lost your papa and nobody to take care of you, why, you're just a baby. But don't you worry none, I know Mister Oliver and Miss Charlotte will help you out all they can, them bein' such fine folks and all. Maybe they could help you find some kinda job or somethin'. Natchez ain't a bad place to live, not at all. There's lotsa fine families here. Can you read and write? Maybe you can find a teachin' position."

"I thank you for trying to help, but I doubt very much if I shall stay in Natchez, not now. I might even go to live in New Orleans." The idea had only just occurred to her, but it wasn't a bad one, at that.

"N'Orleans! Lord, child, that's the devil's own town, for sure! No, ma'am, you will be a heap better off right here in Natchez."

Rebecca smiled. "Well, we shall see."

"Want me to freshen up this dress for you?" Portia held up the black dress.

Rebecca shook her head. "That won't be necessary, Portia, thank you very much. I only wore it for a few hours last night. It should be just fine for the funeral."

Again, suddenly, emotion choked into her throat and tears filled her eyes. Funeral! Her father was dead, she had no money, no family. It was all she could do to keep a rising hysteria from exploding. She would think of something. She must.

"I got breakfast ready downstairs, whenever you feel hungry. Now I'll leave you alone." Portia beamed a bright smile at Rebecca and left the room.

* * *

The funeral was a small, quiet ceremony held underneath a stand of trees very near the river bluff, where Oliver's men had dug a grave, marked by a simple marble headstone, in the shade of a weeping willow. Oliver had also arranged for a fine cedar coffin for her father, which was lowered into the ground as Reverend Dockery said a few words about Mr. Henry Bennett's soul being commended unto heaven.

Rebecca did not cry. Emotion welled up inside her until she thought she would burst, but there were no more tears. Charlotte stood beside her during it all, and took her hand as the first shovel of dirt was thrown in. Then it was all over, and they walked quietly back to the house.

Portia had spread a large table with sumptuous food, in anticipation of visitors, but there were only a few. After all, her father was not known to them, and they came mainly out of respect for Oliver Sebastian.

Sheriff Brown stopped by briefly on his way to Washington, a small town a few miles southeast of Natchez. No, he regretted to report, there were no new developments in the murder case.

Mr. Beckworth, the neighbor, and his wife came in with their son, Charles, who appeared to be about Rebecca's age. He had a round babyish face and large soft hands that had probably never done a day's work. Mrs. Beckworth was a portly woman who tried to offer Rebecca some words of condolence between mouthfuls of Portia's rum cake with butter cream sauce, which kept dripping down her chin and onto her lap. Charles was more interested in the fruit-filled pastries than he was in Rebecca, until Mrs. Beckworth deliberately drew her son over to sit beside them and join the conversation. Then it became painfully clear to Rebecca that the Beckworths were anxious to make a match between their son and her.

After too many minutes of listening to Mrs. Beckworth expound upon her son's sterling qualities, Rebecca became desperate for some fresh air. She excused herself and almost ran out of the house, breathing in gulps of the warm spring air and then setting off for a walk alone. Unconsciously her feet retraced last night's path until she was in sight of the little hill on which stood the gazebo. She stopped in her tracks as a voice hailed her from behind.

"Miss Bennett! Wait for me!"

She turned to see Charles Beckworth following her at a pace, his pudgy body trying hard to catch up to her. She sighed heavily and waited for him. What else could she do?

"Mama says...I am...to walk...with you," he said between huge gasps for breath.

She gritted her teeth. "Thank you, Mr. Beckworth, I was very much in need of someone to walk with me."

He smiled, not recognizing the sarcasm. She had wanted to go sit in the gazebo, where she could think and be alone, but now she must change her plans.

She turned in the opposite direction and began to walk very slowly so that the young man might better match her pace.

"It's a shame about your daddy," he said presently, trying to make conversation. "We woulda come to the funeral, but we wasn't invited."

She stole a glance at him, but his face was untroubled. There was no sarcasm in his words, he was merely stating a fact. "Yes, well, it was a very small service, you see. There was no time to send out invitations." Now why had she said that? There was no need to be rude to this boy. It was just nerves, she hoped.

Charles laughed as though she had just said the funniest thing. "Mama says you ain't got nobody to take care of you now that your daddy is dead. She said you ain't got no money, no home, no family. Why, shucks, Miss Bennett, I got all them things."

Lucky you, she thought to herself, but said nothing.

"What I mean is...could you...I mean...do you think...Miss Bennett, could you stand still for a minute so I can talk to you?"

She stopped in surprise, and turned to face him. "Yes, Mr. Beckworth?"

"Oh, you don't have to call me that. My mama calls me Charles, but you can call me Charlie. Miss Bennett, what I want to ask you is...do you think you could marry me?"

She stared at him for a long moment, then turned and began to walk very quickly back to the house.

"Miss Bennett? D-did I say something wrong?"

He almost had to run to keep up with her, but she did not slow down.

"Mr. Beckworth, I appreciate the kind offer, but I'm afraid I cannot marry you. It is out of the question."

"That's a relief," he said through his gasps. She stopped dead in her tracks and turned to him.

"What did you say?"

"I said that's a relief. It was my mama's idea, really, not mine. She's been tryin' to get me married off for the longest time. Says I eat too much, and I need a wife to cook for me because she's tired of feedin' me."

Rebecca quickly covered her mouth with her hand to stifle a laugh, but couldn't, and burst into laughter.

Charlie grinned broadly.

"Charlie, you are precious," she said when she could talk again. "I can't be your wife, but I can be your friend."

"Why, thank you, Miss Bennett." He beamed.

"You may call me Rebecca."

He actually blushed. "Gosh, I never had a lady friend before. What do we do now?"

"Well, you may offer me your arm and walk with me back to the house. That will do for now."

He very gallantly put out his arm and she took it. Together they walked, slowly this time, back to the house.

"Well! Where have you two been, hmm?" said Charlie's mother with a knowing glance at her son.

"Oh, me and Rebecca went for a little walk, Mama."

"Thank you for walking with me, Charlie."

Mrs. Beckworth was almost beside herself. "Callin' each other by first names, are we? Then it's all settled?"

Charlie gave Rebecca a sly wink. "Yes, Mama, it's all settled."

"Ohh!" she squealed and jumped up. "How marvelous! Get your father, dear. We must be goin' now. And I hope, Miss Bennett - Rebecca? - that we will be seein' a lot more of you?"

"I am in mourning, Mrs. Beckworth, not in hiding," she answered with a smile.

Mrs. Beckworth didn't quite know what to make of this answer, but she was happy enough for the moment. She made her good-byes, and the Beckworths drove away in their carriage.

"What was that all about?" asked Charlotte when she found Rebecca sitting in a chair in the parlor grinning like the cat that swallowed the canary.

"Brace yourself. I have just had a proposal of marriage."

Charlotte's mouth flew open. "What? You mean from Charles Beckworth?"

"The very same. Poor fellow. I feel a bit sorry for him."

"Not sorry enough to marry him, I hope," said Charlotte as she took a seat near Rebecca.

"No, not quite." Rebecca smiled. "He needs to marry a cook, and I'm afraid I'm not very good in the kitchen."

"You saw the way he eats," Charlotte said with a wry grin. "He gets it from his mother, I suppose."

"His 'mama' put him up to proposing to me. She wants him to take a wife so she doesn't have to feed him any more."

"She has a point. That way there will be more for her to eat."

"The only problem is that his mother now thinks that I accepted him. You should have seen her face! She was ecstatic!"

They laughed over this for a long time, sharing the joke. Charlotte told Rebecca about the few times that the Beckworths had been to supper there and how they had nearly driven Portia mad trying to keep food on the table.

"But Mr. Beckworth is a very nice gentleman. He has been a good friend to Oliver."

"I have no doubt of that. Too bad his son did not take after him."

Charlotte was pensive for a moment. "Have you thought about what you will do?"

"I'm not going to marry Charlie, that's for sure."

"No, of course not, that's not what I mean. I mean, now that your father is...I'm sorry, I'm not being very tactful, am I?"

Rebecca stared at a distant spot. "I haven't given it much though, actually. I keep hoping that tomorrow will take care of itself. But tomorrow is here, today, isn't it? I don't know..."

Charlotte cleared her throat.

"Rebecca, why don't you come with us to England?"

The shock must have registered on Rebecca's face, and she gave a violent start.

"Please, Rebecca, it would give me such pleasure to have you by my side. I've only known you for one day, and already I feel we are best friends. I need you. I need you as a companion. I know that sounds rather selfish of me, but I guess I'm just a selfish person. What do you say?"

Rebecca could find no words to convey her feelings.

"I - I am flattered, Charlotte. It is a very kind offer. But I don't see how it is possible..."

"Oh, please don't say no until you've had time to think about it. It is rather sudden, I know. But Oliver is anxious to get back as soon as possible, which means any day now, as soon as all the business is wrapped up. I want you with me. It will be a marvelous opportunity. We'll travel. Have you ever been to Europe? I know all the places to go, and all the right people - and I daresay your chances of finding a suitable match will be much better there than they are here. You shouldn't settle for a Charles Beckworth. Why, I daresay you might end up with a count, or a baronet, or an earl at the least. Oh, I know I'm not making any sense now. I'm too excited about the idea. Just promise me you'll think about it. Promise?"

Charlotte seemed so sincere, she could not bear to hurt her. The truth would certainly hurt her. The idea was totally absurd! Quite unacceptable! And yet...and yet...

The possibilities, the opportunities to be with Oliver made her heart pound. But no, it was impossible. As much as she loved Oliver, she had already made up her mind that they could never be together. She was beginning to love Charlotte, too, and the thought of going behind her back...

No, it was absolutely out of the question.

"Promise?" Charlotte urged.

"I promise I'll think about it," Rebecca replied. In all honesty, although she knew her answer must be no, it was something to think about, to dream about.

"Good. Think about it as long as you like. Take your time making the decision, as long as the decision is yes."

Rebecca smiled at her. "You are a wonderful friend, Charlotte. I will never forget you." That much was true.

"You sound as if you have already made up your mind. You promised to think about it. Now let's not say another word."

Rebecca kept her promise. She did think about it. She could think of nothing else. When they went upstairs for a nap to escape the afternoon heat, she tossed and turned on the bed, her head full of fanciful ideas. Finally she gave up, and left the house for a walk. Maybe there would be a cool breeze coming off the river. She headed for the gazebo.

Far off in the distance sounded the shrill whistle of a steamboat. She sat in the cool shade of the small building, staring at the river, watching for the boat to come into sight around the bend.

So deep in thought was she that she did not notice him until he stepped onto the platform directly in front of her.

"I saw you leave the house. I followed you," said Oliver as he leaned casually against the post.

Her heart leaped into her throat. He was so handsome standing there, outlined against the blue of the sky, in his black suit. She had not seen him since the funeral that morning, but he had been in her thoughts, constantly.

With a rush of feeling, she flew into his arms and he crushed her against his chest.

"Do you know what it is like to be under the same roof with you and not be able to hold you in my arms?" His voice was thick with emotion.

"Yes," she whispered. "I do know. Hold me. Hold me."

He held her as though he would never, could never let her go. All of the sadness rushed back into her heart at the thought of giving him up forever. If only things had been different, but they weren't. She must face the facts and look to her own future. A future without Oliver looked very bleak, indeed, but there was really no alternative.

She finally broke the embrace herself and led him to the bench. "Do you know what Charlotte just asked me? Can you guess?" she said as they sat down very close to one another.

He seemed to hold his breath. "She doesn't know...? She couldn't possibly know about us?"

"No, it's not that."

His relief was visible. "What did she say?"

"She invited me to come along with her to England." She watched his face for reaction.

His immediate reaction was a stunned disbelief. But slowly, as though the wheels in his mind began to turn, he smiled. "That is the best idea I've heard all day."

"What?"

"Darling, that's wonderful! Yes, it's perfect! I wish I had thought of it. Charlotte is a genius! Well, that settles everything."

This was not the reaction she had expected, although he was obviously seeing the same advantages she had. "Oliver, you must be joking. I cannot possibly come to England with you. With you, maybe, but not with you and Charlotte."

"But we could be together -"

"That's the whole point. We cannot be together any more. I will not hurt Charlotte in that fashion."

He stared at her. "You are that fond of her?"

"Yes, I guess I am. But it's more than that. I am not a liar and a cheat. I could not possibly hide the fact from her for very long that I am desperately in love with you. She would find out, Oliver, believe me, and it would crush her. I could not bear to be responsible for that."

He thought for a moment, then shook his head. "I cannot believe you are serious. It is the very solution we need to the problem. Charlotte gets back to England, and you and I are together. What more could you ask?"

She sighed. "I will not share you with any woman. I want you all to myself or not at all. No, Oliver, it is quite out of the question. And you know in your heart that I am right."

He let out a deep breath, and ran a hand over his eyes. "Yes, yes, of course, you are right. For a moment, though, I could not help but think of what it would be like being with you always. God! If I were half a man-"

"But you aren't, Oliver. You aren't half a man. Half a man would have jumped at the opportunity and the devil take the consequences. But you are not like that, my darling. You have honor, and integrity, and you must do the right thing no matter the cost. That's one of the reasons I love you so much. And the reason why we must say good-bye now."

"Now? Are you leaving?"

His anxiety touched her. "Soon. I must. I cannot bear to be so near you and yet so far."

He took her small hands in his large ones and brought them to his lips, kissing her fingertips softly. "This is tearing me apart. I know I must do the right thing, but what is the right thing? If I try to help Charlotte, then I lose you. If I choose you over her, then I lose my self-respect. It is a no-win situation."

She smiled sadly. "I lose the love of my life, but Charlotte gains back her life. That is much more important. This is no place for her. It is not just the climate. She is not suited for this place. She is as anxious to get back home as you are to take her there. Probably the reason she has taken so to me is that she misses her family. I would be as out of place in England as Charlotte is here in Natchez."

"So where do we go from here?"

"I don't know. I guess I must find a job, but that won't be easy. I haven't any skills. I can read and write, though, maybe I could become a schoolteacher. Or a governess. I'll think of something."

"Look, I've just had an idea. Let me take care of you."

"I thought we had settled that!"

"No, no, I mean I could give you some money to live on until something comes along. I could leave a trust fund at the bank for your expenses. It's the least I can do. I feel responsible for you."

"Why should you do that? It wasn't your fault my father was... No, that's very sweet, but how would it look? It would be almost like admitting that we were...no, it's a nice suggestion, but it won't do. I'll find something. I'll get by. I might even get married."

He was horrified. "You aren't serious! No, how stupid of me! Of course you'll get married. It's a wonder you aren't married already."

Unbidden memories of Samuel made her eyes sting with tears. She hadn't told Oliver about Samuel, and now she never would have the chance. It was no longer important, not really. Oliver still believed her to be unspoiled. She would let him continue to believe it.

"Well, I have had a proposal. Today, in fact."

"Today! From whom?"

"Charlie Beckworth."

The relief on his face was gratifying. "I was right. You aren't serious. He's just a boy."

"Compared to you, yes. But don't you think I would make him a fine wife?"

His eyes blazed in sudden passion and he grabbed her by the shoulders. "You are my wife, and don't you forget it. You can marry any man you please, but he will never take my place. I am your true husband."

"That's - that's bigamy."

He laughed. "Nevertheless..."

"So when are you planning to leave for England?"

"I've booked passage for the fifteenth."

"But that's next week!"

"Yes, but you see I booked it as soon as I heard from Mr. Bennett. I was sure there would be no reason why he might not buy the farm. Of course I never dreamed..."

"But have you sold it yet?"

"As a matter of fact, Mr. Beckworth made me an offer this morning. He wants the land to add to his, and he will give the house to Charlie. So you see, maybe you should take Charlie up on his proposal. At least you will be able to live in the house that you came all this way to find."

"Very funny," she said, with a wry smile.

"At any rate, he will have a furnished house to move into. I plan to take nothing back with me to England, except clothing, and a few books. And Portia, of course."

"Portia is going with you?"

"Yes, I don't see how I can leave her behind. She's so devoted to Charlotte, she would never be happy unless she was with her."

"Well, that makes me feel better. It won't be so hard to say no if I know that Portia will be with her. Oh, God, Oliver. I sit here talking so calmly when inside I am falling apart."

Oliver gathered her into his arms, and soothed her with soft, loving words. "I know, my darling, it's not easy for me, either. I almost wish that we had never met. Almost. If we hadn't, I would never have known these sweet lips."

He kissed her tenderly, deeply, not so much with passion as with love. She returned the kiss, holding her breath, taking her sustenance from him. When he kissed her like that, her whole being melted into his. She no longer belonged to herself, she belonged to him, ultimately and totally. It might be only for a few seconds, but in those few seconds everything else faded away. The only reality was the reality of their love.

For a long time, they remained that way, locked in each others arms, until finally she felt the urgent stirring in him that signaled a change to her. His kiss became fiery, and his hand began to roam over her breasts, making her quiver and catch her breath sharply.

Then suddenly they realized that they were not alone.

"Mister Sebastian, sir?"

Oliver jerked around sharply and saw Jeremiah, the nine-year-old, staring at them with open mouth. He got quickly to his feet and went to the child. "Yes? What is it, Jeremiah?" His breathing was still ragged, and Rebecca noticed that he tugged nervously at his cravat.

"It's Mister Beckworth, sir. He come back to the house. He wants to see you about somethin', I reckon. Miss Charlotte sent me to find you because I said I seen you and Miss Bennett walkin' this way."

"Thank you, Jeremiah. I will go directly. Will you stay here with Miss Bennett?"

"Yessir, only Miss Charlotte, she was askin' after Miss Bennett, too. I told them I would find you both. Did I do somethin' wrong, Mister Sebastian?" the boy said as he caught the strained glance between Oliver and Rebecca.

Oliver put an affectionate hand on the boy's head. "No, Jeremiah, you did fine. Well, Miss Bennett, shall we go back to the house?"

Slowly she got to her feet, careful not to look at either of them, lest they see how distraught and shaken she was.

This was the very thing she had hoped to avoid. The situation was completely intolerable.

They walked quickly back to the house, Jeremiah running on ahead to announce their arrival. Mr. Beckworth was sitting on the verandah sipping lemonade. Charlotte sat next to him, fanning herself with a large bamboo fan.

"There you are, Sebastian!" said Mr. Beckworth as they approached. "I know I told you that I would see you later in the week, but my wife insisted that I come on over now and get all the details straightened out. I think she's planning to get Charlie moved in here very soon, although I kept telling her to wait until you all had gone, eh?" He rose politely as Rebecca stepped onto the verandah. "Ah, Miss Bennett, my wife has given me the good news, and I must say, I could not have hoped for a more suitable match for my son."

Rebecca was already in a blush, and this remark deepened her color. She glanced at Charlotte, ready to share the private joke with her, about her supposed engagement to Charlie, but Charlotte stared at her fan, and did not look up.

Quickly Oliver shook hands with Beckworth, took a seat next to him, and began to talk business, thus diverting his attention. Charlotte remained impassively silent. Rebecca was at a loss.

"Do you have another fan, Charlotte? This heat is making me a bit dizzy," she attempted.

"Are you sure it is the heat, my dear?" Charlotte continued to fan herself, not looking at Rebecca.

"Why, yes, of course, what else?"

"What else, indeed."

"What do you mean?" Rebecca struggled to keep her voice low and controlled.

"Shall we go inside?"

CHAPTER NINE

Rebecca followed her into the house, her heart pounding. Charlotte went into the parlor, as far away from the men as she could quickly get. Then she turned to Rebecca with a stern frown.

"What were you doing alone with my husband?"

"I - I was only taking a walk -"

"Again? That's becoming a bit tiresome. I shouldn't think you would be in danger of falling into the river in broad daylight. Well?"

"Please, Charlotte, there is no reason to be angry -"

"Angry? I'm not angry. I am furious!" she nearly shouted. "Jeremiah told me he saw you kissing. Do you think I am blind? Do you think I don't know about you and Oliver?"

Portia came rushing into the room, having heard her mistress raise her voice. "Miss Charlotte, honey! What's the matter?"

Rebecca was too shocked to breathe. "I - I don't know what to say..."

"There is no need. It is written all over your face. What a fool I was, not to have seen it earlier. Oh, I had my suspicions, when Oliver first brought you here. You are just a little too pretty, and he was just a little too generous. But I wanted to give you both the benefit of a doubt. I even began to like you," she said and her voice began to shake under the strain of her emotions.

Portia hurried to Charlotte and put her arms around her shoulders, but Charlotte shrugged her off. "Miss Charlotte, please! Don't say things like that. You'll get yourself all worked up again!"

Charlotte ignored the woman. Her eyes were fixed on Rebecca. "I guess you had a good laugh at my expense, for inviting you to come along with us to England. My God, it's a good thing I see it clearly now. I almost made the mistake of my life!" She made a great effort to compose herself, and drew herself regally erect. "The invitation is, of course, withdrawn. You have no further reason to remain here. You will leave this house immediately."

With that, she turned and left the room.

"Miss Charlotte!" cried Portia, wringing her hands. She glanced nervously at Rebecca, and gave her a crooked smile. "She didn't mean none of it, Miss Bennett. Miss Charlotte - she ain't well..." Portia seemed lost for anything more to say, and finally turned and hurried after Charlotte.

Rebecca stood for a long moment, shaking inside, not knowing what to do now, whether to admit the truth and beg forgiveness or to let the matter take its own course. The thing to do, of course, would be to leave, now. She had known she must from the first, but had found it harder and harder to do. This gave her the impetus she needed to move into action. Secretly she thanked Charlotte for making it easier for her. She went up to her room and changed from the black dress back into the blouse and skirt that were the only wardrobe she had left, the only material things she owned in the whole world.

Things couldn't have worked out better if she had planned them, for when she came down, she found Oliver and Mr. Beckworth gone and Charlie waiting on the verandah.

"Hey, there, Rebecca. Mama told me to come over here and see you. She still thinks we are gettin' hitched. Daddy and Mr. Sebastian are lookin' at barns or somethin', so do you wanna go for a ride in my buggy?"

She couldn't tell Charlie the truth, of course. She only told him that she had decided to go back to Savannah. He very courteously consented to drive her into town where she might book steamboat passage, and even offered to loan her the money she would need. There was not anything he would not do for her. After all, they were friends, weren't they? Only please, Rebecca, reconsider the plan. There was not anything to go back to in Savannah, and at least here she did have friends. Wasn't Charlie her friend?

She smiled warmly at him, gave his hand a pat and then a squeeze. "Of course you are my friend, Charlie, and I am yours. Only it's a very complicated situation. Can you keep a secret?" she asked tentatively.

Charlie looked at her with an expression of admiration. "For you, anything."

She took a deep breath. "I'll probably regret this, but...the truth is, Charlie, that I am in love."

He looked at her and gasped in shock. "You mean, there is another man? Mama will be astonished to death. Who is he? Anyone I know? Or is that why you are goin' back to Savannah?" He gave her a conspiratorial wink.

The image of Samuel popped into her mind. It was very tempting to let him think that she had left a sweetheart back in Savannah and now she was going back to join him. That would satisfy most everyone's curiosity, even his mother's. But she decided against that tack, for she had suddenly remembered another friend she had there in Natchez whom it was just possible might be able to help her.

"Yes, you do know the man. But can we just leave it at that for the moment? I promise I will tell you all about it, one of these days. But right now I have something I need to attend to. Would you be so kind as to drive me to Natchez-Under-the-Hill?"

His astonishment was genuine. "Wh-why you goin' there, Rebecca? That's no place for a lady like you."

"How do you know that?" she teased.

"Well, I - I hear tell, is all. What you wanna go there for?" he persisted.

"I have a friend there whom I am anxious to see. Her name is Mary and she owns the Elysian Fields."

"Oh, you mean Red," he replied and sighed in relief.

"You know her?"

"Sure, everybody knows Red. And if you must know, I have been to Red's place myself. Me and Daddy go there sometimes. But don't breathe a word of it to Mama. She would have a calf if she knew."

Rebecca smiled, gave him a conspiratorial wink. "My lips are sealed."

Charlie deftly handled the horse and buggy over the rutted roads. Not long after, they were driving through the streets of Natchez. Rebecca looked about her, not with the intention of saying good-bye as she had thought a while earlier, but with a new interest. If the Sebastians were going back to England, then there was really no reason why she should not stay in Natchez, at least for a while. She had come this far. Her father had given his life to bring her here. The least she could do was try to make the best of a bad situation.

Rebecca heard the now familiar shrill of a steamboat whistle sounding very close. As they turned down long, muddy Silver Street heading for the bottom of the bluff, she saw another steamboat just butting up to the floating wharf and another boatload of passengers disembarking.

People swarmed everywhere. A small band of black musicians strummed and beat and sang to the visitors in hopes of spare change. Vendors hawked every kind of merchandise imaginable. Young men scurried to assist with luggage in hopes of tips. The place was teeming with activity and excitement.

Rebecca was finding herself more and more fascinated with the river and the people who depended on it, for whatever reasons. Savannah had been rather dull and boring. Natchez was anything but, especially here under the bluff, the infamous Natchez-Under-the-Hill.

Silver Street was just as crowded as it had been yesterday. (Was it only yesterday? It seemed a lifetime ago.) Charlie had to make a slow descent down the rather steep incline so the horse would not run away with them. Finally they reached their destination, and Charlie helped her down from the carriage.

The building in front of her was really rather fine, compared to the buildings that flanked it. The paint was peeling, and the lumber was in need of some repair, but all in all, it had a splendid look to it.

There were ornate carvings along the galleries that spread the width of the place on all three stories that gave it a sort of Oriental look. A faded but still elegant sign declared that this was indeed the Elysian Fields.

Rebecca stared discreetly about her. There were people everywhere, walking, running, lounging, lying, stumbling, talking, laughing, fighting. She got quite a few stares herself, and not such discreet ones at that.

Charlie yelled at a ragged man who was lounging in the mud next to the steps of the building. "Hey! Wanna make a dollar?"

The man quickly got up and came to him.

"Watch my horse and buggy for a while. Now here," he said as he pulled a bill from his pocket and tore it in half. He gave one half to the man and stuffed the other half back into his pocket. "You'll get the other half when I come back. If that horse and buggy are still there."

The man clearly would have preferred to have the whole dollar, but accepted the terms, and Charlie turned to escort Rebecca into the saloon. She gazed at him in admiration. He was a crude boy, no doubt, but that might just be his Mama's fault. There were apparently aspects to his character that just might turn him into a strong, confident man one day.

They entered the building through the open front door. Two men who were then leaving stared hard at her, then turned on their heels and followed them back inside. It was quite dark inside, despite the late afternoon sunshine outside, and it took a moment for her eyes to adjust.

Charlie led her to a table just inside the door and pulled out a chair for her. "Just sit here and I'll go see if I can find Red."

Rebecca became aware of the open stares she was receiving from nearly every man in the house. More than once one would stare lewdly at her, then turn to a companion and make some comment or suggestion that elicited the most raucous laughter and more stares.

Maybe Charlie was right. Maybe Oliver was right. Maybe this was no place for a lady.

To her horror, one of the men who had been staring most ardently actually came over to her table and sat himself down without even a by-your-leave, and began to regale her with tales of his sexual prowess. Her cheeks flamed. She looked around for Charlie, but he was nowhere in sight. The man reached out a dirty hand and tried to touch her cheek, but she recoiled.

Suddenly his hand was slapped away, and the chair on which he had been seated was overturned, spilling him backward onto the hard floor.

"Look, but don't touch," said Red, standing over the man in all her glory, hands on hips and a stern look in her eyes. The man got up and stumbled hastily away. Red turned to Rebecca.

"Forgive them, darlin', some of them ain't never laid eyes on a real lady before. It's good to see you again!" she said brightly and reached to hug Rebecca around the neck. Rebecca returned the embrace, knowing it was genuine.

Red righted the overturned chair and sat down next to Rebecca. "John Henry!" she called, and Rebecca saw the harried bartender look up. "Send over a bottle of brandy. The good stuff. Now tell me all about what's been happenin' to you since I last saw you. Did they ever find the dirty louse that killed your pa?"

Rebecca gave her a sad smile. "No, and they probably never will. I'm pretty sure that whoever did it jumped the boat with the gold."

"Gold? What gold?" Red asked with interest as John Henry placed a beautiful cut glass decanter and two crystal goblets on the table. "Thank you, John Henry. Give Charlie anything he wants. What gold?" She turned her attention back to Rebecca.

"The gold that my father was carrying with him on the boat. I guess I just assumed that everyone knew it."

She took the glass of brandy that was offered and sipped it slowly as she told Red about her father's distrust of banks and how he had been carrying a very large amount of gold on him, to purchase a plantation.

"I can certainly sympathize with him, I don't trust banks either. All my money is hidden in a safe place." She emphasized the word "safe" as though a bank were the last place she would put her money.

"Nevertheless, it proved to be his undoing. I guess he told one person too many about his plans, and he was murdered for the gold. It was everything we had in the world. I don't even have money to live on, to buy clothes, or to get back to Savannah, if I had a mind to."

"If it's money you need, why, I'd be glad -"

"No!" Rebecca cut her off quickly. That was not what she was getting at. "Thank you, but I was thinking more along the lines of...a job?"

Red gave her a thoughtful look for a long moment. "Sure, honey, if I can help you out, I'll be happy to. But just what did you have in mind?"

Rebecca stared into the cloudy amber liquid in the glass and bit her lip. "I don't know, that's just it. There isn't anything I'm trained to do. I thought I might become a schoolteacher. At least I can read and write. Maybe if I could find a position with a good family, I could be a governess to their children, or something. I really don't know. I was kind of hoping you could help me to come up with some ideas." She gave her friend a wan smile without much enthusiasm, as good as admitting that she really had not a hope in the world of making it on her own.

Red smiled at her and patted her arm sympathetically. "Well, never fear, we'll put our two heads together and somethin's bound to pop out. In the meantime, where are you stayin'?"

"I'm not. I mean, I don't have a place to stay. I was thinking about going back to Savannah, but I wanted to see you first."

"Do you want to go back?"

"To Savannah? No, not really. But I'll have no choice unless I come up with something soon."

Just then a whoop and a holler went up as a group of about fifty gentlemen trooped through the door.

"Whiskey and women!" one of them shouted and they all echoed the sentiment, heading straight for the bar. John Henry gave Red a pleading look and began frantically pouring whiskeys into shot glasses.

"Heavens to Betsy," said Red, staring at the frisky group. "And me short-handed, too. Well, I guess I'd better go help John Henry. If he walks out on me too, I'll really be up a creek without a paddle."

"You mean you two run this place by yourselves?"

"Not usually, no, but two of my girls ran off last week with some fancy dudes from Texas. I got some more ladies comin' up from New Orleans, but they won't be here until next week."

"Yes, I remember you telling me that," Rebecca mused.

Red turned to her with a gleam in her eyes. "Listen! You want a job? I mean, really want a job?"

"Well, yes, I suppose so."

"Then how about helpin' me out with this bunch? Right now! I'll pay you."

"But...how? What do you want me to do?"

"Just pour whiskey and smile, darlin'. If these gents have got a dollar on them, and from the cut of their clothes I'd say they're pretty well-to-do, they'd just as soon give it to you as they would to John Henry. Come on, here's your chance to make a few dollars and see what life is like in a saloon. And I know you've always wondered, haven't you? All ladies wonder what it would be like to pour whiskey and be admired by total strangers. Are you game?"

"Well..." Rebecca hesitated.

"Yes or no, honey, I gotta get to work." She got up and turned as if to go to the bar, waiting for Rebecca's reply.

"If you need the help, then sure, I'll help you."

"Good!" she exclaimed, grabbed Rebecca's hand and pulled her along after her to the side of the bar where there was a fold-down counter to prevent anyone who had no business back there from going behind the bar. Red lifted it and closed it again once they were inside.

"Gentlemen, welcome! What is your pleasure?"

One of them reached a hand to Red's face. "You could be, my darlin'." His companions roared with laughter.

"But then what would all these other gentlemen do for amusement? There's only one of me."

"Let them fend for themselves," said the man as he made a lunged for Red over the bar. She deftly avoided his embrace.

"Sorry, gents, all I serve here is whiskey and beer, so which will it be?"

"Well, if you're whiskey, then I guess this other little lady here must be beer." He made a motion for Rebecca, but she shrank from him.

Someone pounded him on the back and said, "She looks more like champagne to me. Champagne for everybody!"

"Sorry, gents, whiskey and beer," shouted Red over the raucous laughter. She began pouring whiskey into shot glasses and handed Rebecca a bottle with instructions to do the same. "A quarter a shot, gents. Pay the little lady."

Rebecca found herself pouring whiskey as fast as she could, for no sooner did she fill a glass than it was downed and another one demanded. Quarters and other coins flew all over the counter, and she managed to scrape most of it off onto the other side of the bar, where it fell to the floor to be picked up in a less hectic moment.

Soon the customers were not satisfied with shots, and called for bottles, and at five dollars a bottle, Rebecca found her hands full of money. Several of them took their ease at the tables and pretty soon some poker games had started up.

She learned from their conversation that most of them were wealthy sugar plantation owners, on their way by steamboat from New Orleans up to St. Louis for a business conference. The steamboat that carried them was docking at Natchez for a few hours only, and soon they would all be getting back on board. But while they were there, they drank freely and spent freely.

When the bar had calmed down to where John Henry could manage it, Rebecca began to make the rounds of the tables, refilling glasses and fetching more bottles or decks of cards from the big box beneath the bar. And every time she did any of these things, she was rewarded, sometimes with small change, sometimes with bank notes, and even once a twenty-dollar gold piece.

Just when she thought it was under control and she could plop down into a vacant chair for a breather, suddenly about forty more men, of the same group based on the greetings they gave one another, burst through the door, and then there was real confusion.

Charlie tried twice to catch her between trips to the bar and the tables, but all she had time for was to say she would talk to him later, and try unsuccessfully to push back a lock of hair that kept falling into her eyes. She sloshed beer and whiskey all over herself and several of the customers, who seemed to think this was immensely funny.

Her hands were filthy, and every time she reached a hand up to that errant lock of hair, or to wipe the perspiration from her face, she left a smudge there. But there was no time to worry about her appearance. There were customers to be served. When she caught glimpses of Red and John Henry, they were working as hard as she, probably harder, since this was their business and they were used to it. She was not.

She was also not used to the pinches on her bottom or the remarks she received from the so-called gentlemen. But every time she pocketed a five-dollar tip that was slipped to her by an appreciative admirer, the liberties got easier to handle.

And then, as though she were saved by the bell, the steamboat whistle blew four sharp, shrill blasts and they all got up and left to go back to the boat and resume their journey. As they left, several of them grabbed Rebecca up into their arms and gave her quick, affectionate little kisses along with remarks about seeing her again in about a week, when they would be heading back for New Orleans. Several of them handed her more money on their way out the door.

Finally the last straggler was gone, and she looked around for Red, who she saw sitting at a table near the bar with John Henry and another gentleman.

Red motioned for her to come over, and she did, dropping exhausted onto a chair. "My gosh! Is it always like this?" She could hardly get her breath.

Red laughed. "No, not always, but I wish to heaven it was. Made quite a bundle off those gents. How did we do, John Henry?"

John Henry thought for a moment, as if adding in his head, then said quietly, "I'd say roughly a thousand. Give or take a hundred or two."

Rebecca's mouth flew open. "You mean you took in one thousand dollars? Just now?"

"If that's what John Henry says we did, then that's what we did," answered Red, demonstrating her total confidence in her bartender. "And I have you to thank for about half of that."

"Me?"

"Yep. Without your help, we couldn't have done it. They would have left here and gone on down the street to some other saloon. Well, honey, what did you think of your first saloon job?"

"It's the hardest work I've ever done in my life," she admitted frankly, with a little laugh. "But it sure pays off." She crammed her hands into her skirt pockets and pulled out wads of money, which she laid on the table. "I hope it's all there, sometimes I wasn't sure if I collected for the drinks or gave them away." She shoved the money toward Red.

Red glanced at John Henry, who gave her a discreet wink. Then she shoved the money back toward Rebecca. "That's yours, honey, you earned it. And here," she reached into her own pocket and pulled out some bills, counted and handed them to Rebecca also. "Here's an extra hundred. I told you I'd pay you for your help."

"A hundred!" Rebecca exclaimed. "You must be kidding. I didn't earn this much money, Red."

"Yes, you did, too. You worked hard for a few hours. I just wish I could get my girls to work that hard. Go on, take it, it's yours."

Rebecca wasn't so sure of that, but Red persisted, and she slowly began to count the money. Someone yelled something about getting a little service around here? and automatically Rebecca made a move to jump up and go to work, when John Henry laid a restraining hand on her arm. "I can handle it now," he said softly, and gave her arm a little pat.

"Relax, honey, it's all over. You can rest now. Did you ever see anything like her, Jim?" Red said to the gentleman at the table, and for the first time Rebecca looked at him.

The man was just about Oliver's age, and had the same sort of aristocratic looks, but his hair was a lighter shade of brown, not the jet-black of Oliver's. His eyes were a piercing blue, and they twinkled with amusement as he gave Rebecca the once-over. He was very attractive.

"No, cain't say as I have, Red. Never did see nothin' like her."

The way his eyes roamed over her made her uncomfortable. Out of nervousness she struggled again with the lock of hair that was in her eyes, rubbed at her nose and then, finally, noticed how dirty were her hands, and flushed with embarrassment.

Quick as a wink, the man pulled out a beautiful silk handkerchief, reached up, and, to her mortification, began to wipe her face of the layers of grime that had accumulated there. She was so astonished she didn't know what to do, so she just sat there and let him do it. Actually, it was a peculiarly pleasant sensation.

"You know, she might be kinda pretty if you could get some of this dirt off of her," he said, and Red laughed.

At this Rebecca finally came to her senses, and not unkindly pushed his hand away. "Thank you, but I am quite capable of cleaning myself," she said as tartly as her fatigue would allow.

He reached up and arrogantly gave her nose one final swipe, as though to disprove her statement, then replaced the handkerchief in his coat pocket. "Where ever did you find her, Red? Not in New Orleans, I gather?"

"Oh, no, certainly not. No, she's a friend I met on a boat. She has had a bit of hard luck, and I'm trying to help her out, is all. No, Jim, put your eyes back in your head. Rebecca is not one of my regular girls. She's only helpin' out in an emergency."

This habit of talking about her as if she wasn't present was becoming annoying.

"Well," he drawled slowly, "she's a looker, I'll say that. Brings a bit of class to this place. Maybe you ought to talk her into stayin'."

"That's somethin' we will talk about, later," said Red, avoiding that topic more for Rebecca's benefit. "Rebecca, what would you say to a good hot meal right about now? I'm gettin' kinda hungry myself. Hmm? Shall I have us a couple of steaks done up, say, medium rare?"

"What I really want now is a bath," answered Rebecca, absently scrubbing her hands against one another.

"Then a bath it is. Come on with me, honey, I've got a room upstairs that's got your name on the door." Red rose from the table and took Rebecca's arm.

"Oh? Do you really?" asked the man she had called Jim.

"Sure do. Wanna know what it says? Private!"

She gave him a knowing look and turned away.

"Oh, wait, miss - er... Miss Private. Don't forget this."

Rebecca turned back and saw him motion to the money.

"Shouldn't leave it layin' around like that. There's many an unscrupulous fella hereabouts. Myself included." He grinned wickedly.

"Thank you," she muttered, and stuffed the money back into her pockets. Then without a single backward glance she followed Red up the stairs to a door that was indeed marked "Private."

"This is my room, honey, but you just make it yours. There's clothes in the wardrobe. Use anything you can find."

"Charlie! I forgot all about Charlie!"

"Don't worry, I told him you would be well-looked after. And you will be. Now get out of those dirty clothes and I'll send Pearly up with some hot water for a bath."

She closed the door behind her, and Rebecca was too tired to do anything but obey. She slipped out of the stained blouse and skirt, and some of the money crammed into the pockets fell to the floor. With a curiosity she had not felt until now, she pulled out all of it, laid it on the dressing table, and began to count.

Finally she had to make stacks, at a hundred dollars per stack, and when she was finished, there were two neat stacks and a third one started, with a pile of loose coins, including the twenty-dollar gold piece. She could hardly believe her eyes, and was tempted to count it again, just to be sure.

By her count, she had two hundred and twenty-seven dollars. And all for only a few hours of work. Red had given her a hundred dollars, which was an outrageous amount, anyway, but which meant that her tips had come to one hundred and twenty-seven dollars. It was really very hard for her to comprehend how those gentlemen could have simply given her that kind of money, for no other reason than that she kept their glasses full. It astonished her, but there it was, in cold, hard cash.

Of course, she was not experienced enough to know that sheer numbers had resulted in her good fortune. One gentleman with a five-dollar tip was one thing, but there had been nearly a hundred men in the saloon, all drinking, carousing, and spending money as though it were nothing.

It struck her suddenly that the sugar plantations of Louisiana were obviously so profitable that these men where rolling in money. Was cotton just as profitable? From all accounts, it was even more so, and therefore the thought of what her father had had in mind to do suddenly made sense to her. There really was a fortune to be made, if one only had the land and the capital to go after it. She felt a pang of remorse that her father should have failed to live to see his dream come true.

But then a new dream seemed to tempt her as she stared at the stacks of money. Was it so easy to make this kind of money? Granted she was exhausted, and had worked very hard, but that was mostly because she was unused to hard work and unused to saloons in particular. But once she had the hang of it, it had really been easy, except for the running back and forth to the bar, the not having time to even wipe her hands.

But if that was all there was to it, she could do it. No doubt. A small fortune lay on that dressing table, and she knew somehow that it was only the beginning. Maybe she would talk to Red, maybe there would be a permanent job for her here; permanent, at least, until she could save up the money for what she had in mind.

Someone knocked on the door, and she opened it. A stout black girl about her own age came in carrying a huge wooden bucket of steaming water. "Red said you wanted a bath. Well, here it is." She poured the water into a waist-high wooden bathtub and turned to leave. "I got some more water on heatin', if that ain't enough. I'll bring it up directly." She was gone before Rebecca could even say thank you.

The water felt wonderful as she slipped naked into the tub. It had a small seat built into it that she sat upon, but there wasn't enough water to cover her breasts. No matter. She began to scrub the grime from her body with a sponge and a large bar of soap that were lying on the edge.

Eventually Rebecca gave up on the scrubbing and simply relaxed in the tub, letting the warm water work its magic on her aching muscles. She let her mind drift, trying hard not to think about her present predicament, and in particular the ugly scene with Charlotte Sebastian. But her mind had a will of its own, and all her thoughts were of Oliver. At the mere remembrance of his touch on her skin, her body tingled.

Unconsciously her own hands began to caress herself just the way he had done. A delicious feeling welled up inside her and she wished with all her heart that Oliver were beside her at that moment. A soft knock on the door almost brought her out of the dreamlike state. She answered lazily, "Come in," expecting it to be the girl with more water.

"If that's an invitation, then move over, I'll join you."

CHAPTER TEN

Rebecca's eyes flew open and she sat bolt upright in the tub, staring at the handsome man called Jim, who entered the room and closed the door behind him. Too late she remembered that the water wasn't quite deep enough, and for an embarrassing moment her naked breasts were exposed for his pleasure. She slithered down into the water as far as she could without drowning.

"What are you doing in here? Get out!" she yelled with a vehemence that surprised him.

"After that charming invitation?" He tossed his high black hat onto the dressing table and stretched his long lean body onto a chair very near, too near, the bathtub. With an arrogance that shocked her, he propped his booted feet upon the edge of the tub, leaned back and stared at her.

"Are you crazy?" Her eyes were wide and panic was striking at her nerves.

"Crazy not to take off my clothes and join you, yes."

His eyes danced with merriment, and he was obviously enjoying her discomfiture.

"Get out!" she repeated with all the dignity her precarious position allowed.

He only stared at her, a sardonic grin tugging crookedly at his full lips. "But you told me to come in," he drawled.

"I -? I did not! I had no idea it was you!"

"Were you expecting someone else, then? Perhaps someone to scrub your back for you?"

"I told you before, I can wash myself! I don't need your help!" Really! The man was a monster! "Now get out of here before I scream!"

"Go ahead, scream, if you think it will do any good. But I can tell you beforehand, you'll be wasting your breath. Remember where you are, Miss - Becky? Was it?"

"I mean it...I shall scream..."

"Oh, well, if it means that much to you..."

For a moment she thought he would give in and leave, but he only crossed his arms over his chest and sat immovable as stone.

In anguish she opened her mouth wide and let out the most bloodcurdling scream she was capable of performing, long and loud, hurting her throat in the process. When all her breath was gone, she gave him a triumphant look, as if to say, so there!

He never flinched. She waited impatiently for the sound of running feet outside the door, and any moment now she was sure she would be rescued. Any moment now...

Any moment now...

Then the horrible realization struck her. No one had heard her scream! Or if they had, they paid no attention, for screams and yells and gunshots and all the other loud noises designed to bring help in any normal place were totally futile here at Natchez-Under-the-Hill. She began to understand more fully why this was no place for a lady.

"Feel better?" he asked, smiling wickedly.

Her nerves were beginning to shatter. She was very near to tears. "You, sir, are no gentleman!" she said with all the desired effect of delivering a deathblow.

He laughed. "I never claimed to be. It's just what they call me. Gentleman Jim, you know. Guess that's the irony of it, eh? I am not a gentleman." He said it as though he was proud of it.

Just then the door opened and the black girl came in carrying another bucket of water. "Was that you doin' the screamin'? What's wrong, is there a water moccasin in your bathtub or what?" Then she saw the man sitting there, or rather lounging there, and with a disgusted look at him, she roughly pushed his feet off the edge of the tub. "Gentleman Jim, what you doin' in here? Didn't know you was even in town. They ain't hanged you yet?"

She poured the water into the tub, and turned to him with her hand on her hip. "Is that why she's screamin'? 'Cause you in here? I don't blame her, I'd scream too. If she don't want you in here, why don't you go on and bother somebody else?"

"Gentleman" Jim smiled at her laconically, and reached over to the money lying on the dressing table. He plucked a five-dollar note from one of the stacks and crumpled it into the girl's fist. "You never saw me," he said.

"Saw who?" she replied with a blank expression, and left the room without another word, closing the door firmly behind her.

"Pearly ain't been the same since she bought her freedom," he remarked conversationally. "Now you have to grease her palm to get any cooperation."

"That - that is my money you are giving away so freely!" she exclaimed.

"Well, did you expect her to bring up your bath water for nothin'?"

"What do I have to do to make you leave me alone?" she pleaded.

"Well, now, that's more like it. Sayin' please would do for a start."

She forced the most piteous, pleading look onto her face as she tried humbly to say, "Please?"

"That's better. By gum, there may be a lady in you after all."

She waited patiently for him to leave. He made no move.

"I said please!" she cried after a moment.

"And I said that would do for a start."

She was at her wits' end. "What else?" she yelled.

"How about a kiss?"

Her outrage was visible. "You are crazy, after all!"

"Crazy enough to do this," he admitted and before she could stop him he reached over, took her head firmly between his hands and pressed his lips to hers. The stolen kiss was interrupted when she hit him squarely on the side of the head with the wet sponge. He looked up in surprise, then his eyes flashed and he grabbed both her wrists and hauled her roughly to her feet.

For a shocked moment she stood naked before him, dripping water. His eyes took in all her beauty hungrily, quickly, then he forced his lips on hers again. Confusion and anger were her immediate responses.

And then suddenly she knew, with a feeling of self-disgust, that she was beginning to enjoy his kiss. Was it because she transposed Oliver onto him, and imagined that it was Oliver kissing her? Oliver holding her, naked and longing? Oliver's tongue, reaching inside, searing her with its desire, forcing her to return the pleasure? Her eyelids fluttered. When she opened them again, to her horror, it was not Oliver, but Gentleman Jim, the man who was no gentleman and was proud of the fact, who held her and looked into her eyes with an expression of wonder. She was so confused and disoriented she thought she would be sick. She slumped in his grasp, all her energy gone.

"My God, I - I never dreamed..." he murmured, but it made no sense to her. She was almost unconscious with confusion.

"I must have you!" she heard him say urgently. She felt his right arm slip under her knees, in an attempt to pick her up out of the tub.

But just at that instant she regained enough composure and strength to push against his chest with her free hand with all her might. He fell backward, off balance, and landed against the chair, which buckled under him. He sprawled flat on the floor.

Quick as a wink she grabbed for one of Red's dressing gowns, pulled it on to cover her nakedness, and stepped out of the tub. Before he could recover from the fall, she had flung open the door and was running blindly down the hall to the long gallery. She flew down the stairs, the dressing gown flowing out behind her.

Suddenly she became aware of the catcalls and whistles being directed at her from the customers in the saloon, and she glanced nervously at the robe she had grabbed in haste. To her horror, she found that it was cut in such a manner that the entire front had to be pulled together very tightly in order to be effective cover, which she had neglected to do in her haste. It certainly left absolutely nothing to the imagination.

Anguished, she clutched at the thin fabric, drawing it tightly to her body, tears beginning to stream down her face. Suddenly Red was at her side, taking her arm, shaking her. "What is it, honey? What's wrong?"

Rebecca couldn't speak, she could only clutch at the fabric with one hand and motion vaguely upstairs with the other. Red glanced up and a certain look of understanding dawned on her face.

"Jim!" she cried. "Have you been molestin' this girl? You naughty boy! Didn't I tell you she ain't one of my regulars?"

Rebecca looked up and saw Jim walking slowly down the stairs, adjusting his immaculate cravat and smoothing his unruffled hair. He spoke not a word as he descended and went straight to the bar, where John Henry poured him a large glass of whiskey, which he downed in one gulp. Then, just as silently, he turned and went out the front door.

Red watched his departure with interest. Then she turned her attention back to Rebecca. "He's gone, honey, everything's all right, now. Come on back upstairs before you drive these men crazy. I must say, that robe does more for you than it ever did for me. Just kiddin'!" she amended quickly at the stricken look Rebecca gave her.

An hour later Rebecca ventured back downstairs, fully dressed this time, in a pretty floral print dress she had found at the back of Red's wardrobe. She was fairly composed now, after the rather confusing encounter with Gentleman Jim. Red had assured her that Jim probably would not be back, for a while at least. He would most likely drink himself into a stupor, or get into an all-night poker game to take his mind off "things". He was a good enough sort, Red asserted, he was just...well, frisky.

Rebecca tried to put the whole ordeal out of her mind. Maybe in about fifty years she could look back and laugh fondly at the memory, but right at the moment it was too embarrassing, too complicated to bear scrutiny. She could not, however, forget the humiliation she felt as she found herself responding to Jim.

At any rate, when she descended the staircase later, her eyes quickly scanned the crowd. But he was not there, so her spirits lifted considerably. She found Red seated at a table with some elderly, tame-looking gentlemen, and when Red motioned to her to join, she did so calmly, despite the whistles and suggestive remarks she received as she crossed the room.

It was all very flattering, of course, in an odd kind of way, but she hoped she was becoming immune to the constant reminders that she was a pretty young woman hanging around a saloon. Never mind that she considered the owner her friend. What business did she have here? None.

But she smiled at Red and smiled again at the gentlemen as Red introduced them, not catching any of the names, but then not really expected to. She sat in the offered chair (how nice to have it pulled out for her by a real gentleman!) and cautiously accepted the glass of whiskey that was pressed into her hand.

"I hope you haven't lost your appetite," said Red, "after that little episode. I've got Pearly fixin' us a couple of steaks that will melt in your mouth."

Not long after, Pearly brought out two sizzling steaks done to such mouth-watering perfection that every gentleman seated at the table ordered one for himself, as well.

Rebecca was ravenous. Lately it seemed that she was going for long periods between meals. She ate with gusto. And she drank with gusto. Besides wine, and the champagne she had shared with Oliver, brandy had been the only other liquor she had ever tasted, but that night she drank whiskey. And lots of it. But with good hearty food inside her, it did not affect her the way it should have. Still, she was feeling no pain.

When the plates had been cleared away, the gentlemen at their table began to talk about a poker game, so Rebecca and Red left them to it. She followed Red closely, more for protection than companionship. It was nighttime, and she could sense that there was a difference in the customers. The very air itself was sparked with elements that were unfamiliar to her.

"Rebecca!" called a male voice and she looked up with trepidation, but it was only Charlie, strolling across the saloon toward her.

"Hi, Charlie!"

"Hey! So how's it goin' here? You gonna stay on here for a while or what?"

"We really ain't had a chance to talk about that yet, Charlie," answered Red for her. "But we will."

"Charlie," Rebecca lowered her voice so only he could hear, "can you believe I made over two hundred dollars today? Two hundred! Why, that's more money than I've ever had in my life. That I could call my own, I mean."

Charlie whistled. "That sure is a lot of money. What'd you have to do, sell your body?"

She was momentarily stunned, but then realized that he was joking. It was a crude joke, but a joke nonetheless.

"Why, do you think it's worth that much?" she teased, and noticed the blush that appeared in his cheeks. He loved to play at being a man, but he was still a boy. "No, I got it from tips, mostly, and helping Red and John

Henry take care of all those gentlemen from the steamboat. You remember, you were here."

"Yeah, I remember. You mean all you did was pour whiskey and beer and made two hundred dollars? Gee, maybe I oughta open up a saloon down here. Sounds like more fun than raisin' cotton."

"You didn't get into any trouble for giving me a ride here, did you?"

He tossed his hand, as though waving that suggestion away. "Nah, nobody knew it. I even beat Daddy home, but I had to avoid Mama because she woulda asked me a lot of questions about what you and me talked about and all. That was the only tricky part."

"Well, I'm glad of that. And I didn't get much of a chance to say thank you, but, thank you. Can I buy you a drink? Whiskey? I'm fabulously rich, now, you know."

"Beer. I only drink beer. Whiskey gives me gas. Sure, you can buy me a beer, I guess."

John Henry set a tall cool one in front of Charlie but refused Rebecca's money.

"Guess your money's no good here, is it?"

"Guess not," she replied, pleased with the treatment she was receiving at the Elysian Fields.

"I reckon you got enough money to buy your own ticket back to Savannah now, huh?"

She paused to reflect. "Yes, I guess I do. But I'm not sure that is what I want to do just yet. I haven't really made up my mind. So is it true that your father is buying Mr. Sebastian's farm and you are going to get the house?" She asked this question with all the innocence she could muster. Actually, she was dying to talk about Oliver.

"Yeah, they supposedly worked it all out today. Daddy is gonna buy it all, but he wants the farm and acres for himself. He says I ain't experienced enough yet to know how to run a farm by myself. I guess he's right, the thought does kinda scare me a little. And I ain't got no intention of movin' into that house until I get married. And you know how I feel about that!"

She smiled. She did indeed.

"But Mama's tryin' to get me moved in right now," he went on. "Mr. Sebastian and his wife are leavin' tomorrow to go back to England. They wasn't supposed to go until next week, but Daddy told Mama that Miss Charlotte had a set-back, or somethin'. She ain't been in good health since they first come here. I reckon she's took a turn for the worse, so they're leavin' right away, now that they worked out what to do with the farm and all. I kinda hate to see them go. I'm gonna miss Mr. Sebastian."

You and me both, Charlie, she thought, but said nothing.

"Oh, that reminds me, didn't you tell Mr. Sebastian that you was leavin' today? Daddy came home sayin' how he was real upset about it. Then Mr. Sebastian himself came over to the house right after that askin' me a lot of questions about you."

Rebecca held her breath. "Like what?"

"Like where did I take you and all that. I told him a lie, I guess, because I told him I took you to town so you could buy a steamboat ticket back to Savannah. That's what you said you was gonna do, then you wanted to come down here and see Red before you left, so I told him you was probably on your way to New Orleans by now. Did I say the right thing? I mean, I didn't know what to tell him. He was so upset I guess I shoulda told him the truth. But I thought I was doin' what you woulda wanted me to do. Was that all right?" He was anxious for her approval. She gave it unreservedly.

"Yes, Charlie, you did exactly as you should have done. And had I not stopped to see Red, I would be on that boat by now. So you did the right thing."

He let out a big sigh. "I'm glad. He sure seemed upset, though."

She had thought she could talk about Oliver calmly now, but she found that she could not. Not enough time had elapsed to dim the memories. And the memories were still painful in the extreme. Painful because they were all she had now, a heart full of memories instead of a real live man.

Well, there was one bright spot. They were leaving tomorrow, so there would be no chance of running into him accidentally or otherwise. She really didn't think she could bear to see him again, not ever. If she did, it might not be so easy to give him up a second time. No, this was the best way. Time would heal the wound, she thought firmly, but without any real hope of it being true.

Rebecca couldn't bear to see him again, she was sure, and yet her eyes kept straying to the door every time someone entered, almost expecting to see him walk in, looking for her. Evidently the whiskey was having some effect, after all, for after an hour and a half of watching and waiting, and no sign of Oliver, she began to be just a little bit angry with him. After all, it was his last night in Natchez. He was downright obliged to find her and make love to her just one more time.

She glanced at the door again. And still he did not come.

Maybe he was looking for her and couldn't find her? But no, if she were still in Natchez at all, he must know that she was at Red's place. Where else would she be? And yet she had a keen desire to go outside, to walk up and down the street, so that if he was looking for her, he would be sure to find her.

But that was foolish. Even in her semi-intoxicated state, she knew that that would be damn near suicide.

John Henry had already broken up two fights just this evening. God only knew what was happening in the street.

No, damn it, he must come to her. Then her mind found another thought to chew on. Maybe he and Charlotte had had a row. Maybe she had confronted him with it, and now he had to stay at home under her watchful eye, lest he come looking for her. That was probably it. But if that were true, then what kind of man was he, after all? Did he love her or not? If he really loved her, really, then it wouldn't matter whether he had a wife or not. Love should be...should be...overwhelming. Yes, that was the word. Overwhelming.

And still he did not come. Charlie had long since disappeared from her side, but she couldn't remember his leaving. He had probably gotten tired of talking to himself, she was so wrapped up in her own thoughts. She hadn't really been fair to Charlie, she knew that. She should have told him the truth. He was on her side; he had demonstrated that fact already. Well, maybe tomorrow, she would tell him all about it. After the Sebastians were gone. She stared at the door.

And still he did not come.

But someone else did. Someone else who made her jump at his sight, for reasons she did not quite understand.

Gentleman Jim strolled calmly through the door. But he was not alone. On his arm was a handsome blonde woman who clung to him as if afraid he might slip away. They paused momentarily at the door, surveying the room. Rebecca was sitting on a barstool at the far end of the bar and half-hidden by customers. He would have to have keen eyes to pick her out, but she shrank anyway, watching him closely.

Satisfied with what he saw, Jim led the woman to a vacant table on the far side of the saloon and they sat down. Red found them as she made her rounds, and greeted them both. Then she went to the bar and brought over the cut-glass decanter and crystal goblets reserved only for herself and very special guests.

This behavior was what confused Rebecca the most. After the scene with the bathtub, she was ready to believe him to be the vilest blackguard on earth. And yet, Red kept telling her that he was really a decent man, just a little frisky was all. Frisky!

Rebecca was ashamed that she wasn't able to turn her attention away from the pair; she felt as if she were peeping through a keyhole. The woman's dress was extremely low-cut, and Jim kept his eyes on her heaving, heavy bosom. When he reached up and lightly trailed a finger against the naked flesh, making the woman wriggle with pleasure, Rebecca could almost feel it herself. Unconsciously she reached a hand to her own bosom, and finally turned her eyes away.

Where the devil was Oliver Sebastian? She needed him, dear God, she needed him!

"What's the matter? You look as if you just lost your best friend." Red stared at her with concern.

"I guess maybe I did," Rebecca admitted with a heavy sigh. "Maybe I'm just tired. Could you - I mean, do you think..."

"If you're tryin' to find out if I can put you up for the night, the answer is yes. I got two whole stories of nothin' but bedrooms, only there ain't usually a whole lotta sleepin' goin' on in them. Fact is, I can put you up for as long as you want to stay. But we'll talk about that tomorrow. Right now you oughta be havin' some fun. I know this place is kinda dull, but it ain't always. Those girls I got comin' up next week are really hot. One plays piano and the other sings, and they both dance. That oughta liven this joint up a bit. But right now I cain't offer you much in the way of entertainment, unless you want to play some poker or somethin'."

"Oh, I don't know how to play poker."

"Ain't nothin' to it, long as it's straight up and no cheatin'. Fact is, I make most of my money from it. Lady Luck has her moments when she wants to smile on me. And I feel like this might be one of those moments. Wanna learn?"

Rebecca stole a glance at the door, then at Jim.

"Sure, why not? A training in saloon life wouldn't be complete without a poker lesson or two. Only please don't win back all the money I made today, I worked hard for that."

In no time Red had commandeered a table and dealt them into a game already in progress. "Don't worry about a thing. I know these gents. They don't cheat," Red whispered into her ear.

Rebecca was much relieved to hear it. It turned out to be rather fun. They were very patient with her, but she found her only real difficulty with the game was learning what-beats-what. After she had that memorized, it was really all a matter of bluffing or calling a bluff.

Still, they kept the bets within reason, and she saw her small stack of money gradually grow. She even went so far as to bet ten dollars once on four queens.

When she showed her cards and raked in the pot, they all gaped at her.

"Did I do something wrong?"

"Why, no, honey, but - Four queens! Why, you could have bet anything you liked on that hand. It's very hard to get four of anything, but queens! That's good luck, for sure! On a riverboat that hand would have netted about ten thousand dollars, no less!"

"Beginner's luck, I guess." She smiled at them.

"'Course playin' with jokers wild helps," Red commented genially. "Serious poker players don't play with wild cards. That's just for fun. And for learnin'."

"Is that so?" said Rebecca, gathering the cards as it was her turn to deal. "Then by all means let's play some serious poker." She took out the two jokers and laid them aside, then shuffled and dealt. When she picked up her hand, she found that she had nothing, nothing at all, on which to bet. "You're right, wild cards do help," she murmured to Red, but the whole table heard it and they all laughed. It was obvious she was going to sit out that hand.

Another bottle of whiskey was brought to the table and Rebecca's glass was refilled. She would have to stop drinking soon. She could barely tell the kings from the jacks as it was. And was that a nine or was it a six turned upside down?

After a hand in which one of the gentlemen at the table raked in a considerable pile, and another of them declared that he was bankrupt, the bankrupt party stated that that was about all he could handle for the night.

"But you can't leave! We have to have a fifth!"

"Sorry, fellas, ladies, I'm all tapped out." He made his good-byes and it looked as if the game was over, for they couldn't tear another player away from a "serious" game.

Rebecca was disappointed. She rather liked the game, and she had actually won some money, not lost everything as she had feared. But most important of all, while she played, her mind was occupied with the cards, and not with other more weighty concerns. For a few hours she had forgotten all that had happened over the past few days, and actually enjoyed herself.

"If you need a fifth, then maybe I'm your man."

At Red's invitation, Gentleman Jim sat down in the vacant seat and the blonde woman hovered next to him, leaning her hip against his shoulder. Jim reached for his wallet and pulled out a wad of money that would choke a mule.

"Aha! Just what we need, fresh blood!" said one of the players.

"I warn you, young man, I intend to take that away from you," said another.

"Maybe you will," drawled Jim, "but you'll have to do it with more than ace high, I can guarantee that."

Rebecca did not look up at him. There was no need. She could feel him staring at her. There was not time to examine her strange, bewildering reactions to this man, as the game again got fully underway. He did not, as she had feared, bait her with remarks to draw her out. He played a serious game, and allowed everyone else to do the same. Soon she could look at him easily, and even raise his bets without feeling self-conscious about it.

But the game was subtly different, somehow. Maybe it was the presence of the blonde woman, leaning suggestively over Jim's shoulder to peek at his cards, or maybe it was the lack of wild cards, but she found it difficult to concentrate. She dropped out when she should have stayed in, and she stayed in when she should have dropped out. Obviously there was more skill to poker than she had acquired in only one lesson.

But when she was dealt three eights, a four and a six, something told her that this was a hand to bet on. Very quietly she called all bets, not arousing any suspicion. Then when Jim asked her how many cards she wanted, she said two, please, discarded the four and six, and slowly picked up the last two cards dealt to her. She hoped fervently that that fourth eight would be there.

The first card was a three. She was disappointed, but not out yet. The next card was also a three. It must have been the whiskey, but it actually took her a second or two to get over her disappointment at not finding the fourth eight and to comprehend that she had, instead, a full house, eights over threes, which was the next best thing to four of a kind.

When she finally realized this, her skin began to tingle with excitement, and she tried with all her might to keep her face expressionless.

The bet from Red was five dollars, and Rebecca put in her five and calmly, she hoped, raised it ten dollars. This fifteen dollar bet went around the table until it was Jim's turn. He eyed her carefully for a moment, but she did not flinch. Then he put in his fifteen and raised it fifty.

"You're bluffin', Jim," Red cajoled him.

"It'll cost you to find out," he retorted.

"No, it won't," she replied, and threw in her cards.

It was now Rebecca's turn again. She hoped desperately that Red was right, that he was indeed bluffing. She was going to put it all on this hand.

She saw his fifty and raised him fifty. The two gentlemen on her left both dropped out. The pot was a bit rich for their blood.

Jim was impassive. He put in another fifty, and raised it by one hundred more. One of the men whistled.

Red said, "Wait a minute, Jim, she's just learned how to play this game, don't give her a lesson the hard way. Lemme see what you got, honey."

Rebecca showed her the cards, and Red nodded her head. "Looks good to me."

Rebecca put in the hundred and then emptied her pockets. She counted all the money she had left, and it came to one hundred and forty-five dollars. She pushed it to the center of the table. "To you, Jim."

Jim was thoughtful for a moment as he studied his cards and her face. But she was determined not to give herself away. Finally he said, "Well, if that's all the money you got, then all I have to do is raise you again, and you'll have to drop out. Unless of course you can get someone to stake you. But that won't be necessary. I'll call." He counted out one hundred and forty-five dollars and tossed it onto the mountain of money on the table.

They all looked at Rebecca, and she laid her cards down, face up. "Full house, eights over threes." The other two gentlemen breathed a sigh of relief. Red smiled. They waited.

Jim gave her a long look, then grinned. "Not good enough." He showed his cards. "Aces over tens."

There was general astonishment all around. Two full houses in the same hand! But no one was as astonished as Rebecca herself. She watched in horror as he wrapped his long arms around the pile of money and hauled it toward him. Every dollar that she had made that day now belonged to him. She couldn't believe it. The other players were all very sympathetic, of course. Fickle thing, Lady Luck. What a rotten ending to a fun evening. Rebecca thought she was going to be sick, and it wasn't just from the whiskey.

"I guess I gave you some bad advice, honey. I'm awful sorry." Red patted her shoulder gently and looked as if she really meant it.

Rebecca tried to smile at her. "Oh, it wasn't your fault. It's just the nature of the beast, that's all," and she looked pointedly at Jim, who was gathering up all that money while the blonde woman laughed into his ear.

The game did break up at that point. No one seemed to have any stomach for it anymore. It was most gratifying, their condolences, but it didn't replace the money. The money was gone. And she had no one to blame but herself.

Feeling more than a little sick, Rebecca asked to be excused. Red told her to just stay in her own room tonight, since she knew where it was and all her things were in there for her to use. They would sort out a room for her tomorrow.

"Yes, tomorrow," Rebecca muttered as she walked slowly away and up the stairs.

At the top, she paused and leaned for support on the gallery railing. She looked down, and saw Jim stuffing some money into the blonde woman's bosom, who smiled and gave him a big kiss. Rebecca almost choked on the bile in her throat. It had been her money. Now she was poor and alone again.

CHAPTER ELEVEN

She ran to her room, shut the door behind her, and leaned heavily against it. For a long moment she stood there, trying very hard to control the shakes that wracked her body. Sweat popped out on her forehead. She went quickly over to the washstand, poured some cool but dirty-looking water into the basin, and splashed her face. After a moment, she felt better, physically, but inside she was so shaken she had to sit down.

In the past few days she had experienced more than most people do in a lifetime. And it was beginning to take its toll on her. Excitement she had wanted, and excitement she had got. But she was beginning to wonder if she was really up to it. Could she handle any more? That quiet existence with her father in Savannah which she had once found dull seemed very welcome at the moment.

Someone knocked softly at the door. She really didn't feel like talking, but there was no reason to be rude to Red, so she opened the door.

"May I come in?" said Jim, with a smile.

"No," she answered simply and tried to shut the door in his face. But he put out an arm and prevented it.

"Just for a minute, please. See, I said please."

Rebecca was nearly in tears. "What do you want?"

Jim pushed his way gently but firmly into the room and closed the door behind him.

"I just want to give you this." He held out his hand.

Rebecca stared through blurry eyes at the wad of money he was holding. "Why?"

"Because it isn't mine. It's yours. I cheated." He held the money closer to her, wanting her to take it.

"What?" She was confused.

"I cheated," he repeated, simply stating a fact. "It was all a joke, really. I had every intention of giving it back to you. I only wanted to teach you a lesson, that's all."

She stared at him, not understanding, but beginning to be very upset.

"I'm a professional gambler, Miss Becky. I do this sorta thing for a livin'. And I'm not a rare animal, there are thousands of us out there, all waitin' to pounce upon some poor sucker."

"Like me," she said, her lips twisting in irony.

"Well, not exactly. I usually make it a practice never to play with beautiful women. They are either total innocents, or total cheats. And for some strange reason, women seem to be better cheats at cards than men. But you, Miss Becky, are a total innocent. And I mean for you to have this back." He tried to press the money into her palms, but she pulled her hands away.

"And how do you know that I didn't have aces up my sleeve?" she asked angrily.

"Well, for one thing, you ain't wearin' sleeves." He reached out a hand and ran his finger lightly across her bare arm, sending shivers over it. She jerked out of his reach.

"If you're goin' to hide aces in your sleeves, it's imperative that you have sleeves that hide 'em well." He put his right hand to his left, pulled up the bit of lace that dangled there, and revealed a thin leather band strapped to his wrist, securely holding several playing cards. He pulled them out and showed them to her. They were all aces.

Her mouth fell open in amazement. Of course she had heard about such things, who hadn't? But she had never thought she would come face to face with a real live professional card sharp. She stared at him.

"I mean for you to have this back," he said firmly. Grabbing her hand, he forced her fingers closed around the money. "There. Now I can sleep peacefully," he added with a wry grin.

"I don't know what to say..."

"Say thank you."

"Thank you," she murmured mechanically. Inside her heart was beating very hard and fast, and she was thrilled to have the money back. Honor forbade her accepting it otherwise, but if he admitted to cheating her out of it, well, then...

"Can I confess somethin' to you, Miss Becky? See, I had this picture in my head. I had planned to come up here and make love to you, and then leave the money lyin' on a table or somethin'." He gave her what she imagined was an embarrassed smile. "But I couldn't insult you like that."

Charlie's prophetic words about her selling her body raced through her mind. She was grateful to Jim for not carrying out his original plan.

"Insult me by paying me, or insult me by making love to me?" Her words astonished her as much as they did him. She blushed fiercely as she saw his eyes light up with unmistakable desire.

"Miss Becky, it would be a great honor if you would allow me to share your bed tonight."

Her mind whirled wildly. "What about the woman I saw you with, the blonde? Won't she do?"

He laughed nervously. "Sure, in a pinch. But I sent her packin'. I have a taste for a real lady tonight."

With those words, he slipped his arms around her waist and drew her against his chest.

"Do you know any real ladies?" she said for lack of anything better.

"I'm lookin' at one," he said gently. He didn't crush her to him and assault her as she feared he might. In fact, she rather wished he had, then she could have rallied and forced him away. Instead he very slowly and tenderly began to press his lips to her cheeks, to her eyelids, her forehead, her temples, covering her entire face with sweet little kisses that demanded nothing from her but that she receive them.

Something inside of her broke under the strain. What she really wanted was for it to be Oliver holding her in his arms, but he had not come. Still, she needed someone to hold her. Anyone.

Her hands found their way around his neck and she sought his lips with her own. Her kiss was fiery and desperate, and surprising in its intensity so that it was a long second before the man returned it, hungrily.

He pulled himself away, looked at her with smoldering eyes, then went quickly to the door, throwing the latch and locking the world out. Then he was back in her arms, and the kiss he gave her made her quake inside. In an instant, she was carried to the bed and he loomed over her majestically.

"My sweet lady," he crooned as he lifted her skirt and unfastened his trousers. Before she knew it, he was upon her, thrusting inside, taking her with a power she had not expected.

She could not respond. This was so unlike what she had experienced with Oliver that she could only lie there, motionless, feeling nothing but the sheer physicality of the act.

Almost as soon as it had begun, it was over. He lay on top of her, breathing heavily. She lay beneath him, feeling nothing but a sad loss.

He was so still that she closed her eyes and instantly fell asleep. But she found no solace there. Oliver invaded her dreams. She dreamed that he told her to leave his house at once, that he loved his wife and would not ever leave her. And Charlotte stood smiling triumphantly.

She stirred, came awake, and realized that Jim was still in her bed, lying beside her, not asleep, but staring at her.

"I've been watchin' you sleep," he said. "Did you have a bad dream? You were tossin' and turnin' and moanin' out loud."

She couldn't look at him. There was nothing to be said. Slowly, so as not to jar her aching head unduly, she started to rise from the bed. But he grabbed her arm.

"Where you goin'?"

"I have to take off my dress," she mumbled, not sure if she was awake or still asleep.

"Then let me do that."

She had not the strength to resist as he expertly stripped her of her clothing, until she lay naked under his gaze.

"My beautiful, sweet lady," he murmured softly, then leaned and placed a kiss on first one breast then the other. He took off his own clothing, and lay beside her, staring at her.

"I've never known anybody like you. I've never known a real lady."

"Am I a real lady?" she asked caustically, as a picture flashed through her mind, of Oliver and his "real lady". Had Oliver become as obsessed as Jim over the prospect of having a "real lady"?

"'Course you are, darlin'. And that makes all the difference in the world to me. There are plenty of women who would jump into my bed, but not many that I would want there. You belong to the second group, as far as I'm concerned."

He kissed her gently on the lips. She tried desperately to put Oliver out of her mind, but the memory of his lovemaking lingered. If only Jim could excite those same feelings in her...

Almost as though reading her thoughts, he moved his head down, and began to shower her body with tiny kisses, nipping with sharp little bites at the tender flesh that ached for satisfaction.

But satisfaction was the one thing that Jim could not give her. His mouth and hands did indeed bring her to an excited state, a state where she found herself clinging to him and hastening him into giving her the ultimate gift a man can give a woman, but there he fell short of the mark.

It wasn't his fault, and it wasn't hers. It was Oliver's. She knew with a grim certainty that Oliver had spoken the truth when he had told her that she could marry anyone she liked, but no one could ever replace him. He was her true husband, the one that could take her to such dizzying heights of fulfillment.

Those dizzying heights were what she needed, and Jim simply was not capable of supplying them. Oh, there was nothing wrong with his technique. But she did not love him, and to her that made all the difference in the world.

But Jim did not give up. He kept trying. All night he kept trying. Several times he seemed almost to sense his failure, and asked her what could he do to pleasure her? Rather than tell him the truth, which would have been the best thing, of course, she only smiled at him meekly and went into his arms again. It was enough for her if he would simply hold her. He fell into an exhausted sleep with a smile on his face and his arms wrapped tightly around her.

She lay still for a long time, tears spilling quietly onto her cheeks, wondering if she would ever be the same again. She had gone through so many changes lately, she hardly knew who she was anymore. But finally she fell asleep again, and found a certain amount of peace, because she dreamed no more.

Daylight streaming through the window and falling warmly on her face woke her the next morning. She opened her eyes slowly, her lashes thick with dried tears, and squinted at her surroundings. She was alone in the bed. Her dress lay in a heap on the floor where it had been tossed, and a pile of money lay on the dressing table. She focused her eyes on the small ornate clock and noted with surprise that it was after eleven o'clock. She had never slept so late in her life, but then she had never had a night like last night, either. Her body ached not a little.

Slowly she got out of bed, slowly because her head felt like it was stuffed with wet cotton that shifted painfully with every move. She pulled on Red's dressing gown and picked up the stack of money. Quickly she made a rough count of it, out of curiosity, and found that to her surprise there was about a thousand dollars there. Now why would Jim give her more money than she had started with? Granted she had won a little from Red and the other players before he started, but that only amounted to a hundred or so. But then he had admitted that he had cheated on that final hand. So by all rights the money that he had bet with was hers too.

This logic seemed to placate her sense of honesty, so she hid the money away in a safe place and thought no more about it.

The ever-present whistle of a steamboat reminded her of something, and she went over to the window, which she found looked out over Silver Street and down over the riverfront. She could see a huge steamboat moored there, and crewmen casting off the ropes preparing to get underway. A couple of late-boarding passengers jumped onto the deck just as the boat pulled away from the dock.

Were Oliver and Charlotte on that boat? Or would they be on a later one? Or had they taken an earlier one? From her internal feeling of emptiness and loneliness, she guessed that they were already gone.

Maybe it was best that way. Maybe it had been a blessing that she had slept so late. Otherwise she might have been tempted to do something rash, like running down to the dock and searching for Oliver. But her instincts told her it was too late. He was gone.

She took her time dressing, and when she went downstairs later, the saloon was empty except for John Henry behind the bar polishing glasses.

"Good morning, John Henry," she said with the brightest smile she could manage.

"Good morning," replied the softly-spoken man, returning the smile. Did she only imagine that the words held a certain inflection? Suddenly embarrassed, she wondered if he knew that she had spent the night with Jim. How could he? But how could he not? He knew everything that went on at the Elysian Fields. He made it his business to know. But he also kept it to himself. She had nothing to worry about there.

He offered her coffee, which he poured from a silver pot into a china cup. That was just what she needed, and the steaming liquid helped to revive her flagging spirits.

"Where is Red this morning?"

"Sleepin' late, as usual, I reckon. She never gets up before two o'clock in the afternoon. But then she don't get to bed before dawn either."

"Dawn! You mean this place stays open all night?"

"Why, yes, ma'am, that's when we do the most business. And we don't open until noon. That's to keep out the riffraff that's been up all night already and are lookin' for a place to sleep. Soon as I open them doors this place will be busy again. It never stops."

"I guess it's a good thing it doesn't stop."

"Sometimes, yeah. But I tell you, I wish I could take me a little holiday away from all this. It's been almost two years since I've been able to take any time off. But I guess it's no matter, I'd probably end up in New Orleans in another saloon. It's in my blood, I guess."

She smiled at him, and they talked for a while. He told her that he had no family, no wife and children that is, because saloon life was not compatible with a home life. This caused an unexpected pang within her, and she wondered if she would ever get married and have children. Or was she destined to be like Red, or John Henry? Was it in her blood, too? Her father had been a merchant. Wasn't it very close to the same thing, supplying the public with what they wanted? And what was the difference if it was yard goods or whiskey?

John Henry consulted his pocket watch, then replaced it in his vest pocket with a sigh. "Well, I guess it's about time."

As soon as he unlocked the front doors, they were thrown open from the outside and three men rushed in, hollering for whiskey. Before John Henry could get back behind the bar, four more had entered, and the place was busy again.

"See what I mean?" he said to Rebecca with a grimace.

She could only smile.

Suddenly a large bouquet of flowers was thrust under her nose. She turned, and Jim stood there, grinning like a schoolboy, holding out the flowers to her as though they were precious jewels.

"For you," he said proudly, as if it weren't obvious.

Graciously she accepted them, and breathed in their subtle fragrance. "They're beautiful, Jim. Thank you."

"Thank old widow Throckmorton. She grew them. I only picked them."

"Jim!" she admonished, but only half-heartedly. At least he was being honest. Rebecca glanced up and caught John Henry watching them, but he only grinned and shook his head slightly, then went back to pouring whiskey.

"Thank you for last night," said Jim in a low, intimate voice. "Good Lord, listen to me. That's the first time I've ever said anything like that. It's usually the other way around." And he gave her that mischievous grin again.

Was he implying that she should thank him? If so, he was in for a disappointment.

But Jim was full of energy and good cheer. He wanted to take her to a fancy restaurant up on the bluff, so they drove up the steep road in his open carriage pulled by a beautiful, spirited black stallion.

When they walked into the restaurant, they got the kind of stares that made her believe that they made a handsome couple.

He was extravagant with the menu, and ordered several more dishes than they could possibly have eaten, along with a bottle of the best wine that was offered.

Nothing was too good for his lady, he kept saying. He was obviously known as a big tipper, too, because the service was impeccable. Rebecca felt like a queen.

The only damper to the enjoyable outing came when Sheriff Brown walked in and noticed them. He came over and said a few polite words to Rebecca, but she had the distinct feeling that he was really more interested in her companion. He did not tarry long, and bid them both good day, but she caught a backward glance as he turned away that had her wondering if he didn't approve of Gentleman Jim at all.

They left the restaurant and took a long drive along the spectacularly scenic bluff. At a highly likely place, Jim pulled up the horse and they sat on the grass in the shade of an oak, staring out across the muddy Mississippi River.

They talked of many things, but it was Jim who did most of the talking. He seemed to want to tell her every single thing he had ever done in his life. And she was anything but disinterested. From his accounts, he had led a fascinating, if dangerous, life. He lived on the outside of the law, as some men do, so talented in his craft that he always avoided detection. And despite the fact that she could not, certainly, condone his lawlessness, still, she was captivated by it, by the courage to take hold of life and wring it for all it was worth. She listened raptly, asking questions when he paused, and nodding at the appropriate times.

Then it was her turn. But she had little to say, really. How could she make this man understand the simple, quiet life she had lived up until now? Samuel's betrayal was something she would never tell anybody about. Falling in love with Oliver was still too painful to think about. Besides, Jim didn't want to hear about the other men in her life. As far as he was concerned, he was the only one, now or ever.

She told him instead about the steamboat accident, and about her father's murder, but she only said that he had died on the journey from Savannah. She told him they had come here to buy a farm, but she did not mention whose farm. He didn't ask her any pertinent questions, only accepted what she told him, for which she was grateful.

When all the talking seemed to have been done for the moment, they sat silently for a while, staring at the swift waters of the river, until he took her in his arms as she knew he would sooner or later. The kisses were sweet and loving on his part, and desperate and longing on hers.

She found that she was responding not to the man himself but to the needs of her own heart, a heart which had been opened up to the glories of love and then suddenly deprived of them, and which drove her now into seeking those glories wherever she might find them. She needed someone to hold her, to kiss her, to love her, and Jim was the man of the moment. She could have done worse, much worse. Jim worshipped her, and demonstrated that fact every second he was with her. Was there anything really wrong with being loved by a man even if she didn't, couldn't, love him back?

When his kisses became ardent, she forestalled any further physical expression of his love for her. For one thing, it was broad daylight and they were not exactly out of sight of any curious eyes. For another, she was anxious to get back to Red's place. There were plans about her future that she needed to finalize.

Jim was flatteringly disappointed in the interruption of his lovemaking, but also eager to please her in any way.

The saloon was bustling with business when they returned. Red greeted them heartily as they entered, and Rebecca felt a real warmth from this woman whom she now considered her friend.

"I see you two have patched things up," she said with a lift of her eyebrows.

"What do you mean?"

"After the - umm - bathtub incident, I mean."

"Oh." Rebecca blushed. "Well, you said it yourself, he's harmless, just frisky."

Jim gave them both a look. "If you ladies are goin' to talk about me as though I wasn't here, then maybe I ought not to be here. Excuse me, I think I spy a sucker who needs to be relieved of his wallet." He tipped his hat, and left them alone.

Rebecca watched as he went over to a table of four gentlemen and soon had them talked into a "friendly" game of poker.

"So are you and Gentleman Jim more than friends?"

Rebecca didn't reply.

"Come on, honey, this is Red, remember? You can tell me anything. As if I didn't already know that he stayed in your room last night."

"I - I hope you're not angry with me."

Red grinned. "Why should I be angry? You're a grown woman, you do as you like. My place is yours, I told you that. No, I'm not angry a bit. I only hope you know what you're doin'."

"You said he was all right."

"And he is. Up to a point. I trust him, but then he's never done anything against me. But I cain't speak for everybody. You know what he is, of course?"

"You mean do I know that he is a professional gambler? And a cheat? Yes, I know that. But do you know that he admitted cheating me out of that final poker hand last night and even gave me back my money, plus what I would have won, legitimately?"

Red whistled softly between her teeth. "He must have it bad for you, then. That man is a rake and a scoundrel, even if he is a friend of mine. I've never known him to do a thing like that before. Well, all I got to say is, heaven help you if he is in love with you."

"Why do you say that?"

"Because that man ain't normal when it comes to women he takes a shine to. He'll treat you like a queen and sit in your lap like a puppy. And jealous! Honey, he puts a new definition to the word! God help a stranger that looks twice at you. He's got a temper that the devil himself would be proud of. Listen to me, givin' you advice on matters of the heart, when I ain't got room to talk." She stopped suddenly, deep in thought.

"No, go on, I appreciate your telling me these things. How else will I learn? I know nothing of love..." That wasn't exactly true, she reminded herself.

Red seemed sadly thoughtful. "Neither did I at your age. Oh, I thought I was head over heels a few times. Even had a few fellas wanted to marry me. Can you imagine me with a husband, cookin' supper and darnin' socks and havin' babies? No, no, I'm happy right where I'm at. But I tell you, there was one man that I would have followed to the end of the earth if he had asked me to. But he never did ask me, and that's a pity. He couldn't really, you see, because..." She gave a short, humorless laugh. "...because he was already married."

Rebecca's heart leaped into her throat. She knew exactly how Red must have felt. Exactly.

"But he was really somethin'. Handsomest man I ever laid eyes on. I tell you the truth, Gentleman Jim Brogan ain't got nothin' on him. And he was a real gentleman, not just a nickname. God, I was so in love with him. But I guess you don't want to hear about me."

"Oh, but I do," Rebecca answered quickly. She had her own reasons for wanting to know more. "So what did you do? How did you handle the situation?"

"There was nothin' I could do, seein' as how he had a wife that he loved. At least he kept tellin' me that he loved her. But you know I always had some little naggin' doubt in the back of my mind, that he really didn't love her at all, or at least not as much as he declared he did. But he was an honorable man, and he never did nothin' that he couldn't go home and tell his wife about. Well, leastwise that I know of. So I finally had to give it up. It wasn't easy, believe me. I kept right on lovin' him, only I quit tellin' him so. It was enough just to see him once in a while, when he would come in here for a drink."

"Did he love you at all?"

"I tried to pretend that he did. But I think he just didn't want to hurt me, is all. He was the finest man I ever knew. I practically threw myself at him, and he didn't want me, but he let me down gently. He was really somethin'."

"So where is he now?"

"Oh, he's gone. He's not around to tempt me anymore." She gave Rebecca a sad smile. "I guess it's a good thing. Eventually I would have made a fool of myself, I just know it. I still want him. I probably always will."

"That's very sad."

"Ain't it?" Red agreed with an attempt at cheerfulness. "The worst part of it is that it's still so fresh on my mind. It's gonna take a long time to get over him. He only left town today."

Rebecca looked up sharply. Could it be?

"Today?"

Red smiled wryly. "Figured it out yet, honey? The man I fell head over heels for took his beloved little wife back to England today. Guess we just weren't good enough for her."

Rebecca could hardly breathe for the lump in her throat. Red noticed her discomfort, but did not know the reason for it. How could she?

"I'm talkin' about Oliver Sebastian," said Red as if that were necessary. "I fell in love with that man the first time I ever laid eyes on him. But he's gone, now. Guess I'll just have to get over it. I even thought I might have a go at good old Jim, but it seems you've beat me to it. Anyway, I hope things work out for you two, and I really mean that." Red patted Rebecca's hand affectionately.

Rebecca was stunned. Her mind raced back to the time when she had first seen Red, on the steamboat, when Oliver had gone for the bottle of champagne, and come out of the bar with Red trying to hold him back. He had given her a sad smile and refused her invitation.

It was all clear to her now. She and Red were both in love with the same man!

CHAPTER TWELVE

Now Rebecca had a new dilemma. Should she tell Red the truth? Or would that only hurt Red more, when the smartest thing for them both was to simply try to forget Oliver? She did not want to cause Red any more pain. The truth would hurt, she knew that instinctively. And the truth was that Oliver had turned down Red's affections but accepted Rebecca's. How did one woman break it to another, tactfully, that the man they both loved was actually in love with her?

Or had he really loved her at all? For the first time, there was real doubt. Was he in the habit of going around breaking hearts, because he was safely tied down to a frail wife and therefore could not be expected to fulfill any other obligations? The thought filled her with horror.

"Red..." she began tentatively, and the other woman waited patiently for her to go on. "You know that my father and I were coming to Natchez to buy Oliver Sebastian's farm?"

"Yes, I know that. Oliver told me himself. I even thought about buyin' it, but what would I do with a cotton farm? I like my saloon."

"Oliver has been very kind to me. He buried my father on his land and he said he would put it in the deed that it should never be disturbed."

"Didn't I tell you he was a fine man?" said Red a bit triumphantly.

"Yes, he is. And his wife really is a fine lady. She was very good to me when I stayed with them."

Until she found out, she almost said, but stopped. There was no need to go on. She had decided that there was really no point in telling Red the truth. If Red was astute enough to guess, then that was one thing. But Rebecca would not deliberately add to this woman's pain. Red had been too good to her to repay her in that fashion. Maybe someday they could laugh about it, but it was too soon, now, to laugh.

"So now you have no cotton farm to live on, and no father to look after you, and no money except what you have in your pockets," said Red. "Would you like to stay on here for a while? I can sure use the help, honey, and judgin' from the way you handled that crowd yesterday, I'd swear you were born for this kinda thing. There's money to be made, and plenty of it. And free room and board for as long as you like. Unless of course you end up marryin' Jim. Then the Lord only knows what will become of you."

Rebecca stared at her hands.

"On the other hand," Red continued, "you just might be what old Jim needs, to get him to finally settle down. There ain't no tellin' how much money he's got stashed away somewhere. Why, he could have the finest house and plantation in the country if he had a mind to. And the right woman to put in it. You just might be that woman."

Rebecca smiled. "I don't know about that. But there is something I've been thinking about. If I could make enough money, I'd like to buy that farm. It would mean a lot to me, I think, to kind of fulfill my father's dream. He never even got to see it. And his grave is there. I would like to be near him."

"Honey, that sounds like a wonderful idea to me. It would make your papa proud, I think. But ain't it already sold?"

"Yes, Oliver - Mr. Sebastian - sold it to Mr. Beckworth, Charlie's father. He wants the land, but he's giving the house to Charlie for his own. It's really the house and the grave that I'm interested in. I know even less about cotton than you do. I was just wondering whether I couldn't get Charlie to sell it to me, if I could come up with the money somehow."

"I think that's a very good idea you've got there, and I don't see why Charlie wouldn't sell it to you. Seems to me like he would do anything you asked him to, judgin' from the way he was fawnin' at your heels yesterday. Charlie's really a sweet boy, and seein' as how your papa is buried there and all, I don't see how he could say no. Have you talked to him about it?"

"No, not yet, but then I've only just now made up my mind that that is what I want to do. And I hope you're right. I feel that he will be happy to sell it to me, that is, if his mama will let him. She wants him to get married, and I'm sure she's behind his father giving Charlie the house in hopes that that will lure some unsuspecting young lady."

"Sounds like you've met the whole family. Well, if I were you, I'd talk to Charlie, the sooner the better, before he does find a wife and settle in. Then it might be a little difficult to uproot him."

"You're absolutely right. I will talk to him as soon as I get the chance. In the meantime, I've got to figure out a way to come up with the money to buy the place. Now are you sure about your offer? To let me work here, I mean? I would be happy to pay you room and board."

"No way! You are welcome to stay here, for free, as long as you like. This place is paid for, thank goodness. It's all mine, I can do as I please. Besides, it's really to my advantage to have you workin' here. You're a pretty girl and pretty girls are worth their weight in gold in a place like this. You'll bring in enough customers that it'll pay me to keep you around. I found that out yesterday.

"And there's another thing. I noticed that you don't care much for the pinches on the - shall we say - derriere. Well, the way to get around that is to keep Jim around you. I told you, that man will guard you like you was some priceless treasure if you let him. He'll see to it that no one bothers you. And from the tips you made yesterday, and the luck you had at poker, I wouldn't be surprised if you didn't have that money in no time flat."

As it turned out, Red's words were prophetic on all but one count.

Charlie was no problem at all. He was willing to give her the house if that was what she wanted, only his mama was pretty upset with her for breaking off the engagement and skipping town. Charlie had told his parents that Rebecca had gone back to Savannah. But he assured her that just as soon as his father put the deed to the house in Charlie's name, then he would be more than happy to sell it to her. He had never really wanted it in the first place.

Charlie and Rebecca agreed upon an appropriate price, based on what Mr. Beckworth had paid Mr. Sebastian for the entire plantation. Charlie even drove Rebecca out to the farm, so she could put flowers on her father's grave.

Red was right about another thing, too. Gentleman Jim Brogan became attached to her like a leech, and it was all too easy for Rebecca to allow it to happen.

Jim settled in at the Elysian Fields, playing poker with unsuspecting visitors from steamboats and keeping a watchful eye on Rebecca.

It was true that he never allowed anyone to bother her. Sometimes she wondered if he didn't have a sixth sense about her, because at times he would come out of nowhere and send an offender packing, often with a black eye or broken jaw as a souvenir. It seemed to Rebecca a small price to pay, if all Jim wanted in return was the honor of sharing her bed. He slept with her every night, and did his best to satisfy her desperate need for love.

The only point on which Red had been wrong was the most important one, and that was money. Oh, there was money enough to be made, but nothing like what she had made on that first day. But then every well-dressed gentleman that walked through those doors was not a wealthy cotton or sugar plantation owner. Some of them were gamblers like Jim, looking for their own suckers to cheat.

So except for the occasional steamboat full of millionaires docking at Natchez, she was not making as much money as she had hoped to make, even though she could save virtually every dollar, having no other expenses.

The only thing she really seemed to be lucky at was poker. She grew to love the game, and in the odd moments when the saloon was quiet, or she was not needed to work, she found great enjoyment in playing. It took her mind off her troubles and also added, little by little, to her capital, as long as she was careful to choose the right game to join, and didn't get taken by a professional card sharp.

When the game was fair and square, she was as lucky as any one person had a right to be. And she was also becoming more skilled. She became adept at reading faces, and knowing when a person was bluffing. Of course, she had Jim to thank for most of her knowledge. He very patiently taught her all she needed to know about poker, even how to spot the card sharps. And he would deliberately refrain from joining in a game in which she participated if he knew that it was fair. He knew that she wanted to be left to her own devices to hone her skills. But he kept a watchful eye on her, at all times.

Once she became very frightened when an innocuous-seeming gentleman took her for almost a thousand dollars with four aces to her flush. As he was pulling the pot toward him, two more aces fell from his sleeve, and all hell broke loose. Jim jumped up, pulled out a pistol, accused him of cheating, and demanded that he empty his pockets and leave at once. When the man refused, he was hustled out of the saloon and never seen again. Rebecca got up the courage to ask Jim what had become of the man, but his answer that the man was now catfish food sent a chill down her spine. She never questioned him again.

Life might have gone on in that manner indefinitely, but it was brought to an abrupt halt about a week later, when the two women that Red had engaged in New Orleans finally arrived in Natchez. The Elysian Fields took on a whole new aspect then. Until then, the only entertainment they had been able to offer was whiskey and poker, but now the customers were treated to song and dance as well.

Dixie and Florrie, Rebecca found out, were experienced dance hall girls who had made a name for themselves in New Orleans. Red had obviously been able to convince them that the cotton tycoons around Natchez would be even more generous than the wealthy sugar plantation owners in Louisiana.

The atmosphere at the Elysian Fields changed considerably. Rebecca found herself having to compete with Dixie and Florrie for the tips that were passed around, and in that department Rebecca fell short, because she still was not willing to allow her body to be fondled by complete strangers, even for a decent tip.

The other two girls had no such compunction. It soon became apparent that two women in revealing clothing who didn't mind sitting on a man's lap were much preferred to one who was only willing to serve them whiskey and beer. Rebecca found herself with less and less to do, and more and more often she was engaged in a poker game simply to pass the time.

Finally it reached the point where the only money she was making was at poker. It was definitely time to rethink her strategy, as she still was far from having the money to buy Charlie's house, and time was running out. He had lately been seeing quite a bit of a certain neighbor's daughter who seemed very willing to become Mrs. Charles Beckworth, and Charlie's mother was pressuring him to move into his own house. Rebecca had to act quickly or she would lose the opportunity to get the house she so desperately wanted.

So she began in earnest to hone her poker skills and to learn everything she possibly could about the game. She began to ask Jim questions about his gambling tricks, and he was more than willing to teach her everything, including how to conceal extra cards on her body, how to shuffle and deal from the bottom of the deck, and even how to mark a deck of cards so that she knew at a glance who held what. She was an eager and adept student, for a plan was formulating in her mind that, if it worked, would supply her with all the money she would need to fulfill her dream.

She would become a professional gambler, a card sharp, with this difference: she would only play against other card sharps, and take from them the money that they had taken from other poor innocents. Integrity forbade her cheating an innocent party, but to her mind cheating a cheater was only giving him what he deserved. In her heart, she fully believed that her father had been murdered for his gold. It seemed to her poetic justice if she were able to get back the money her father had lost, by taking it away from the sort of people who would stop at nothing, not even murder, for the love of money.

When she presented this plan to Jim, he was vaguely surprised at her fervent determination, but helped her all he could. She never told him why she wanted to do it, only that she had her heart set on buying her own home and this seemed like a good way to get the money. He never asked her for details, and even offered to buy the house for her himself, as a gift, but of course that was not part of her plan. No, this was something she had to do alone.

And besides, she knew that Jim was not the love of her life. She could not see herself living with him for the rest of her life. If she couldn't have Oliver, then she didn't want anyone. She would rather be alone. But she would use Jim in the meantime, without, of course, letting him know that he was being used.

Jim told her that if she was to learn to be a card sharp, then she would have to learn to play against them, to learn all their tricks, to learn how to recognize them, and to learn how to protect herself from being caught. He suggested that New Orleans would be a good place to begin her education, as that city was well known for its professional gamblers.

Riverboats, too, were good hunting grounds. Many an hour of a long trip on the river was passed with poker, as Rebecca was well aware.

The plan finally took shape in her mind on one particular evening when Dixie and Florrie were entertaining the customers and Rebecca was engrossed in a poker game. One of the players in the game, a rough man who's clothing was impeccable but who's manner was anything but, started tossing hundred-dollar gold pieces onto the pile instead of the usual bank notes.

Rebecca was suddenly overwhelmed with emotion, and stared openly at the man. He seemed to have several of those gold pieces, and won and lost them over and over. She managed to acquire one, herself, in a winning hand, and held it in her palm, tightly, as though it might speak to her. She did not recognize the man as having been on the steamboat "Lucky Star," but then there had been hundreds of passengers, and she had had no reason, at first, to be curious. It was entirely possible that the man sitting across the table from her had been the same man to put a knife to her father's throat and cut short his life.

The very next day that same man was found near the river's edge with a bullet through his head, and all his money gone.

Sheriff Brown made the required investigation, but of course there was nothing he could do. No one had seen or heard anything. It was just another unexplained murder, and they were common enough at Natchez-Under. But Sheriff Brown's visit upset Rebecca in a different way. The sheriff seemed anxious to know why she was still staying on at Red's place, and why she was living in sin with Gentleman Jim Brogan.

She told him bluntly that it was none of his business. She had no use for the man, anyway. He had made not the first effort to find out who had killed her father. This did not faze the sheriff, who told her just as bluntly that she was heading for trouble if she did not watch her step. She thanked him for his concern, but assured him strongly that it was totally unnecessary. She was capable of taking care of herself.

He gave her a stern look and a deep harrumph! but left her alone.

The very next day, Rebecca and Gentleman Jim boarded a steamboat for New Orleans.

The trip downriver to New Orleans was uneventful, and Rebecca contented herself to sit with Jim in the bar and watch him play poker against the other men on board. Jim did not have the qualms that she had about taking money from an innocent person, and proceeded to strip large sums of money from every one that he played.

By the time they reached New Orleans, he had won a small fortune, and they proceeded to have a high time in that city.

They stayed in the finest hotels and ate in the finest restaurants. Jim took her to the most exclusive dressmaker in town and paid for a complete new wardrobe, more befitting to his "lady". Then they would while away the hours in the best saloons, Jim playing poker as she watched carefully.

In their hotel room, she would practice "stacking" the deck, as Jim called it, and dealing from the bottom, under his watchful gaze. After all, he was a master at the art. If she couldn't fool him, what hope had she of fooling another card sharp? Soon she was able to deal out exactly the hands she intended without him catching her at anything underhanded. It gave her a certain vicarious pleasure.

She even picked up a few new tricks of her own, with which even Jim himself was not familiar. It was not long, then, before she had the confidence to try it herself.

Jim helped her to fashion a lovely velvet wristband that, when tucked away under the voluminous lacy sleeves that her new gowns now sported, was totally undetectable and would hold almost half a deck of cards without appearing bulky.

The first time she played under these new conditions she was so nervous that Jim had to make her stop, before she did something foolish and gave herself away. She sat nearby and watched him playing, using the same tricks, until she was ready to try it again. But still it took a huge, stout gulp of brandy to steady her nerves to the point where her hands stopped shaking.

It amazed her that the men she played against, all professional gamblers themselves, she made sure of that, never caught on to her. Evidently a woman card sharp was virtually unheard of, even in the roughest places, and they trusted her to the point of carelessness. Oh, they still used their own tricks, to be sure, and she lost a few hands because of them, but all in all they seemed totally unaware that she was cheating them at their own game. It therefore became very easy to join in any game that looked likely enough, as the men were always eager for female companionship, even at the poker table.

This went on for several days, and Rebecca made a lot of money. She was very clever about it, too. She knew that it was smart to lose a few hands, to keep the game going, and even found herself betting upwards of a thousand dollars on nothing more than a pair of deuces, when she knew full well that someone at the table held a full house, because she had dealt the cards herself.

But this strategy paid off, because later when she was able to get the winning hand, and knew it, she could bet any amount she chose, and they would call, on the assumption that she might be bluffing or that they could beat her hand. In this way, it was only a matter of a few days before she had accumulated several thousand dollars.

Sometimes she and Jim would play in the same game together, though more often they did not. But when they did, they would help each other out of tight spots, when they found that they were playing against some particularly sharp gamblers, and then they would split the winnings between them. It was becoming a very profitable partnership.

It was not long, then, before Rebecca had made up her mind that she now had enough money to buy Charlie's house, and that her career as a professional gambler was coming to an end. If she was lucky, the return trip to Natchez would supply her with just that extra amount of money to see her safely through a couple of years until she could develop her next plan. She had no intention of being a gambler the rest of her life. She had the nerves for it by now, but not the stomach. It was still cheating, no matter how she looked at it. Her father might approve her tenacity and her ingenuity, but he could never condone her methods.

She mentioned none of this to Jim, only told him that she was tired of New Orleans and was ready to go home.

Home. Was Natchez really her home now? It must be, it was where her heart was, as the old saying went. She also knew that soon she must say good-bye to Jim.

She had no intention of ever marrying him, and she was painfully aware that the fact that they were virtually living together made her appear to be a common woman.

And she was not a common woman, she was a smart woman. She knew when to keep a man around and when to get rid of him. Jim was fast outliving his usefulness.

Jim booked passage for them on the "Golden Promise," a luxuriously appointed steamboat that was painted almost entirely in gold. So luxurious was it, in fact, that Rebecca and Jim were among only a handful of passengers who could afford the steep fare.

In the bar her experienced eye told her that the only card sharps on board were Jim and herself. All the other passengers were businessmen or wealthy gentlemen of leisure, and not the sort that she was, by now, used to playing against.

Jim's hungry eye, however, saw it differently. It mattered not to him whether he played against another professional like himself or against any other ordinary person. They were all suckers ripe for plucking. When he muttered something to her about the prospects of this trip looking mighty good, she sighed. She was getting tired of it all, very tired.

But when Jim could only interest three of their fellow passengers in a game of poker, he insisted that she join them. Five was the normal number of players, and besides, with a beautiful woman playing too, attentions could be easily distracted. She tried to tell Jim that she had no stomach for it anymore, but he took her arm and squeezed it brutally, saying she owed it to him and all he expected was for her to just help him out if he needed it and to sit there and be charming.

On riverboats the customary poker game was played not with a full deck but with only twenty-five cards, ace through ten, among four players. All the cards were dealt out and one had to play what one was dealt, there was no discarding and drawing. This restricted the game severely, to the point where, if the cards were dealt out in a certain manner, an ace-king combination might take the whole pot. It was also possible, in this way, to get four of a kind or even a royal flush. Even though she had her qualms about this game, she had left her cabin prepared. In her sleeve was a stack of cards that she could resort to if need be. But the need didn't arise. Jim saw to that, with his expert manipulation of the cards.

One of the tricks that they used when playing together was for her to pretend that she knew nothing whatsoever about cards. Asking for help from the others was a good way to draw their attention, and to convince them that she was totally innocent of any underhandedness. This even worked with professionals, although they should have been more alert to possible tricks. But for this game, she had already made up her mind that although she could resort to the cards up her sleeve, she would not do so. As a matter of honor, she was not going to cheat these men; let Jim do as he wished.

So charmingly did she perform this little theatrical that three other gentlemen in the bar who had declined to play now were attracted to the table and came and gathered around her and began to talk to Rebecca and advise her on her cards. Jim eyed them carefully, ever watching out for her, but seemed satisfied that they meant no harm. She amused them as well as herself by asking them what she should do with a certain hand, and then following their instructions. They were soon convinced that she was indeed unfamiliar with the game, as she kept constantly asking "what beats what?"

But it was all in fun. She was a charming woman and they all enjoyed her little joke. Even Jim relaxed a bit, as those three other harmless gentlemen pulled up chairs and surrounded her, eager to be of service.

She played fairly, and did not cheat, although Jim got more than a little perturbed at her and kicked her once under the table with a viciousness that surprised and enraged her. She had told him she would not cheat these men. It was not fair to try to force her to do something which she adamantly did not wish to do. Yes, it was time to get rid of Gentleman Jim Brogan, and the sooner the better.

When Jim suggested that it was time for a new deck of cards, he got up himself and went over to the bar. When he came back, he had a wrapped deck in one hand and a bottle of whiskey in the other. He tore the wrapper from the deck as the bottle was passed around. Rebecca was not fooled. She had seen him mark and rewrap that same deck in their cabin. The pattern on the back of the cards exactly matched the cards she had hidden up her sleeve.

So when he dealt the hand, she could see right away that he dealt himself four aces. But he was a little careless with the rest of the cards, and when she peeked at hers, privately, she saw that she held the king, queen, jack and ten of spades, along with the ten of diamonds.

She was on the verge of asking her mentors whether she ought to bet on two tens when an idea struck her, almost as violently as Jim's kick under the table. The top card on the stack in her sleeve was the ace of spades.

As innocently as she could manage, she fumbled with her cards and dropped the king and jack of spades to the floor. When one of the gentlemen seated behind her reached to retrieve them, she very skillfully withdrew the ace of spades from her sleeve and hid away the ten of diamonds, so that when she had all her cards together again, she was holding a royal flush. She turned to the men behind her and asked very demurely if they would advise her to bet on that hand?

To a man their mouths dropped and their eyes grew wide in amazement, and they assured her fervently, with all their hearts, that yes, indeed, that was a hand most definitely upon which to bet. She seemed satisfied, and when it came her turn to bet, she bet every dollar that was lying on the table in front of her.

The bet went around to Jim, who eyed her suspiciously, but raised the bet, as he was holding, he supposed, the winning hand. Jim's bet went around the table until it was Rebecca's turn again, and after consulting with her mentors, she reached into her velvet reticule and pulled out more money. And she raised Jim's bet again.

This time the other men dropped out, as the stakes were now too high, and they were convinced, from the encouragement that Rebecca's helpers were giving her, that she had the winning hand. Jim was not to be done in so easily. He saw her bet and raised her a thousand.

"Gentlemen, what do you think?" she asked them again, and they assured her that she had absolutely nothing to worry about. So she tossed a thousand dollars on the table and said, "I call."

They all looked at Jim, whose face broke into a big smile as he laid down his cards. "Four aces. Beat that, if you can."

Someone behind her gasped in surprise, and after thinking for a second, Rebecca replied, "I guess you win," and tossed her cards onto the pile of discards.

The gentlemen at her side all were astonished at her behavior. She rose from the table and said, "If you all will excuse me, please, I should like to bow out of this game." They excused her, and she turned away and went to the bar.

The three men who had been watching all this stared at one another, then followed her.

"My dear! Why on earth did you do that? You had him beat by a long shot!"

Rebecca started to explain, but then the steamboat whistle blew two shrill blasts signaling that they would soon be pulling over to the shore to wood up, so she suggested that they take a stroll out onto the deck.

Jim gave her a stern look as she passed him, which she did not return. It was time he learned that she was her own woman.

They leaned against the railing and watched as the boat pulled over and gently bumped the shore, then one of the gentlemen at her side could contain himself no longer and asked again why she had done such a thing?

"Gentlemen," she said in a low, intimate voice, which made them all lean toward her. "You saw the hand that I held?"

They all agreed that they had, certainly.

"A royal flush? Including the ace of spades?"

Yes, of course.

"Then how do you suppose it is possible that someone else could have had four aces when I held one of them myself?"

Before they could reply in outrage, she stopped them. "Gentlemen, it is clear that someone at that table is not playing honestly. Now, I know what you are thinking, but please, do me the honor of not making a to-do about it. I abhor dishonesty and I refuse to play with a cheat. So let us leave it at that, shall we?"

They protested, gallantly, that they were willing, very willing, to call the scoundrel out. But she staved them off. She had no desire for that, she explained. She abhorred violence as much as she did cheating.

"Now, would anyone like to bet against me that the price of a cord of wood will be two dollars?"

One of them took that bet, more in fun than seriously, which was her intention, after all. They waited for the captain to complete the ritual, and soon they heard him call out, "Got any wood for sale?"

The man on the shore spat into the river and replied, "Reckon it might be possible."

"How do you sell it a cord?"

"Three dollars."

"Three dollars!" cried Rebecca in unison with the captain. "Why, that's a dollar a cord too much!"

"Prices has gone up," replied the man, and they all burst into laughter. Rebecca reached into her reticule and paid her bet with good humor. "Let that be a lesson to me," she said almost to herself, "nothing in this world is for certain."

They watched as several of the crew ran down the planks connecting the boat to the shore and began to haul wood back on board.

Suddenly a man rushed by them and flew down the stairs, his coat tails flapping out behind him. Before they knew what was happening, the poker players from the bar ran outside and started pursuing. But the man was too quick for them. By the time they had reached the bottom of the stairs, he had bounded across the planks and disappeared into the night.

One of them pulled out a pistol and aimed it, but just at that instant, another one pushed his arm above his head, so that the pistol fired harmlessly into the air. Everyone ducked their heads.

"What the devil is going on?"

"A cheater! A lying, filthy no-good card sharp! That's what!"

Rebecca's mouth fell open. She should have recognized him, of course, but it had all been so sudden that she hadn't expected it to be Jim that came running out of the bar, and that now was somewhere in the dark woods beyond the river with a pistol shot ringing in his ears.

One of the offended players explained. "How would you feel if you were dealt two aces of spades in the same hand?"

Her companions stared at Rebecca, but she made a slight motion of her hand that said, please, no more of this.

Another of the hapless victims declared that he had had enough poker for one day, and Rebecca declared how terrible to be deprived of playing so delightful a game, simply because someone had been cheating.

"It is a pity, because I was just beginning to get the hang of the game. But, there it is," she said with a little toss of her head which they found charming. As if on cue, they suggested a game of poker among themselves, a fair game this time.

"But gentlemen, please don't do this on my account."

They assured her they were not, that they were all interested in playing, and all entirely on the up and up.

She consented, and as they all went back inside, she unobtrusively divested herself of the extra cards up her sleeve, dropping velvet band and all into the waters of the Mississippi. Her cheating days were officially ended, then and there. She would play with them, but she would play fair.

Not only did she play fair, but she won fair. She made such a charming companion that they did not mind losing to her, especially as they were convinced that she really knew very little of the game and it was obvious that lady luck was definitely on her side.

There was a lot of luck involved, certainly, but there was also skill. She took great pleasure in winning a hand by her own talents. It wasn't long before she had accumulated nearly two thousand dollars more to add to her savings.

Finally Rebecca excused herself, saying that she had had enough excitement for one day, and was going to her cabin for a good night's sleep.

And that's exactly what she got, a good night's sleep. She had not slept alone since the first night she had met Jim, and it was strangely comforting not to have his arms around her for a change. Oh, yes, he had served his purpose, she thought with a cold heart, but she was finished with him now. If she never saw him again, it would be too soon.

CHAPTER THIRTEEN

Immediately upon arriving in Natchez the next day, without even stopping in at the Elysian Fields, Rebecca went straight to the bank, where she added the money she had acquired on the trip to New Orleans to what she had deposited there before. It came to a considerable sum. Then she hired a carriage to drive her out to the Beckworth place to see Charlie, and she even carried her trunk of new clothes with her. If they could settle everything today, and she could move in right away, that would suit her just fine.

When she got to the Beckworth place, she was told by the servant at the door that Master Charles was out at the moment, but that he was expected home for dinner. The servan as her if she would she care to wait.

Rebecca assented, and was shown inside and conducted to a pleasant room with large windows that afforded a beautiful view of a nice green lawn and gardens. The Beckworths had a very fine home, with all the acceptable trappings of wealth, but without the cultivation. Still she could find no fault with that; it meant that Mr. Beckworth had probably started with little or nothing, and had worked hard to get where he was. This was exactly what her father had dreamed of doing.

It wasn't long before she heard voices in the hall outside. When the door opened, Mrs. Beckworth came in with a very puzzled expression on her face.

"Why, Miss Bennett! Am I ever surprised to see you! We thought you had gone back to Savannah!"

Rebecca rose out of courtesy and presented her hand to the woman.

"Hello, Mrs. Beckworth. I owe you an apology, I expect. You see, I had indeed intended to go back to Savannah, but there was a last minute change in plans, and I find that I wish to stay on in Natchez indefinitely. I trust you and your family are all well?"

Her dignified manner and her polite conversation quite put Mrs. Beckworth beside herself. She had been all prepared to upbraid this sassy young woman for leaving her son Charles waiting on the church steps, as it were, but she found her anger slipping away. After all, what harm had been done, really? Charles had found another potential bride, and her plans for him had not been completely shattered.

So they spent a few minutes in innocuous small talk before Mrs. Beckworth finally got around to asking her why she had come there.

"Oh, I just wanted to see Charlie about something," Rebecca answered evasively, not knowing how much Charlie had told his mother of their agreement.

"Why, whatever could you want to see Charles about, my dear Miss Bennett?"

The inflection in her voice told Rebecca that the woman was a bit nervous at her appearance now after the way she had run off so suddenly. Was she worried that Rebecca might try to throw a kink in her plans for getting Charlie married? Was she here to accept Charlie's proposal, now, when it would be damned awkward to do so?

Rebecca thought quickly and put Mrs. Beckworth at ease by answering, "I only wanted permission to visit my father's grave, Mrs. Beckworth. You see I'm not in the habit of trespassing."

Mrs. Beckworth was visibly relieved. "Oh! My dear! Well, of course you have permission. Imagine not giving you permission to visit your dear old father's resting place! I assure you, Miss Bennett, that you may visit as often as you like. But my dear, is that dress exactly...well...suitable for a daughter in mourning?"

Rebecca resented the woman's remark, but she was right of course. Rebecca should be dressed in nothing but black for her period of mourning. And here she was, making social calls, dressed in one of the finest gowns north of New Orleans.

"Yes, of course, you are right, Mrs. Beckworth, and I have not any excuse to give you, except to say that black does not become me."

This was not the answer Mrs. Beckworth wanted to hear, not at all. Rebecca could sense that the former esteem the woman had held for her had just fallen considerably. Mrs. Beckworth's nose rose perceptibly, and she looked down it at Rebecca with all the haughty demeanor of a queen to a scullery maid.

Thankfully, Rebecca was spared any further embarrassment when Charlie walked into the room. The welcome smile on his face when he saw her was quite uplifting. She went into his outstretched arms and returned the big, warm hug that he gave her.

"Rebecca! My God, I've missed you! Where on earth have you been?"

"Oh, I took a little trip down to New Orleans, but I'm back now, safe and sound. I'm glad you missed me. I missed you, too." It was true, she had missed Charlie. He and Red were the only true friends she had.

Mrs. Beckworth watched this exchange with a puzzled expression, but Charlie made no effort to enlighten her. Instead he took Rebecca's hand and said, "Come on, let's get out of here so we can talk."

The carriage that she had hired in town was still waiting for her in the drive. "You know why I'm here, don't you, Charlie?"

"To buy the house, I guess. Did you come up with the money?"

"Yes, all of it. I can pay you today, if it can be arranged. See, I even brought my trunk. I'm ready to take possession immediately."

He laughed. "It may not be that easy, Rebecca. I don't know much about these things, but I do know there's a hell of a lot of paperwork and lawyers involved. I always did hate lawyers. I cain't never understand a thing they say. But never you mind, I have the deed to the house and a few acres of pasture, includin' your daddy's grave, and it's all in my name, nice and legal. So I can do anything with it that I please, and nobody can stop me. It's legal," he repeated with his chest thrust out proudly.

"Oh, Charlie, that's wonderful! Well, then, can we do it as soon as possible? I guess it is too late today, the bank is probably closed by now. How about first thing in the morning?"

"Sure, whatever you wish. I know, why don't you send that carriage back to town, and I'll drive you over there right now. You can even spend the night there, if you want to, if you think you won't be scared."

"Scared? Of what? Charlie, that is my home. It has been ever since I said good-bye to Savannah. It only took a while to get moved in, that's all. And if you are talking about ghosts, why, don't you know that my father's ghost is there waiting for me? And he would never hurt me. So what is there to be scared of?"

She had meant the talk of ghosts as a joke, but the look on Charlie's face was anything but amused. "Please don't talk about such things, Rebecca. It gives me the creeps."

Rebecca paid the driver (how good it felt to have her own money!) and her trunk was transferred to Charlie's buggy. He drove her the short distance to the house, and when she got her first glimpse of it between the trees, a lump rose in her throat that made it hard to swallow, even to breathe.

The place had become very dear to her, and not just because of her father. Memories of the things that had happened here, things that were still very fresh in her mind, would not be quiet.

She remembered the first day she had come, with Oliver, and little Jeremiah running out to them, his face all lit up at sight of his master. As Charlie unlocked the front door she almost expected to see Portia standing there, with that big, toothy smile.

"You can see, the Sebastians left the house just like it was. I don't think they took nothin' with them but a couple of trunks." He threw open the library doors, and if she had seen Oliver Sebastian sitting there reading a newspaper and smoking a cigar, she would not have been surprised at all. The memories were very fresh indeed.

She could almost feel his presence in the house. Everywhere she looked, something reminded her of him. She began to feel a little lightheaded. Maybe this hadn't been such a good idea after all. Sure, she wanted the house for her father's sake, but she hadn't realized the effect it would have on her, knowing that Oliver had sat in that chair, had read that book, had eaten at that table.

There was no denying it. She was still very much in love with Oliver Sebastian.

The room that really got to her, though, was the master bedroom, the room he had shared with Charlotte. Everything else in the house had been left exactly as it was, but this room was a mess. She noticed a couple of broken crystal bottles or vases, it was hard to tell which, as they lay in shatters next to a dressing table that was still littered with some of Charlotte's personal toiletries. Perhaps they had been broken in the haste of packing, or perhaps they had been flung to the floor by a distressed wife. Or even, perhaps, by a distressed husband?

The bed was a marvelous four-poster of heavy mahogany, but it was in shambles, the sheets tumbled wildly and pillows lying on the floor. It was surprising that the rest of the house was so immaculate, yet this room had been abandoned in such disarray.

She wandered over to the tall mahogany wardrobes and noticed that they were all empty. There was a door between two of them that she had not noticed when she first entered the room, and she opened it now. It led to a small, dark area that appeared to be a bathroom. There was the same kind of waist-high wooden bathtub that she had used at Red's, as well as mirrors and a washstand with pitcher and basin. But what drew her attention was a long velvet-covered sofa against the far wall that was also littered with sheets and pillows.

For a moment she accepted the idea that Portia had slept here, in order to be near her mistress if she was needed. But then she remembered that she had already seen Portia's room, downstairs next to the kitchen. So if Portia hadn't slept there, who had?

She walked over and saw a long white silk ascot that had been overlooked lying tangled among the bedding. She picked it up slowly, her fingers tingling, and pressed it against her face. Her knees suddenly felt as if they were made of butter, as she inhaled the rich, very masculine scent that lingered still on the scarf. She sat down on the sofa, and buried her face in the sheets, breathing in the smell of Oliver Sebastian.

Tears fell unchecked down her cheeks, and she felt as if her heart would break.

She smelled him, sensed his presence, heard his footsteps in the hall.

Her head jerked up. There were footsteps in the hall! Her heart began to pound fiercely.

"Rebecca? Where are you?"

It was only Charlie. She sighed, almost a sob, and dried her tears on the scarf. "Yes, Charlie, I'll be right out."

Then, impulsively, she stuffed the scarf between her breasts, out of sight, but close to her heart. It was all she had left, now.

The sun had slipped beyond the horizon as they walked back downstairs, but it was not quite dark yet. Charlie asked her if she was sure she wanted to stay there that night, and for a moment her resolve weakened. He didn't mind, of course, it was only that, well, the house had been empty for a while now, and she would be all alone, and helpless if anything should happen. There were highwaymen in the area, and they might try to come in. He would feel a lot better, he declared, if she would wait until she was the proper owner, and had gotten a housekeeper or someone to stay with her. He didn't like the idea of her staying there all by herself, no, ma'am, he did not like it at all.

When she still seemed unable to make up her mind, he even offered to stay with her. This made her smile.

"Well, I guess if you feel that strongly about it, I could go back into town and stay with Red tonight. I didn't even stop to say hello to her today, I wanted to come and see you first. All right, Charlie, you win. But promise me that first thing in the morning we get all the paperwork and lawyers out of the way. Then it will be mine, all legal, and I intend to stay here even if I have to sleep with a gun under my pillow."

* * *

When Rebecca and Charlie walked into the Elysian Fields, Red's greeting was warm.

"Honey! Glad to have you back! So tell me all about your trip to New Orleans. Where is Jim?"

"Jim had to make a fast getaway. I'll tell you all about it, later. First I want to buy my friend Charlie a drink to celebrate."

"Celebrate what?"

"Tomorrow I will become landed gentry."

"That's wonderful! You got the money you went after, then. Honey, I'm proud of you. Yes, that certainly calls for a drink. But keep your money in your purse. The drinks are on me."

Charlie accepted the beer that John Henry set before him, but declined another one. He was expected back at home in time for supper, but he promised to fetch Rebecca first thing in the morning, to complete the deal on the house. Then he bid them all goodnight.

When Charlie had gone, Rebecca felt more comfortable telling Red what had happened with Jim. It wasn't that she didn't trust Charlie, rather she was embarrassed for him to know how she had gotten the money. She was proud of having figured out a way to buy the house for herself, but she was not proud of how she had gone about it. Charlie's was one friendship that she did not want tarnished with knowledge of her activities.

Red, however, was a different story. She listened eagerly as Rebecca recounted her adventures into gambling, wanting to know every single detail. She passed no judgment on Rebecca for what she had done, for Red was as guilty as anyone. The only thing that did upset her somewhat was when Rebecca told her what happened on the "Golden Promise" when Jim had had to beat a hasty retreat.

Red laughed heartily at the picture Rebecca's words conjured up, but then her face took on a grave look.

"What I'm wonderin' is how Jim is takin' it right now."

"What do you mean?"

"Well, I mean, from the way you tell it, he wasn't aware that you had thrown away that extra ace of spades back into the same deck. Whatever possessed you to do such a thing?"

"I honestly don't know," Rebecca replied truthfully. "It just seemed like a good idea at the time. Besides, I guess I was angry with him. I told him I was tired of being a cheat, and I wanted to stop. He wouldn't let me, though. He kicked me under the table. Hard."

"But, honey, was that kick worth riskin' Jim's life?"

"I thought so at the time," Rebecca answered with a sheepish grin. "Oh, Red, I was tired of it, that's all. Tired of cheating, tired of having to be so very careful not to get caught. And most of all, tired of Jim."

Red gave her a thoughtful look. "I see. Well, if you wanted to get rid of him, you couldn't have done a better job if you'd planned it. The thing that worries me, though, is will he let it go at that? Knowin' Jim the way I do, I heartily doubt it. If he really loves you, he'll be back and he'll forgive you. If not, he'll be back anyway, to get even with you for what you did."

Rebecca felt a shiver run down her spine. "In that case, the smart thing to do is not to let him find me. I'm going to move into my house tomorrow, and Jim won't know where to look for me, because I never told him about it. I only told him I was planning to buy a house, but there are thousands of houses around here. How will he know which one?"

Red gave her young friend a sad smile. "Oh, honey, you don't know split beans from coffee if you think that will stop Gentleman Jim Brogan. Don't you know that any time a piece of property is bought or sold that the deed is registered and becomes public knowledge? All he has to do is make a few inquiries and he'll find you, make no mistake about that."

"Red, stop it, you're frightening me. Do you honestly think he'll come looking for me?"

"Yes, I do. I've known Jim a long time. He'll stop at nothin'."

"Then what on earth am I going to do?" Rebecca cried. "I don't want to see him again, ever. It's over between us. As a matter of fact, there never really was anything serious. Oh, I know, I made a stupid mistake and let him think there was something between us, but that was because I needed a man at the time, and Jim did teach me a lot of things. Because of him, I can buy that house now. But that's all I wanted from him. I don't want him now."

"Honey, you've got a lot to learn about men," said Red, shaking her head. "But never mind that. Right now you got more important things to think about. Now, it seems to me that you might be better off if you just let Jim find you and then apologize to him. If he still has any feelings for you, and unless I'm sadly mistaken, he does, then he'll accept your apology and that will be that. I don't know how you're gonna get rid of him, though. That's another problem altogether. It could be that once you get moved into your house that he'll stay gone most of the time. I really cain't see him settlin' down, not for any length of time, anyhow. He's got ramblin' and gamblin' in his blood. He won't be happy bein' a househusband."

Rebecca was thoughtful. "I suppose you're right. I hope he doesn't find me, but if he does, it might be best to apologize, and then hope that he gets so bored he'll leave of his own accord. Red, I don't know what I'd do without you."

"Shucks, honey, it ain't nothin'. What are friends for?"

Still, Rebecca was uneasy, and kept glancing at the door, fearful that Jim might show up there. Red tried to get her interested in a poker game, but she declined. She had had enough poker to last the rest of her life.

There was really nothing to do until morning, so she asked Red if she would mind her staying the night there. Red replied of course not; there was no need to even ask. Rebecca thanked her and went upstairs, but after thinking about it for a moment, she went on up to the third floor, where she knew there were several empty bedrooms. She needed to be alone, away from everybody.

Her trunk had been left at the house, so she lay down on the bed fully dressed, convinced that she would not sleep anyway. The silk scarf at her bosom rustled softly when she rolled over. She pulled it out and pressed it again to her face. She could still smell him, and the tears began to fall again. If only he were there. He would protect her from Jim, from everything.

She cried into the scarf for a long time, until exhaustion took its toll and she fell into an uneasy sleep.

She awoke early the next morning as the first light of dawn crept into the dark little room, almost surprised that she was still in one piece. The scarf was still clutched tightly in her hand, and there were tear stains on the soft silk. She rose, her body stiff, and tidied herself as best she could, in preparation for her meeting with Charlie. The scarf was tucked back in its hiding place between her breasts, next to her heart. It gave her some small measure of comfort to feel the softness against her skin. Even though it was only a piece of fabric, it had belonged to Oliver, and that made it precious.

The household would all be asleep at this early hour, and the front doors locked and barred. But she was familiar with the building and knew that the door at the end of the hall led out onto the top gallery, and a stairway led from there to the street. So she went outside and stood against the rail, breathing in the soft morning air, and waited for Charlie.

It wasn't long before he pulled up in his buggy.

Her heart lifted. He had kept his promise. She called down to him from above, then raced down the stairs.

They drove up Silver Street into town to the office of the lawyer who handled all of Mr. Beckworth's legal affairs, who was only just arriving and was surprised to see them so early in the morning. Charlie assured him that it was urgent, and gave the lawyer his instructions.

The man's only comment was a rather personal and direct question as to whether Charlie had his father's permission to do this? Charlie straightened his shoulders and told the man that it was none of his business, that the property was legally his, and he could do with it as he damned well pleased.

The lawyer was startled by this answer, but reasoned wisely that it was no concern of his. After a moment, he told them that it would take a little time to prepare the necessary documents, and would they care to wait?

Rebecca suggested that it might be a good idea to go to the bank and get that part of the deal settled. The bank was only just down the street, so they walked the distance. Rebecca made the withdrawal from her account, and Charlie transferred it into his own. Now all that needed to be done was to sign the papers and the house would be all hers.

When they returned to the lawyer's office, the papers were ready. Her signature, as buyer, Charlie's signature, as seller, and the lawyer's signature, as witness, made the transaction final. She felt a wondrous pride as she held the important piece of paper in her hand. Finally, after all the trouble she and her father had gone through, it was hers. The sad part was that her father was not there to share in her accomplishment.

Charlie drove her back out to the house, and at the front door, handed her the keys.

"Here," he said. "I thought you might like the honor of unlockin' your own house."

She smiled at him. "Dear Charlie, you know me pretty well by now, don't you?"

This question only made him blush. She unlocked the door and opened it wide. "And I want you to have the honor of being my first guest. Enter, Master Beckworth." She dropped him an elegant little curtsey.

"After you, my lady," he replied with a gallant bow and a sweep of his arm. They both giggled like children playing at being grown-ups.

"I can't believe it's mine, Charlie. You don't know how much it means to me."

"Oh, I think I do know. You've told me often enough."

"I don't know what to do first. I suppose I ought to hire someone to do the cooking and housekeeping. I'm not very good at that sort of thing. And there's probably nothing to eat here. Maybe we should have bought some provisions before we left town. I'm afraid my mind is not working properly at the moment, I'm too excited."

She did find a container of coffee, though, in the kitchen. Charlie brought in some firewood, showed her how to build a fire in the large cast iron stove, and soon a kettle of water was boiling.

"I'm afraid I can't find any sugar," she said as she placed two steaming cups on the kitchen table.

"That's all right, I take it plain, like my Daddy. Oh! I almost forgot. I want you to have this. For protection."

He reached inside his coat and withdrew a pistol.

Rebecca stared at it. "Charlie, I was only kidding about sleeping with a gun under my pillow. I'll be fine, don't worry."

"I won't worry, if you have this with you. Well, not so much, anyway. You need some kinda protection, Rebecca. You cain't just stay here all by your lonesome. Take the pistol. It's loaded and everything. Here, I brought some extra caps and balls, I'll show you how to reload it."

"Charlie, I don't know anything about guns, and I've never handled a pistol before in my life."

"There ain't nothin' to it. I'll teach you."

Despite her protestations, he did teach her everything she needed to know about the gun. She had no intention of ever using it, but it did give her a tiny bit of comfort, knowing that it was there, should the need arise.

The first day in her new home was spent in getting her trunk unpacked and the master bedroom cleaned up. She had thought that she would not be able to stand sleeping in the same room, indeed the same bed, that Oliver and Charlotte had shared. But on second thought, why should she not? It was her home now, not Charlotte's, and the sooner she got used to the notion the better off she would be.

She found a broom and a dustpan in the pantry and swept up the broken glass, and cleared away all the abandoned personal effects. She heated a large kettle of water on the wood stove and washed all the sheets and linens, and hung them out in the bright sunshine to dry and to soak up that unmistakable clean-air smell that she loved.

While she was doing all this, Charlie went back into town to pick up some food. Just as he was leaving, she stopped him. "Charlie, if you don't mind, I'd...I'd like to kind of keep it a secret that I am living out here."

He nodded. "That's good thinkin'. If anybody knew you was all alone, they might try to bother you."

"That's right. So if anybody should ask you where I am, you won't tell them, will you?"

"You can count on me, Rebecca. It'll be our little secret. 'Course Mama and Daddy will have to find out sooner or later. But I'll keep it from them as long as I can. Now, just keep that pistol handy, and I'll be back before you know it."

His return wasn't quite that soon, but he did come back before she had run out of chores and had time to think about being nervous again. She could not shake the conviction that Jim would find her, sooner or later. She almost wished it would be sooner; the suspense was killing her.

Charlie had done a proper job of buying food, and she set about preparing a meal to show her appreciation, but she found it more difficult than she had imagined.

Her father had employed a live-in housekeeper and cook back in Savannah. Rebecca had never had to learn anything in the kitchen.

The over-cooked eggs and the under-cooked bacon were hardly the meal she would have liked to present to Charlie, but he ate heartily, and she ended up giving him her portion as well. She had no stomach for her own cooking, but with practice, she thought, maybe she would get used to the wood-burning stove that seemed to be hotter than necessary, no matter how she adjusted the vents and flues.

After eating, Charlie settled into a chair on the shady verandah and took a nap. She used the time to stroll out to her father's grave, and pulled weeds that had begun to grow there, replacing them with wildflowers that she gathered nearby.

It soothed her spirit to be able to talk out loud, privately, with no one around her, and to tell her father everything that had happened to her since he had passed away. As long as she could come out here and be close to him whenever she needed, she would feel better. It seemed to be the only place she could find real peace.

Charlie was still napping when she returned, so she brought in the bed linens and made up the bed in the master bedroom. It was her bedroom now, so shouldn't it be the mistress bedroom? She was mistress in her own home. The thought gave her more than a little pleasure. Then she went down and began to heat another kettle of water for a bath.

The noise must have awakened Charlie. He found her and said that it was getting late and he should be heading for home. His parents never really worried when he was away all day, but they did expect him to put in an appearance at the supper table. He was happy enough to oblige them in that respect, being always eager for a meal, and finding it a small price to pay for the freedom to come and go as he chose.

But he was still clearly concerned for her safety, and asked her again if she would like for him to stay with her. She appreciated his kindness, and all that he had done for her, but it was time she stood on her own two feet. She would be just fine, she assured him.

When he said that he wasn't so sure about that, and thought that maybe he might ride over again after supper to check on her, she told him firmly no. If she heard a horse approaching after dark, it would scare her to death, and she just might shoot him accidentally with that pistol, and how would she explain that to his mama?

He was still clearly anxious for her, but he left with a smile on his face. She made sure the doors were all securely locked then carried the bath water upstairs, lit a candle in the small bathroom, and took a long, leisurely bath until the water turned so cool it gave her goosebumps when she finally stepped out.

She slipped between the cool, crisp, fresh-smelling sheets, then suddenly got back out of bed and impulsively knelt on the floor beside it.

Because it was the only prayer she could remember, she recited the old standard she had learned as a child: "Now I lay me down to sleep", with her hands pressed together reverently. When she came to the "God bless" part, she had a short but sincere list, that included Father, Mother, Charlie, Red, John Henry...Charlotte...and finally Oliver, whose name she repeated twice. Amen.

Then she crawled back beneath the covers and curled up into a tiny ball. The last thing she did before she fell into a deep, unbroken, peaceful sleep was to place a tender kiss on the white silk scarf that she was wearing around her neck.

CHAPTER FOURTEEN

Warm sunlight streamed into the room through the tall wide windows and fell caressingly on her face. Rebecca awoke to the sweet sounds of mockingbirds serenading her just outside in a huge oak tree, and she smiled.

It was good to be alive, and she was happy for the first time in ages. She lay in her new bed listening to the chorus of birds as if it were the songs of angels. Then she sat bolt upright, straining to hear.

Their sweet music had been joined by another sound, the sound of hoofbeats. Someone was coming up the drive at a fast clip.

She threw off the covers and reached quickly for her robe, her heart beginning to pound. But then she made herself calm down. It was probably just Charlie.

He was so concerned for her welfare that he had probably ridden over first thing to see if she was all right. She drew the robe around her and forced herself to walk calmly down the stairs.

Before she reached the bottom step, she saw the figure of a man through the tall narrow windows that flanked the door, and he was not Charlie, of that much she was certain. Her heart began to pound in earnest now, as the man knocked loudly on the door and then tried the knob. It was still locked, thank goodness.

Then he seemed to examine the windows to see if he could find an entrance that way, but gave that up and pounded on the door again.

"Becky! Open the door! I know you're in there! Becky! Open up, Becky!"

Rebecca's scalp tingled with fear. It was Jim. He was the only one who called her Becky, but she knew the voice, just the same. What should she do? She didn't want him to come in, but unless she let him in, he would break in, she was certain. How did he know where to find her? She worried frantically, but there was no time for speculation. The only thing to do was to let him in.

"Jim? Is - is that you, Jim?"

"Becky? Open up! You know it's me, damn it! Open this door or by God I'll break it down!"

She went quickly and unlocked the door. He thrust it open, almost knocking Rebecca backwards. Jim stood there glowering at her with a black rage in his eyes that terrified her, really terrified her. Slowly, never taking his eyes from hers, he closed the door behind him. She began to shake.

"Jim! I - I'm so glad you're all right! I was w-worried about you!" It was a pathetic act, but at the moment, it was her only choice.

His eyes held hers as he came toward her. She was almost ready to scream with fear. Quick as lightening he grabbed her arm so tightly that it bruised the skin and he brought his other hand up with a vicious backhand across her face that sent her head spinning wildly.

Stars exploded behind her eyes, and the pain was excruciating. He loosened his grip and she crumpled to the floor like a rag doll.

Through the blinding pain she could hear his footsteps as he walked away from her and seemed to be surveying the rooms and the house. Her ears rang loudly but she was aware he was talking to her, saying something about what a fine house she had, and how he was going to enjoy living there. She touched her lip tenderly with shaking fingers, and saw blood on them.

"Yes, this will do nicely. You've done well, my darlin'. Only you should have told me sooner. Then there would have been no need for the trip to New Orleans, would there? I could have bought this place four times over. But you wanted to surprise me, didn't you, darlin'? And what a nice surprise, too! I shall cherish it always. Just like I shall cherish havin' to run for my life after you pulled that stupid -stupid!- trick on the riverboat!" His voice had gone from irony to rage, and Rebecca stayed where she was, afraid to move, afraid even to look up.

He paced back and forth in front of her. "How could you have done such a thing? If I hadn't been quick on my feet, I'd be floatin' in the river now, facedown. Is that what you wanted? Is it? After all I've done for you? That's a fine way to repay me. You knew how dangerous it could be. Did you want to see me get killed? Answer me!"

She was silent. He took a menacing step toward her and she shrank away, covering her face with her arms.

"Answer me!" he bellowed.

"I'm sorry!" she cried, tears spilling down her face. "I never meant-"

"You're sorry," he repeated disbelievingly. "Is that supposed to cure everything?"

"What do you want me to say, that I did it on purpose? Well, I did! Yes! I did it! I wanted to beat you at your own game! And that's what really galls you, isn't it? You taught me all the tricks and then I pull one that you never thought of! I beat you at your own game!"

His body stiffened with rage, and he took another step toward her. She cowered, bracing herself for another blow. "Please don't hit me again," she whimpered, and burst into sobs.

But the expected blow did not come. Instead, after a long moment, she felt herself being pulled up from the floor and into his arms. He cradled her head against his chest and stroked her hair.

"Oh, my darling, I won't hit you again. I'm sorry I hit you at all, but you gotta understand how I felt. It took me two days to get back here, and I could think of nothin' but how much I wanted to hurt you. But it's over now, I won't hurt you again. I love you, don't you know that?"

He raised her tear-streaked face up to his and kissed her. It made her lip hurt, and her jaw felt like it was broken. If she had had the pistol in her hand, she would have shot him through the heart, right in the middle of his words of love. Love! He didn't know the meaning of the word.

But wisely she said nothing, only let him finish with what he had to say. He seemed genuinely repentant, now that his anger had died away. But how long would it be before he tried something like that again? She shuddered, hating him with every fiber of her being.

She was lifeless in his arms as he carried her upstairs and found the open door to the bedroom. When he walked into the room, he whistled in admiration of the magnificent four-poster bed. "Nothin's too good for my lady," he crooned as he laid her gently on the bed and pulled her robe and nightgown from her body. Then he stripped off his own clothes and climbed on top of her.

She lay like a stone beneath him, unable to respond to his lovemaking. No, that was wrong, she did respond, but the response was not one he would welcome. She wanted to kill him.

When he was finished he rolled over to her side and stroked her breasts. His touch made her skin crawl.

"Very pretty," he said, fingering the silk scarf that still hung from her neck.

She snatched it from him a little too quickly, and he gave her a bewildered look.

"It - it's just a scarf," she said meekly. He stared at her for a long moment, then rose abruptly from the bed.

"Fix me somethin' to eat. I'm starved. I'll be back in a little while. I got somethin' to take care of. Oh, and there's a fella comin' out to see me about some business. Put on one of them pretty dresses I bought you and make him feel at home, will you?"

She wanted to scream how dare he! It was her house, not his! But she was in no hurry to get another slap like the first one. She waited as he put his clothes on, and bent over and kissed her. Then he left the room, but she didn't stir until she heard the front door open and close behind him.

Last night's bath water was still in the tub, icy cold by now, but she didn't care. She felt filthy from his touch. She got into the water and scrubbed until her skin was raw, and still she felt dirty.

She was in the kitchen holding the pistol in her hand, wondering if she had the nerve to use it, when she heard her name called, and she started violently.

"Rebecca? Where are you?"

She breathed a sigh of relief. Charlie walked into the kitchen with a big grin for her. "There you are! Well, I see you made it through your first night all right. Were you scared?"

She replaced the pistol in the flour canister where she had hidden it earlier and said, "No, not a bit, Charlie. Last night was very peaceful." It was this morning that she was distressed about, but she didn't tell him that. Out of embarrassment she kept her face turned away from him. The mirror in the bathroom had shown her an ugly black and blue bruise on the whole side of her face and she kept licking at the dried blood on the crack in her lip.

"Want some coffee?"

"Sure. Rebecca, you know you told me that you wanted to keep it a secret, about you bein' here and all? And that if anybody asked me if I knew where you were, to tell them no?"

She stiffened. Dear God, not Charlie!

"Well, there was somebody askin' about you. He came to the house last night after I got home. Said he had just got back into town and he wanted to know where he could find you."

She set the coffee cup down in front of Charlie and then turned her face fully to him. "He found me, Charlie."

Charlie gasped at the sight. He seemed speechless for a long moment. "You mean, he did that to you? I cain't hardly believe it."

"Believe it, Charlie."

"But I always thought Mr. Sebastian was a good man."

Rebecca's jaw dropped painfully. Her breath caught in her lungs. "Did...did you..." she stammered.

"I swear I didn't tell him nothin', Rebecca. I don't know how he found out, because I didn't tell -"

"Charlie!" she cried. "Did you say...Mr. Sebastian...?"

"Why, yeah, ain't that who we're talkin' about?"

The relief was almost painful. Oliver was back! She started laughing uncontrollably from sheer nerves, and Charlie stared at her wide-eyed.

"Rebecca? Are you all right?"

"I am now, Charlie," she said between gasps for breath. Oliver! "But how...? I thought he left for England."

"He did. But his wife died on the way and they never even made it to New York. So he turned around and come back. Rebecca, I didn't tell him you were here. Why did he hit you?"

"Oh, Charlie, he didn't hit me. Someone else did. I haven't seen Oliver - Mr. Sebastian. You did just fine. It isn't your fault."

"Well, I'm glad of that, anyway. But who hit you, Rebecca?"

She sighed. "It's a very long story, Charlie, one that I should have told you a long time ago. You are my friend, and I should have told you the truth. The fact is -"

The sound of footsteps brought her to an abrupt halt. She jumped to her feet, and only had time to whisper quickly, "Go get Oliver!" before Jim walked into the room.

Jim stared coldly at them both, and cocked a hand menacingly near the pistol stuck into his belt. "Well, ain't this a fine howdy-do. And just who is this fella here? One of your lovers?"

Rebecca blushed fiercely, more for Charlie's sake than her own. "This is Charlie, Jim. He's the one who sold me the house. He just came over to see if everything was all right."

Jim eyed him boldly. "And is everything all right, Charlie?"

Charlie was nervous, but not foolish. "Sure, I guess so."

"Darlin', I'm surprised at you. He ain't your type at all. Or maybe he's got more between his legs than he's got between his ears. Is that it, eh, Charlie? Got somethin' down there to please the ladies with?"

"Jim!" she cried. "He's just a boy, for God's sake!"

"Yeah? Well, he don't look like no boy to me. You just skeedaddle on home, boy, you ain't got no more business here."

Charlie looked at Rebecca but she pleaded with her eyes for him to do as he was told. "I reckon I'll see you later, Rebecca -"

"No, you won't," Jim interrupted. "I told you, you ain't got no business here. Now go on and don't let me catch you sniffin' around here again."

When she heard Charlie's buggy going down the drive and knew that he had gotten safely away, she turned to Jim in fury.

"That was totally uncalled for!"

"Shut up!" He sneered. "I cain't trust you for a minute, can I? I turn my back and you got some other man makin' puppy eyes at you. What's the matter? Cain't you get enough?" He took a step toward her but she backed away. "Shall I take you upstairs again? And prove to you that I'm the only man you'll ever need?"

Dear God, she couldn't bear that, not again.

"H-here, I've made you some coffee. N-now sit down and eat." She busied herself with setting out a plate for him, and he stared at her for a long time, but his hunger got the best of him, and he sat down and ate poorly-cooked eggs and bacon, a replica of the meal she had served Charlie the night before.

"God, this is horrible! Cain't you even cook? Cain't you do anything except drive me insane?"

She was silent, her eyes fixed to a spot on the table. The flour canister was on the cupboard directly behind her. If she could get to the pistol without him knowing it...

But that was a foolhardy notion, just at the moment. He had his own pistol in his belt, and she was sure that her inexperienced fingers would bungle the job and he would have the jump on her. No, she must wait for the right opportunity.

Hoofbeats sounded out in the drive. Her heart leaped. Could it be?

Jim listened carefully, then rose to his feet. He stood facing the door, the pistol in his hand. She made a motion to get up.

"Don't move," he commanded, pointing the pistol directly at her. Footsteps told them someone was inside the house. "Who's there?"

"Jim?"

He let out a sigh of relief and replaced the pistol in his belt. "In here."

Rebecca gasped with shock. She expected to see any man in the world walk into that room except him, that man from the Sentinel, the one who had made her skin crawl from his unwanted attentions, the one who she was convinced had something to do with her father's death.

"Well, this ain't bad at all, Jimmy boy. How'd you manage to get your hands on a place like this?" said Mr. Latimer.

"Compliments of the little lady," Jim replied sarcastically.

Latimer noticed her, then, and his eyes grew wide. "Why, if it ain't Miss Bennett. How-do, Miss Bennett! You're lookin' just as pretty as ever. Jim, you old dog, you. You didn't tell me -" He stopped abruptly, and a stab of fear crossed his face. "Wait a minute. What's goin' on here, Jim?"

"Nothin' that's any of your business, Latimer. Let's go into the other room and settle up. Then I want you to hightail it outta here. You don't need to be seen around here."

"But, Jim, that's Miss Bennett, she's -"

"What!" he shouted. "Don't tell me you've had her too?" He turned to Rebecca with a look that made her blood curdle. "And here I thought you were my woman. Have you been with every man up and down the entire Mississippi?"

"What are you talkin' about, Jim?" Latimer cut in. "Look, I don't know what kinda deal you got goin' here, but I know one thing. It scares the piss out of me. Let's settle up and then I'm gone."

"Come on," Jim said, grabbing Rebecca by the arm. "I cain't let you out of my sight."

The grip on her arm was painful, but she had no choice but to follow. They went into the library and Jim pushed her roughly into a chair. Then he pulled something heavy from where he had hidden it beneath the desk.

"I was goin' to leave it hidden for a bit longer, just to be sure. But Becky changed my plans, didn't you, Becky?" He glared at her. "Had me runnin' for my life, but as it turned out..." Jim picked it up and placed it on the desk. "...it was excellent timin'. Put me off just at the right place."

Rebecca's heart was beating so hard she thought it must surely explode. The object that Jim had placed on the desk was the small brass chest that her father had used to carry his gold from Savannah to Natchez.

Jim opened it, and Latimer crowded up close, eager to see the gold and also to make sure that Jim didn't try to cheat him.

Rebecca's throat constricted so tightly that she could only rasp out, "That - that's my father's!"

Jim gave her a look, but turned back to the business of counting. Could she be mistaken? Brass chests were common enough. But something in the pit of her stomach told her that this was indeed her father's own.

"Jim!" she cried, her nerves stretched to breaking.

He stared at her. "What now?"

"Is that...is that my father's money?"

Latimer shuffled his feet and glanced nervously from one to the other, but she paid no attention to him. Her eyes were fixed on Jim.

"Darlin', that's the craziest thing I ever heard. What makes you think this is your father's money?" he drawled, picking up one of the gold pieces and tossing it into the air. "This is our money, me and Latimer's, but if you're a real good girl and keep your mouth shut, there just might be somethin' in it for you too." He flipped the coin to her, but it fell unheeded to the floor. She knew without looking that it was a hundred-dollar gold piece.

"What's the matter, darlin'? Ain't my money good enough for you?"

"It's not your money!" she cried. "Jim...did you kill my father?"

Latimer cleared his throat nervously. Jim stared at her. "What are you talkin' about? I don't even know your father."

"That's his money," she said quickly, while she still had the courage to speak. "It was stolen from him on the steamboat. Jim," she pleaded, "please...did you kill him?"

Jim gave her a confused look, then turned to Latimer, who was scuffing the toe of his boot against a desk leg. "Do you have any idea what she's talkin' about?"

"That's what I been tryin' to tell you, Jim, you hard-headed bastard. That man that we took this off of? Well, that was Miss Bennett here's father."

Jim stared at him in disbelief. A bitter bile rose in Rebecca's throat.

"So it's true," she whispered.

Jim gave her a long, strange look, then crossed his arms over his chest and leaned against the desk. "Well," he said slowly, "this puts the situation in a whole new light."

"What are we gonna do, Jim?" Latimer asked, looking to him for guidance.

Jim thought about it carefully, then replied, "We go ahead with our original plan. You take your half of the gold and get as far away as you can. I can handle her."

Her stomach constricted. "W-what do you mean by that?" she asked shakily.

"I mean, my love, that you will marry me, as a sort of, shall we say, insurance, and we will forget about the whole business, or..."

"Or what?"

"Or I'll have to kill you."

"I think you better go on and kill her now, Jim. I don't trust her."

"I don't care what you think!" Jim bellowed. "I said I can handle her. Now, here, let's finish this up." He turned back to counting, but gave that up and scooped out roughly half the gold, spilling it onto the desk.

Latimer was torn between keeping an eye on Rebecca and keeping an eye on Jim. But he needn't have worried about her. Rebecca was rooted to the spot and couldn't have moved even if an earthquake had struck.

"This is yours," Jim said, closing the lid of the chest. "Take it, and get rid of that chest as soon as you can. You don't need to be caught with it. No one can accuse you of anythin' just for havin' gold on you, but that box could be incriminatin'. Do you understand?"

"Yeah, Jim, sure."

"Now get out of here."

Latimer picked up the chest and headed for the door, but just at that moment, they heard hoofbeats pounding up the drive. Rebecca's heart leaped in hope. Surely Charlie had found Oliver, or at the very least he would have gone for help of some kind.

"Somebody's comin', Jim," Latimer said nervously.

Jim crossed quickly to the window and pulled the curtains apart just enough to peek out.

"One man on a horse," he said. "I don't recognize him. You better wait a minute, Latimer. Hide that chest."

Latimer put the chest back under the desk, and Jim raked the pile of gold that was his share of the booty from the desktop into a drawer. Then he whipped out the pistol and waited.

They could hear the man outside as he walked up onto the verandah and knocked at the door. Rebecca glanced at Jim, but he made a motion with the gun that she should not move. After a moment, a knock sounded again.

"Miss Bennett?" called a voice, and Rebecca almost fainted with relief. It was Oliver!

"Miss Bennett? Is anyone home?" he called again.

Rebecca jumped up and would have rushed to the door, but Jim was quicker. He grabbed her arm and shoved the pistol painfully into her ribs.

"Miss Bennett? I'm not leaving until you open this door, Miss Bennett."

Rebecca looked at Jim.

"Miss Bennett!"

"All right," Jim whispered fiercely, "Answer the door and get rid of him. And don't do anythin' stupid," he added, shoving the gun deeper into her ribcage.

He kept the pistol on her as they walked slowly toward the door. She unlocked it and pulled it open a fraction, Jim standing just out of sight on the other side.

When she saw Oliver Sebastian's handsome, welcome face she nearly fainted with joy. For a second she almost forgot the gun in her side, and wanted nothing so much as to rush into his arms.

"There you are, Miss Bennett!" Oliver said genially, calmly. "May I come in?"

She took a deep breath, willing him desperately to read the message in her eyes. The pistol was pushed harder against her. "M-Mr. Sebastian, th-this is a surprise. B-but I'm afraid you've caught me at a rather bad time. I'm sorry, but I c-cannot invite you in." Why couldn't he see the desperation in her eyes?

"Oh? Well, please forgive me, Miss Bennett, I only wanted to come in for a moment, to get some of the things that I, unfortunately, had to leave behind."

His voice was calm, but his eyes twinkled at her, and in her heart she knew with conviction that she was one of the things that he had, unfortunately, had to leave behind. And now he had come back for her. Her heart went out to him.

But the gun in her side brought her back to her senses. "I-I'm sorry, that's impossible." She made a move to shut the door in his face, but he quickly prevented it.

"It will only take a moment, I assure you."

Jim shoved her roughly aside and jerked the door open. "If you wanna come in that bad, then by all means, come right on in," he said, brandishing the pistol at Oliver's chest.

"You should have told me you had company, Miss Bennett, I would not have been so insistent," Oliver said smoothly as he moved inside the door and reached for her hand, which he squeezed lovingly as if to give her courage. Luckily Jim did not catch the movement. His jealousy over her would have meant instant death to Oliver.

Jim closed and locked the door. "Cut out the sweet talk and get in there, both of you." He motioned toward the library and followed them inside.

Latimer stared open-mouthed at Oliver. "You!"

"Mr. Latimer. We meet again."

"You two friends or somethin'?" asked Jim, eyeing them both curiously.

Latimer spat in the direction of Oliver's boot. "I swore I'd kill this slimy English bastard."

"You may get your wish," Jim replied, shoving Rebecca into a chair and pushing Oliver against the wall.

"Wait a minute," said Latimer, his face almost contorted with thought. "It's all fallin' into place now. Mr. Bennett said he was comin' to Natchez to buy a farm. It was your farm, wasn't it? So this must be it, here."

"Well done," Oliver replied calmly. "I congratulate you on your astuteness."

"Shut up!" hissed Jim savagely. "Get your hands in the air. Up!"

Oliver raised his arms over his head and Jim searched him for a concealed weapon, keeping the gun pointed into his chest at all times. "Just as I thought," he said, pulling out a pistol from behind Oliver's coat, and jamming it into his own belt.

"Now explain to me why you would pay a social call on Miss Bennett here, totin' a gun."

Oliver nonchalantly adjusted the sleeves of his coat. "Isn't it customary to carry a gun for protection? After all, one never knows the kind of low-life ruffian one might happen to meet."

"Like me?" Jim said, and he gave Oliver a sharp blow across the mouth. Rebecca flinched.

"Just so," Oliver replied, his eyes glittering dangerously.

"I'd watch that mouth, if I were you, otherwise you might find the barrel of this gun in it." Jim touched the end of the pistol to Oliver's lip, where a single drop of blood had formed.

Oliver said nothing. Jim backed away, smiling, but keeping the pistol trained on him. He came over to Rebecca's chair and placed his free arm around her shoulders.

"He's a mighty handsome fella, darlin'. Is he a close friend of yours?"

Rebecca said nothing, knowing that this was a dangerous question.

"Jim, we ain't got time to play games," cut in Latimer. "What are we gonna do about these two?"

"Well, now," Jim drawled, stroking her hair gently. "I guess that all depends on Miss Bennett here. We gotta kill him, that's for sure. But she's a different story. How about it, darlin'? Are you goin' to cooperate or not?"

She was silent just a second longer than pleased him, and he grabbed her hair and yanked her head back hard against the chair. Oliver took a quick step toward them, but Jim jerked the gun back up.

"You ready to die now, Englishman? Then back off!"

"Jim, please!" she begged, nearly in tears.

Latimer was nervous. "Look, do what you gotta do, but I'm gettin' outta here now." He pulled the brass chest out from under the desk.

"I thought you wanted to kill this Englishman."

Oliver saw the chest. "Kill me, like you killed her father?" he asked accusingly, drawing Jim's attention away from Rebecca.

Jim looked at him in surprise, and released his grip on Rebecca's hair. "Yeah, that's right. Just like her father. Only you got it wrong, Englishman. I didn't kill her father. I didn't know nothin' about it until today. I only took the gold. I ain't got nothin' to do with no murder."

"Jim!" cried Latimer. "What are you sayin'? Why, you're the one that told me to -"

Oliver looked pointedly at Latimer.

"I didn't have no choice! I thought he was asleep, but he woke up and found us in his cabin. I had to kill him before he yelled for help."

"You brainless warthog," Jim spat at him. "That's the last dealin's I'll ever have with you. It should have been a simple robbery, and now you got me mixed up in murder."

"Jim! Why are you doin' this? You were there!"

"Obviously he intends to lay the whole blame on you, Latimer," said Oliver. He looked at Jim. "Were you on the boat the whole time, or did you come on board when we stopped for wood?" he asked, almost conversationally.

"If it's any of your business, Englishman, I came on when it stopped to wood up. It's easy enough to do, I've done it hundreds of times. I met Latimer here on board, and he told me about this sucker - pardon the expression, darlin' - that had all this gold on him just waitin' to be relieved of it, so I relieved him. Then I got off the next time the boat stopped for wood, and hid the chest. Latimer stayed on board, so as not to arouse any suspicion, and me and him would split the money later. And that's all I know. If Latimer killed the man, then that's his business, not mine. I only robbed him."

"But it makes you an accessory to murder, and just as guilty, in the eyes of the law," Oliver replied.

"The law! Ha! Well, the law ain't never gonna find out about it, because nobody's gonna be alive to tell them. Now enough talk. Get over here."

He motioned with the gun and Oliver walked over to Rebecca.

"We're gonna take a little walk down to the river. I'd just as soon shoot you both right now and get it over with, but I made the mistake of lettin' that boy leave this mornin' and if they find your bodies here, they might put two and two together. So we'll just go down to the river, shall we? Maybe your bodies will wash up down in the Gulf of Mexico. Come on."

Oliver took her hands and pulled her to her feet. "Don't be afraid, my love," he said gently, looking deep into her eyes, trying to convey strength to her.

"What did you say, Englishman?"

Oliver did not have to answer this question, for just then they heard a booming voice from outside.

"Jim Brogan! This is Sheriff Brown! The house is surrounded! Throw down your weapons and come out with your hands up!"

"Jim!" cried Latimer.

Jim made a move to go to the window, but as he did, he took his eyes from Oliver, and Oliver grasped the opportunity. He grabbed Jim's hand and forced it into the air. The gun went off, the bullet embedding harmlessly into the ceiling. Then Oliver quickly grabbed the other pistol from Jim's belt and held him at gunpoint.

Latimer made a move toward them, but Oliver's tone stopped him. "I wouldn't do that if I were you." Then he spoke to Jim. "I don't suppose you noticed it, but your gun was a cap-and-ball, with only one shot, which you have just spent. This is a six-shot revolver, and believe me, I know how to use it."

Jim glared at him angrily, but dropped the useless gun to the floor. Oliver moved a few feet away to where he could cover both men.

"Sheriff!" he shouted. "This is Oliver Sebastian! I have them under cover. Come on in. Miss Bennett will open the door for you." He pointed the gun at Jim's head. "Go on, my love. Let them in."

She did not hesitate but moved quickly to the front door and opened it. "Hold your fire! It's Miss Bennett!" the sheriff yelled.

In a flash a dozen or so armed men rushed past her and entered the house. "Are you all right, Miss Bennett?" Sheriff Brown asked her gently.

"I am now, sheriff," she replied honestly. Sheriff Brown winced as he saw the ugly mark on the side of her face, but said nothing else, and walked into the library.

"They're all yours, sheriff," Oliver said, replacing his gun beneath his coat.

Jim and Latimer were surrounded by guns, and they lifted their arms above their heads.

"Those are the men who murdered my father, sheriff," Rebecca said as she came into the room. "The money is in that chest there, and also in one of the drawers."

"Thank you, Miss Bennett. Brogan, Latimer, you're both under arrest for the murder of Henry Bennett."

"You ain't got no proof, sheriff," Jim said.

"I heard them confess it, and I will say so in a court of law," Oliver replied.

"And I will deny it!" Jim spat. "You cain't prove it!"

"Sheriff, maybe I can help," Rebecca said. "If you will be so kind as to open that chest..."

The sheriff motioned to one of his men, who pulled the chest out into the center of the floor. Rebecca knelt beside it, lifted the lid and dumped the gold inside onto the rug. Then she held up the chest for the sheriff to see.

"There is my father's calling card. He always placed one of his cards inside most everything that he sold, just as a reminder to his customers of where they had purchased it. It was designed to bring in repeat business."

Sheriff Brown looked inside the chest and saw a small white card, stained brown from the river water, stuck in the corner that read "Bennett Mercantile, Henry H. Bennett, Proprietor, Savannah, Georgia."

"Your father was a farsighted man, Miss Bennett. I wonder if he knew that it would also help to catch his murderers. That's enough for me. Come along, you two. We will need to take the chest and money along, too, Miss Bennett, for evidence."

"Of course."

"You are one dead Englishman," Jim snarled threateningly at Oliver. "And you've got somethin' comin' to you, too, darlin'. I swear I will kill you both."

"Shut up, Brogan. You'll be swingin' from a rope before you can hurt any more innocent folks. Get them out of here."

Jim and Latimer were escorted roughly from the room. "I may need you to testify," Sheriff Brown said to Oliver and Rebecca both. Oliver nodded in understanding. "Well, good day."

"Good day, sheriff, and thank you."

Neither of them moved until they heard the sheriff and his men ride away. Then suddenly the release of tension was too much for her, and she turned to Oliver.

He said not a word, only held out his open arms to her and she flew into them, clinging tightly and sobbing into his chest. It was hard to believe the nightmare was over and she had him back again.

Oliver held her for a long time, crushed against him, as her body shook with sobs. Finally he raised her tear-streaked face and stared at the horrid mark there.

"My beloved Rebecca," he murmured, stroking the tender flesh gently. "You've been through rather a tough time, haven't you? I should never have left you. Despite everything, I should never have left you. Can you forgive me?"

"You're back, that's all that matters," she whispered tearfully.

"And I shall never leave you again, I swear it. Oh, Rebecca, I've missed you so much -" He cut off his own words, kissing her deeply. Her eyes closed and she melted into him, wanting to join with him and become one with him. He was everything to her, even life itself. Her fingers entangled in his hair, pulling his mouth closer to her own. Her tongue reached for the sweetness that she knew was there, tasted it, and her whole being instantly was alive and full, full of love for him, and full of his love for her. She was complete once more.

CHAPTER FIFTEEN

Rebecca poured a steaming cup of coffee for him and he complained. "Don't you have any tea? After all, I am an Englishman, am I not?"

Oliver dodged the towel that she flung playfully at him.

"Sorry, fresh out. You'll have to drink coffee and like it."

"I'll drink it," he grumbled, "but I won't like it. I don't suppose I could have some sugar, to kill the taste?"

She gave him a longsuffering look and shook her head.

"Guess I'll have to get used to these barbarities," he sighed and sipped the hot, black liquid, making a face as he did so.

She smiled at him over her own cup of coffee. It was such a fresh joy, having him back. She could hardly keep her spirit under control. It kept wanting to soar.

"So tell me everything that has happened since I left. And mind you, leave nothing out. I want to hear it all."

"You'll have to wait. I want to know about you, first. Charlie said that...that Charlotte died."

"Yes," he replied sadly, staring into his cup. "She was hysterical the day she threw you out. Oh, yes, she told me all about it. I could have wrung her neck. I tried to catch you, you know. But I must have been one step behind you. Where did you go after you left?"

"To Red's."

"Ah. I should have guessed that. If I had gotten a chance, I might have gone there looking for you. As it was, I never got a chance. Charlotte was beside herself with anger. She accused me of all sorts of ugly things, the most of which came from her own head. I did not deny that I was attracted to you. But I wasn't exactly sure if I loved you. I mean, we are being completely honest, here, aren't we?"

She nodded. "We are."

"Later, there was no doubt in my mind, no doubt at all, that I loved you with all my heart. But at the time, the only thing I could think of was Charlotte and that I owed it to her to follow through on the plans of going back to England. It was her idea to leave the next day. She had poor Portia running in circles, trying to get everything ready. And on top of that, she collapsed from her own emotional outburst. Portia stayed up with her until dawn. I couldn't leave her sight, either, not for a second. If I even went down to the kitchen for tea, she accused me of leaving and going to find you. I did manage to slip out once, for a moment, and I went to talk to Charlie. He told me you were planning to go back to Savannah, but somehow I just couldn't believe that.

"Anyway, we boarded a steamboat early the next morning. Charlotte never really recovered. She was sick all the way to New Orleans. I almost put off taking that ship to New York, hoping she would get better. A long sea voyage for someone who is already sick is not the ideal situation. But she was determined. She wanted to go home. So we left."

He raked his hand across his eyes. "We made it as far as Roanoke. I was on deck watching the landing. When I went back to the cabin, she was dead. Portia was hysterical. She was devoted to Charlotte. I informed the captain, and Charlotte was buried near Roanoke. So Portia and I turned around and came back. And here I am."

"Where is Portia now?"

"Her people are here. She's with them. She only consented to go to England because of Charlotte. She'll be just fine now."

"And how about you? Will you be just fine now?"

He gave her a tender smile that melted her heart. "When I'm with you, my love, the whole world is just fine."

"So how did you find me? I mean, how did you know I was here? I own this place now."

"Yes, I know. Charlie told me. I stopped in at the Beckworth house last night to inquire, but he wouldn't tell me anything then, although I could tell he knew more than he was saying. So this morning I was on my way to see Charlie again, to beat it out of him, if need be, when I met him on the road. He told me where you were, and that there was a man here with a gun. Charlie was scared stiff, but he volunteered to come back with me to the house. He must be very fond of you."

"We've been through rather a lot together," she replied.

"I sent Charlie after the sheriff, and you know the rest. Did he do that to you?" Oliver reached up and gently stroked the ugly bruise on her cheek. His touch was almost healing.

"Yes."

"I should have killed him when I had the chance. No one will ever lay a hand on you again, I swear."

She smiled. She believed him.

"Now, pour me another cup of this stumpwater you call coffee, and then tell me what other excitement I have missed, if you please."

"If you don't stop complaining about my cooking, I'm going to give you something to really complain about. I'll fix you some bacon and eggs!" she threatened as she poured him another cup.

"What's that supposed to mean?"

"Never mind. Just stick around and you'll find out."

"That is exactly what I intend to do. You are never going to leave my side again. Now, tell me how you came to fall in with a couple of criminals. I'm bursting with curiosity."

"Criminals? Yes. Only I didn't know it at the time. And I only fell in with one, not two, thank you. The second one was rather a surprise to me, too. I never expected to see him again."

"And which one was that, my love?"

"Latimer, of course! Don't tease. I knew there was something wrong with that slimy weasel when I first laid eyes on him."

"You're dying to say I told you so, aren't you? So go ahead. Say it."

She glared at him, but took a certain pride in saying, "Yes, I told you so. I told the sheriff, too, didn't I? I knew it. I don't know how I knew it, but I knew it. The day I left here, I went to Red's, and she put me to work. You wouldn't believe the kind of money I made serving whiskey and beer. Well, that's when I got the idea to buy this house. Charlie agreed to sell it to me if I could save up the money. So that was my plan, to work at Red's place and save my money. And it worked. For a while. Then I sort of lost my appeal at the Elysian Fields when these two...women...came up from New Orleans and started working there. So then I had to think of something else. And that's when I sort of fell in with Jim."

"Sort of?"

"Do you want the truth?"

"And nothing but."

She grinned, almost embarrassed. "He was a substitute for you. A poor one, I'll admit, but a substitute, nonetheless. I was so devastated at losing you, I guess I sort of took the first man I ran across. Does that make me cheap?"

"My darling, in my eyes you could never be cheap. I understand how you felt, believe me. I felt the same way at losing you. But I had Charlotte. You had no one."

"And I desperately needed someone, anyone. I thought, I really thought, that Jim was different from what I later found him to be. But by then it was too late."

She went on to tell Oliver everything, about the time Jim had come in while she was bathing, about the nights they spent together and how she had wished with all her heart that it had been Oliver instead of Jim, about the gambling tricks, about the trip to New Orleans, and finally about how she had tricked him on the "Golden Promise" and how he had had to run for his life.

"I came back to Natchez and lost no time in buying the house from Charlie. I guess it was my intention to hide out from Jim, but as you can see, that plan failed. But the strange part of it is that Jim had to leave the "Golden Promise" very near the same spot where he had also gotten off the "Lucky Star" and hidden my father's gold. If Latimer hadn't shown up looking for him, I might never have found out that they were responsible for Father's death. I shudder to think what would have happened to me if you hadn't arrived when you did. You saved my life."

His fingers closed around hers reassuringly. "It's all over now, my love. Jim will never hurt you again."

"Oh, Oliver, I'm so glad you came back to me. Can we really be together? Forever?"

"Forever."

"And no ghosts?"

"None."

"I feel really sorry for Charlotte. I honestly liked her, you know."

"I know. And she honestly liked you, too."

"Honestly?"

"Honestly. Portia told me that practically her last words were for you, how she was sorry she had treated you so badly."

Rebecca felt tears springing into her eyes. "It was I who treated her so badly. I shouldn't have fallen in love with her husband."

"Are you sorry you did?"

"No! Of course not! I'm just sorry that things couldn't have been different, that's all. Do you still love her?"

"No. Well, yes, I suppose so. I don't know. I used to love her, very much, at least I thought I did. But not like I love you. I'm beginning to think that I have never really loved anyone before you."

"Oliver, I have to ask you a rather personal question. Forgive me, but I simply have to know. I found the sofa in the bathroom upstairs. Were you -"

"Was I sleeping on it instead of with my wife? Yes, I was. I hadn't slept with Charlotte for a long time, mostly because of her physical condition, and the risk of her conceiving a child. But now I realize that we were also drifting apart. Now are there any more personal questions that you simply have to ask?"

She smiled. "No. There's nothing else I need to know, except how much you love me."

"So much that the earth isn't big enough to contain it all," he answered.

"How about the universe?"

"Well, there's always hope, isn't there?" he teased.

The next few days were blissful heaven. They spent all their time together, rediscovering their love, walking along the riverbank in the moonlight, running through the meadows in the sunshine, making love in the gazebo, the library, the kitchen, sometimes even the bed, wherever they happened to be when the spark flashed between them and the urge to meld into one body and soul was the most important and consuming thing in the world.

Charlie came by once to check on her, and found her to be happier than he had ever seen her, and in very good hands.

They ate in restaurants in town. She was not about to spoil the honeymoon-like atmosphere with her terrible cooking. They even went down to Red's place for a couple of Pearly's delicious steaks, but the look on Red's face when she saw them walk in together tore at Rebecca's heart, and she almost wished that they had not come. She had not forgotten that Red had also been in love with Oliver. But Red was a big-hearted soul who took life's little disappointments in stride, and, to Rebecca's eternal gratitude, welcomed them both with open arms.

The only real fly in the soup came from an unexpected quarter: Mrs. Beckworth. Charlie's mother made the trip over one day because she had seen Rebecca and Oliver returning from town and was curious to see just what was going on in Charlie's house. Charlie had not yet told them about selling it, but had been looking for the right opportunity to do so, honestly he had. Mrs. Beckworth was outraged to the point of apoplexy. She was convinced that Rebecca had somehow tricked her poor son out of the house.

And the shocking behavior! Why, Rebecca should still be in mourning, and for that matter, so should Oliver. Yet these two heathens were living together, openly, in sin! It wasn't long before the entire town knew about it, and although Rebecca was able to ignore the whispers and stares and innuendoes because she really couldn't have cared less what they thought of her, still it pained her for Oliver's sake. He had enjoyed a stainless reputation and distinction during the years he had been in Natchez, one of the few real gentlemen around, and although he professed that it didn't matter to him what people thought, she was not convinced.

It wasn't long before they were making plans to be married, but not in Natchez. She was determined that the new life they would start should be completely new, in all respects, which meant moving away from Natchez.

He couldn't understand her position on that point. Wasn't she happy here? Wasn't she glad to be near her friends Charlie and Red and near her father? Of course she was, she reassured him; that wasn't the point. It was simply that they were too well known now to find any semblance of a community life. It would be years before they would be accepted as anything but social outcasts, if ever.

No, the only solution was to leave, to start all over in a place where they had never heard of Gentleman Jim Brogan, and where a lady's shady past might remain in the past. When Oliver finally could see her point, he offered a suggestion...

...Europe?

Her imagination soared with that idea, and very soon they were making plans to leave for Paris.

Rebecca offered to sell the house back to Charlie at the same price. Luckily the money was still intact in Charlie's bank account, and it pleased her to see the relief on his face at getting the property back. His parents, his mother in particular, had given him absolute hell over what he had done. He wasn't sorry for doing it, by any means, and would do it again, if Rebecca decided she wanted it back, but it would get him clearly off the hook with Mama and Daddy. And Mama was still pressuring him to get married. Maybe it was time he settled down, after all. And of course, Mr. Bennett's grave would be well taken care of; that went without saying.

There was still something bothering her, though. The money she had used to buy the house was definitely ill-gotten gain. If she were going to make a clean break with her past then that meant tying up all the loose ends.

Oliver applauded her idea of giving the money to a charity there in Natchez, as a fund for distressed orphans, of whatever age. She would not ever forget how lack of money had more or less forced her into doing some things she would never had dreamed of doing. If she had only had some sort of recourse, things might have been very different. This fund would be her way of righting a wrong. And she didn't need the money anyway, now that her father's gold was recovered. And Oliver Sebastian was a very wealthy man.

So it was all settled. Rebecca sold the house back to Charlie and set up the trust fund with the charity in town.

Oliver went and talked to Sheriff Brown, who seemed to think that their testimony would most likely not be needed in court. Gentleman Jim was suspected of being involved in half a dozen other crimes there in Natchez, and the Lord only knew what else up and down the Mississippi. If they didn't hang him for Mr. Bennett's murder, then they would hang him for something else, rest assured.

Oliver and Rebecca were scheduled to board a steamboat the next day for New Orleans, where they would take a sailing ship to New York, and another to London, then on to Paris. She was so excited about the trip she could hardly contain herself, and Oliver laughed at her good-naturedly. He had already seen much of the world, but he would take a delicious delight in showing it to her.

"Oh, Oliver, I can hardly believe this is happening. That we really leave for Paris in the morning. Is it real, or is it just a dream? Pinch me. Ouch! I was only kidding!"

He smiled at her and grabbed her arms, pulling her down beside him where he lay on the bed. "I love you," he said and kissed the tip of her nose. "I think we should be married in Paris. What do you think?"

"I think it wouldn't matter if it were the North Pole, as long as we are together. I love you, too."

She pulled his head toward hers until their lips met in a warm, sweet kiss that deepened into a mutual longing. His hands began to roam over her body, sending unmistakable signals to the appropriate regions. She gasped for breath. "Oliver! I haven't finished packing! I've got a million things to take care of before morning."

"And I'm one of them," he growled. There was no time for further protest, she was as caught up in desire as he. His lips captured hers, devouring, tasting the sweetness that was there for him alone. The past was gone, the future was a bright promise, but the present was all consuming.

He stripped off her clothing and his own, and covered her naked body with his. "I can't get enough of you," he murmured hungrily, and her heart echoed the sentiment.

His tongue left trails of blazing fire as he explored her body as if for the first time. Every time was like the first time, and Rebecca wondered with not a little bit of awe if they would ever become used to one another, to the point of taking each other for granted, of losing that passion that was so overwhelming. Her heart answered for her: no, they would not ever become used to one another. They would continually find new territory to explore, new boundaries to cross, and new depths to plumb.

Oliver pulled his familiar but still devastating ploy of satisfying her first with his tongue, and later with his body, so that her pleasure was doubled. She almost felt guilty at having so much ecstasy thrust on her, and giving only a small amount in return, but when she told him so, he only laughed, and said that giving her pleasure gave him pleasure, and that was enough for him.

But it was not enough for her, and when he had exhausted himself with proving his love, she took over, and showed him, to his astonishment, just how intensely she loved him, so that they both had double pleasure, and were equal. His joy was extremely gratifying, and she began to understand how giving pleasure to her brought pleasure to him, because it worked both ways.

She curled up into his arms and fell into a peaceful sleep.

Several hours later Rebecca woke with Oliver's arm lying protectively across her breasts. His breathing was deep and regular, and he slept peacefully. There were so many things still to be done before morning. Very slowly and without disturbing him, she moved his arm and got out of bed. If she was very quiet she could finish packing and never wake him up.

She lit a candle and reached for her robe. If she was going to be up half the night finishing the packing, then she needed some tea for stamina. They had bought plenty of tea and sugar in town, as Oliver still refused to drink her vile coffee.

Holding the candle high for light, she slipped quietly out of the room and made her way downstairs. It had been late afternoon when they had fallen asleep after their lovemaking, but it was quite dark now. The candle was her only light as she went into the kitchen and fumbled for the lamp, found it, and lit it from the candle. As the lamp wick took fire, she blew out the candle, and settled the glass globe back onto the lamp. The kitchen was immediately lit up, and she moved toward the stove to start a kettle of water.

Just as she reached for a match, suddenly a hand was clamped down roughly across her mouth, stifling the scream that rose there in panic.

"Don't move," whispered a male voice harshly against her ear.

Her heart leaped into her throat and stuck there. Dear God! It was Jim!

CHAPTER SIXTEEN

Rebecca struggled to pull Jim's hand away from her mouth so she could scream for Oliver, but he held her even tighter and thrust something hard and cold between her ribs.

"Be still or I kill you now," he whispered. "Thought you'd never see me again, didn't you? Will wonders never cease. I been layin' up in that rathole of a jail just thinkin' of the sweet revenge I'm gonna have. And I'm gonna have it, darlin', believe me. That English bastard is a dead man. Oh, yeah, I know all about you and him shackin' up here and all. He's dead, do you hear me? Dead! And you're gonna be dead too if you don't cooperate. Now I'm gonna take my hand away and you're not gonna scream, are you, because if you do I'll blow your head off."

She knew that he would do it, too, so when he withdrew his hand she turned to him. "Why have you come back?" she whispered. If Oliver were to hear, he would come down to investigate and they would both be dead.

"I told you, darlin', for revenge, pure and simple."

"B-but you're supposed to be in jail!"

"I was, thanks to you. But I broke out. Sheriff Brown ought to choose his deputies with more care. It was easy as pie to get that key away from him. Too bad he was stupid and pulled a gun. Latimer took that shot but I killed him for it."

"You k-killed a deputy?"

"He killed Latimer, and he woulda killed me! You wouldn't want to see me dead, would you?"

Her stomach churned. "What is it that you want here?"

"I want you, darlin'. I've had a lot of time to think about that Englishman, him with his hands all over you. And I couldn't stand it. You're my woman. You're either mine, or you're dead, is that clear enough for you?"

"Jim, please," she begged, "don't hurt Oliver. Do as you like to me, but please let him live."

In the lamplight she could see his eyes grow hard and cold, and he raised the gun up to her face. "He's a dead man. And you're comin' with me. I got us a couple of horses hidden out back, and I reckon we can make it across the river into Louisiana before the sheriff even knows what happened. Then we'll head for Mexico. They'll never catch me there." He smiled at the simplicity of his own plan.

"Jim, please, I beg you, don't do this."

"Enough talk," he said and grabbed her roughly by the arm. "Now where is he? It's time for him to die."

"No, Jim!"

"Where is he?" He shook her hard, and she motioned upstairs with her head. Maybe she could think of something before they got there, maybe trip him on the stairs or something. Tears formed in her eyes. She must think of some way to save Oliver, to save them both, for there was no way she would ever leave with this man. If he killed Oliver, then he might as well kill her too. There would be nothing left to live for.

"Come on." He pulled her to him and they took a step toward the door then suddenly stopped.

"Rebecca? Are you down there?" Oliver called from upstairs. His voice sounded calm. He did not know the desperate situation she was in, the danger he was in.

"Rebecca? You're not making coffee, I hope."

He was coming closer. Any second now he would walk into the kitchen to his death. She opened her mouth to yell at him, but Jim quickly prevented that with his hand. Tears rolled down her cheeks and across his fingers. She was helpless to prevent a murder.

Oliver took one step into the kitchen and froze. He stood naked in the lamplight, staring at Jim and the gun that was leveled at his chest.

"Well, now, if this ain't a fine specimen of a man, I don't know who is. Gotta hand it to you, darlin', you sure can pick 'em."

"What the devil are you doing here? Let her go!"

"You don't give orders to me, you English bastard, you take them. And right now I'm orderin' you to die."

Jim raised the gun and fired. Oliver leaped to the side, and the bullet caught him in the arm instead of the heart. He sprawled to the floor clutching his arm, and to Rebecca's horror she saw blood gushing out from the wound.

She bit hard into Jim's hand and he withdrew it just long enough so she could dash toward Oliver, but Jim caught her by the robe and jerked her backward. She fell heavily against the cupboard.

"Do you wanna die with him?" Jim spat at her. "Stay back! I'm gonna finish this bastard now."

The kitchen table partially blocked Oliver from Jim's view. Jim took a few steps around the table, toward him, his back to Rebecca.

"I took your advice, Englishman," Jim drawled. "This here gun is not a cap-and-ball like the one I had before. This is a six-shot revolver. The sheriff makes sure his men got all the latest weapons for law enforcement," he chuckled. "So if the first shot didn't kill you, it's for damn sure one of the five I got left will." He raised the gun and pointed it at Oliver's head.

Cap-and-ball, cap-and-ball...Something nagged at Rebecca's brain. Of course! Charlie's gun, the gun he had given her when she stayed her first night in the house alone! It was a cap-and-ball and it was still hidden in the flour canister where she had put it away and forgotten it.

There was not a moment to lose. She reached for the canister and jerked off the lid, which crashed to the floor. As Jim turned around at the noise, she pulled out the gun and pointed it at him.

"Darlin'-?" he said with a look of wonderment on his face. She cocked the pistol. He raised his own gun and pointed it at her, but it was too late.

She fired. The bullet hit him squarely in the neck, and the awful expression that crossed his face would haunt her to her grave. He dropped the gun and clutched with both hands at his neck, but blood was gushing like a waterfall, and in another two seconds he fell to the floor, and breathed his last.

Rebecca stared at the body for a long moment before she finally dropped the pistol and rushed over to Oliver's side.

"Oliver, you're hurt." But Oliver's wound was not fatal, as Jim's had been.

"I'll be all right. He only grazed me. Are you all right?"

Strangely enough, she was very calm. Her nerves that had been at fever-pitch only a few moments ago now were calm and serene. The danger was over. "Yes, I'm all right," she answered quietly.

Heavy footsteps sounded on the verandah and they heard another familiar voice.

"Miss Bennett? Sebastian? It's Sheriff Brown."

"In here, sheriff," Oliver called, and struggled to his feet. He yanked the tablecloth from the table and wrapped it around his nakedness. Rebecca got a towel and bandaged his arm to stop the blood.

"I came to warn you-" said the sheriff as he walked into the kitchen, but the sight of blood on Oliver's arm stopped him.

"You're a bit late, sheriff," Oliver said and pointed to Jim's body.

The sheriff walked around the table and looked, then let out a deep sigh. "You folks all right?"

"Yes, just a flesh wound. Did he hurt you, my love?" Oliver asked, caressing Rebecca's face with his free hand.

"No, I'm all right," she replied calmly. "I killed him, sheriff. You can hang me for it, but I'm not sorry I did it."

The sheriff knelt and examined the body, then stood up again. "I don't reckon there's no need to hang anybody, Miss Bennett. He killed one of my deputies in his escape. I figured he'd be headin' this way, that's why I came. No, Miss Bennett, I reckon you did us all a mighty big favor, and saved the taxpayers from havin' to pay for a hangin'."

"He would have killed us both," Rebecca said in that strangely calm voice.

"Then I reckon it was self-defense, plain and simple. I'll get my men to clean up this mess. You better see about that arm, Oliver."

"Thank you, sheriff," Oliver replied. Sheriff Brown called to his men, who came in and hauled the body outside. They even took some towels and washed up the blood on the floor, erasing the evidence of what had happened.

Rebecca made Oliver sit down and she attended to his wound. Luckily the bleeding had stopped, and on closer inspection, it appeared to be only a flesh wound after all. He had been lucky, very lucky.

"You folks still plannin' on leavin' tomorrow?" asked the sheriff at the door.

Rebecca stared into Oliver's eyes, saw the love reflected back to her. "Yes, sheriff, we're going to Paris. To be married."

"Well, I wish you a lot of happiness. Reckon you've both had enough trouble to last a lifetime. I hope you find some peace with each other. Good luck to you."

When Sheriff Brown and his men had gone, Oliver pulled her into his lap. "Guess that makes us even."

"What makes us even?"

"I saved your life, and you saved mine. You were wonderful, my love. But you never told me you had a gun hidden in the flour canister. Are there any more secrets you're keeping from me?"

"Charlie gave me that, for protection. I never thought I'd have to use it."

"You only had one shot, you know. Good thing you didn't miss."

She shuddered, remembering the look on Jim's face. "I couldn't miss. Your life was at stake. It was him...or you."

"I'm glad it was that simple. And I'll be eternally grateful to Charlie for giving you that pistol. I love you, you know."

"I know. And I love you, too."

He kissed her deeply, warmly, then pushed her off his lap and picked her up in his arms.

"Oliver, your wound! You'll hurt yourself!"

"Never mind that. It's still a long time before morning," he said as he carried her out of the kitchen and up the stairs. "Let's go back to bed."

"I don't think I can sleep," she said. "But in a way I'm glad it happened. Now we can both be fully free of the past.!

"So you're glad I was shot, are you? No, no, I am only teasing, my love. I'm sorry you had to kill him, but you'e right, we are free. And for going back to bed, darling Rebecca, who said anything about sleep?" He swept her up into his arms, and carried her up the stairs, and to their blissful new life together.

If you love romance, then Domhan is the place for you. From sizzling contemporaries to sensual sagas, look no further than these pages....
All prices are in Us dollars and pounds sterling and are correct at the time of press.
Domhan Books:
USA: 9511 Shore Road, Suite 514 Brookyln, NY 11209
Rest of World: 3 Killyvilly Grove Tempo Road Enniskillen Co. Fermanagh BT 74 4RT N. Ireland

The Wildest Heart Jacinta Carey $12.95/£6.99

Rebecca Whitaker is struggling to keep her family ranch from foreclosure by trading with the Indians, working in a saloon, and raising horses. Enter the mysterious Walker Pritchard, claiming he wishes to stay with Reb to leave the memories of the war behind and learn about the ways of the west. They fall in love, but can Reb trust Walker? What are his real motives for coming to the Bar T, and how did he know there would be gold in those hills? Reb must fight to save him and her ranch, before everything she loves is destroyed by the men from Walker's shady past.

Heart's Desire by Sorcha MacMurrough $10.00/£4.99

Nurse Sinead Thomas rescues the hospital's handsome architect Austin Riordan from a life-threatening situation. She accepts his offer to be his private nurse over the Christmas holidays, but gets more than she bargained for as they grow ever closer. A young widow, she never wants to go through the torment of being in love again. But Austin is nothing if not persistent. Can they fight the demons from her past, to secure their hearts' desire?

Star Attraction by Sorcha MacMurrough $10.00/£4.99

Zaira Darcy literally bumps into the man of her dreams in an elevator. Dashing Brad Clarke, Hollywood's hottest new director, working alongside her in New York, is everything she could want in a man, and more. But the secrets from her past, and the double life she leads, threaten to destroy any chance of happiness the two might have. Zaira must lock horns with her ex-husband Jonathan one last time to save Brad's life, even if it means sacrificing her own.

Ghost From the Past by Sorcha MacMurrough $10.00/£4.99

Biochemist Clarissa Vincent's fiance Julian Simmons was killed in a terrible explosion five years ago. Or was he? Taking a new job in Portland, Oregon, Clarissa sees a man at the airport who could be Julian's double, and is suddenly propelled into a nightmarish world of espionage and intrigue. She must struggle to save her family and the man she has always loved from the ruthless people who will stop at nothing to achieve world domination.

The Hart and the Harp by Sorcha MacMurrough $12.95/£6.99
Ireland, 1149

Shive MacDermot and Tiernan O'Hara agree to wed to end a five-year feud between their clans. Though an unlikely alliance at first, Shive begins to fall in love with her new husband. She soon realises the murderer of her brother is a member of her own clan. How can she win Tiernan's love and prove to him she is not the enemy?
Shive undertakes an epic struggle to save her lands and Tiernan's from the ambitious Muireadach O'Rourke, determined to kill anyone who opposes his bid to become highking of all Ireland. Will she prove worthy of Tiernan, or will he believe all of the vicious lies about her supposed love for another, and become her enemy himself?

The Fire's Centre by Sorcha MacMurrough $12.95/£6.99
Riona Connolly is willing to do anything to save her family from starvation during the Potato Famine. So when she meets the handsome Dr. Lucien Woulfe, who offers her post at his clinic, it seems a dream come true. But their growing attraction is forbidden in the straight-laced society of Victorian Dublin. Riona and Lucien must walk through the fire's centre to secure their happiness before it is destroyed by the evil Dr. O'Carroll and the vagaries of Fate.

Hunger for Love by Sorcha MacMurrough $12.95/£6.99
Ireland and Canada, 1847
Emer Nugent and her family are evicted from their home at the height of the Potato Famine in Ireland. Forced to emigrate to Canada, they endure a harrowing journey on board a coffin ship bound for Grosse Ile. Emer, working as a cabin boy to help her family's financial situation, meets the enigmatic Dalton Randolph, the ship's only gentleman passenger, who is not all that he seems. They fall in love, but darker forces are at work against them. Emer's duty to her family forces Dalton and she to separate. Will they ever be able to overcome the obstacles in their path to true love?
This incredible saga of love, adventure and intrigue continues in the second volume The Hungry Heart, also available from Domhan Books.

The Hungry Heart by Sorcha MacMurrough $12.95/£6.99
Canada and Ireland 1847-1849
Emer Nugent leaves her lover Dalton Randall to search for her family in the hell of the Grosse Ile quarantine station. The land of opportunity is nearly the death of them all. Dalton is deceived into thinking Emer is dead by his father, and is about to marry the daughter of a business rival when he meets Emer again. Outraged that his plans for keeping the two apart have failed, Dalton's father has Emer arrested on false charges and transported back to Ireland.
But the Ireland she returns to is on the brink of civil war. Emer finds herself unwittingly embroiled in the 1848 rebellion, and is put on trial for her life. Dalton must travel half way across the world to try to save her before it is too late.

Scars Upon Her Heart by Sorcha MacMurrough $12.95/£6.99
Lady Vevina Joyce and her brother Wilfred are forced to flee Ireland after being falsely accused of treason. On the road with Wellington's army, they meet an unexpected ally in the enigmatic Major Stewart Fitzgerald. Side by side they fight with their comrades in some of the most bitter battles of the Napoleonic Wars. Can Vevina clear her name, protect those she loves, and stop the Grand Army from taking over the whole of Europe in a bold and daring move engineered by the person responsible for her family's disgrace?
Is Stewart really all that he seems? Appearances can be deceptive....

The Sea of Love by Sorcha Mac Murrough hardcover $25.00/£14.00 paperback $15.00/£8.00
Ireland 1546
Wrongfully accused of murder, Aidanna O'Flaherty's only ally against her evil brother-in-law Donal is the dashing English-bred aristocrat Declan Burke. Saving him from certain death, they fall in love, only to be separated when Declan is falsely accused of treason. Languishing in the Tower, Declan is powerless to assist his beloved Aidanna as she undertakes an epic struggle to expose her enemy and save her family and friends. She must race against time to prevent all she loves from being swept aside in a thunderous tide of foreign invasion....

In From the Cold by Carolyn Stone $12.95/£6.99
Cambridge scientist Sophie Ruskin is propelled into a world of espionage and intrigue when her father disappears on his way to an important advanced-technology conference. Adrian Vaughan, handsome, enigmatic, but haunted by his past, is assigned to train her as a spy to win her father's freedom, or destroy his work before his kidnappers can create the ultimate weapon. But Adrian's fate soon lies in Sophie's hands, as she travels two continents to save his life, win his love, and fight for the freedom of the oppressed, war-torn Russian Republic of Chechnya.

The Art of Love by Evelyn Trimborn $10.00/£4.99
Struggling Dublin artist Shannon Butler gives a hugely successful show. Enter her adopted brother Marius Winters, hell-bent on revenge. He accuses her of robbing him of his share of their dead father's estate. Thrown together by circumstances, they try to make up for the mistakes of the past. Despite all their differences, they grow ever closer. But Marius' lying ex-wife threatens any chance of happiness they might have. How can Shannon prevent her new-found love from leaving her forever?

Castles in the Air by Evelyn Trimborn $10.00/£4.99
Poverty-stricken aristocrat Alanna Lacy is at her wits' end. Enter property developer Bran Ryan, who offers her a way out of her desperate financial situation-marry him! Faced with her father's disapproval, and Bran's spiteful ex-fiancee, can they build a future together, or will all their dreams go up in smoke?

Science Fiction/Fantast/Paranormal Romance:
The Wizard Woman by Shanna Murchison hardcover $25.00/£14.00 paperback $15.00/£8.00
Ireland 1169
The great Celtic myth of the Wheel of Fate is played out against the backdrop of the first Norman invasion of Ireland in 1169. Dairinn is made the wizard's woman, chosen by the gods to be the wife of the handsome but mysterious Senan. Through him she discovers her own innate powers, and the truth behind her family history. She must bargain with the Morrigan, the goddess of death, if she is ever to achieve happiness with the man she loves. But how high a price will she have to pay for Senan's life?

Wages of Justice: The Archons of Nublis by Kate Saundby $12.95/£6.99
The first volume of the Julian Trilogy
In the Fifth Millennium, a young tourist visiting the small planet of Nublis is about to be tried for murder by its mysterious chief judge or archon. Always masked, the Nublian archon is blindfolded whenever he presides over the court and, except for the evidence presented, he knows nothing about the circumstances of any case before him. The accused is unconcerned because he knows his powerful father Augustus Veniston, who is the Interplanetary Synod's Chief Justice, is on his way to rescue him.
But the prisoner's lofty connections mean nothing to the Archon. Damon Veniston's fate sets off a cataclysmic chain reaction, the consequences of which threaten the safety of the Emperor Julian and the entire royal family, and all of Nublis itself

Wages of Sin: Rules of War by Kate Saundby $12.95/£6.99
The second volume of the Julian Trilogy
The adventures of the Emperor Julian and his family, and his beloved brother Cassius continue. Augustus Veniston, still determined to get revenge for the death of his son Damon, hounds the intrepid pair of brothers. Only by forming an unholy alliance with the terrorist Enoch Kane can Julian hope to save his planet from a deadly weapon

Veniston has perfected.

Wages of Greed The Sixth Plutarch by Kate Saundby $12.95/£6.99
The third volume of The Julian Trilogy
Thamar is wed to Ephraim the smuggler, who befriends Cassius and his brother the Emperor Julian of Nublis. Defying all prophecies, he and his new friends risk all they hold most dear to destroy the evil political system of his homeland and put Ephraim on the throne of the planet Seira.

Golden Silence by Kate Saundby $12.95/£6.99
This is abridging novel between the Julian and the Felix Trilogies by Kate Saundby. Duke Adrian of Ceila, born without vocal chords, is cheated out of his birthright by his conniving cousin Philip and his shrew of a wife Abigail. But he soon discovers that living well is the best revenge.

Fortune's Hostage by Kate Saundby $12.95/£6.99
The two countries of Illyria and Lodebar suddenly call a truce after years of intense fighting. Prince Darius of Lodebar is Fortune's Hostage, kept by the Interplantary synod as surety for his father's good behaviour. But dark forces are at work in both countries, as the struggle for power threatened to rip even the entire Synod apart.

Christian Historical Romances:
The Way Found by Nina J. Lechiara $14.95/8.99
Matteo and Gianna search for love and truth in university studies, religion and philosophy, from Padua and Venice to Egypt and Arabia. They find it unexpectedly in Yahshua, in the one place they have never looked, the Scriptures. They learn both the truth and the meaning of love and marriage. Despite organised religions and societies which persecute true believers, they become teachers and shining examples of Yahvah's way.

To Seek the Way by Nina J. Lechiara $14.95/8.99
Stefano, son of Gianna and Matteo, raised in the Word of Yahvah from birth, and Alanna Ann, raised in religious confusion during the reign of Queen Elizabeth I of England, meet and realize the emptiness and tragedy of life without Yahshua. Troubles at home from political enemies and marriage force them to separate and live in the larger world, where they meet again. Alanna Ann becomes a famed dancer of Scriptural stories, and Stephano a swordsman and statesman for righteousness. Having found happiness in mariage, they must learn how to trust and how to surrender all, even their beloved spouse, to Yahvah through Yahshua.

Come Unto Me Nina J. Lechiara $14.95/8.99
Peter, an orphan whose estates in New Grenada have been confiscated, and Briana, only child and hope for an heir of an Austrian Count, marry. But the Count's plan for a marriage of convenience to produce an heir during the Thirty Years' War is thwarted by their steadfast love and commitment to Yahshua. From Austria to the New World of South America, though they are persecuted, they serve as wintesses for the Messiah.

9 781583 450086